WHEN WE LEAST EXPECT IT

A MR. INCONVENIENT NOVEL

STEPHANIE ROWE

AUTHENTICITY PLAYGROUND PRESS

PRAISE FOR STEPHANIE ROWE

"Stephanie is a master at weaving a great romcom filled with adventure, mishaps, laughter, intrigue, and love. This story made me feel all the feels and I look forward to the series as it unfolds." ~5-star Goodreads Review (Heidi)

"I love how Stephanie Rowe builds a story. First, you become so captivated and involved with the characters, that you become their first row cheering section. Then she creates a story that sucks you in from the beginning and with the twists and turns that occur, you can't put the book down until it's finished...I love this more light-hearted, humorous, yet emotional spin-off from the Hart family series. There's lots of excitement, intrigue, emotions, and humor; all classic elements of a Stephanie Rowe story that combine for a five-star read." ~5-star Goodreads Review (Elizabeth)

"Stephanie Rowe hit another one out of the park!" 5-star Goodreads Review (Denise P)

"Stephanie Rowe has a way of grabbing your attention from page one and before you know it hours have passed and the book is finished." ~5-star Goodreads Review (KReid09)

"I cannot ever say enough about the genius of Stephanie Rowe. I've loved all her books across all the genres she writes… This book has it all. Laughs, cries, finger-biting. Everything. Lovers of mysteries, cozy mysteries, romance and books in general will love reading this installment. I can't recommend it highly enough. Can I make it 5+ stars? 6? 100? I would if I could." 5-star Goodreads Review (Jeanne S.)

"This one grabbed me from the first sentence and took me along for a hilarious and twisty ride. This was a stay up too late because I could not put it down kind of book." 5-star Goodreads Review (Tammy M.)

"This book is pure genius. Hilariously funny all the way through and with a fantastic storyline too." 5-star Goodreads Review (Nikki P)

"OMG!!! The best yet!! Stephanie has outdone herself! I am in love with this book. I was on an emotional roller coaster. I just love the banter, love and laughter." ~5-star Goodreads Review (Cindy A)

"I laughed, I cried, I had to stop and compose myself. But I had a hard time putting it down." 5-star Goodreads Review (Laura C.)

"Masterful… tugged at my heart." 5-star Goodreads Review (Elizabeth)

"I fell head over heels for Leila and Dash! Their story made me laugh, cry, and swoon!" 5 stars, Jessie's Reading Corner

"Exquisitely beautiful!! All the feels. This is a do not pass up book. Perfectly written :)." 5-star Goodreads Review (Jann)

STEPHANIE ROWE BOOKS

MYSTERY

MIA MURPHY SERIES
(COZY MYSTERY)
Double Twist
Top Notch
Gone Rogue
Triple Trouble
Margarita Mayhem

CONTEMPORARY ROMANCE

MR. INCONVENIENT SERIES
ROMANTIC COMEDY
LINKED TO THE HART RANCH BILLIONAIRES SERIES
When We Least Expect It
When We Take a Chance

THE HART RANCH BILLIONAIRES SERIES
(CONTEMPORARY WESTERN ROMANCE)
A Rogue Cowboy's Second Chance

(PARANORMAL ROMANCE)
Dark Wolf Rising
Dark Wolf Unbound

STANDALONE PARANORMAL ROMANCE
Leopard's Kiss
Not Quite Dead

FUNNY URBAN FANTASY
Guardian of Magic
The Demon You Trust

DEVILISHLY SEXY SERIES
(FUNNY PARANORMAL ROMANCE)
Not Quite a Devil

ROMANTIC SUSPENSE

ALASKA HEAT SERIES
(ROMANTIC SUSPENSE)
Ice
Chill
Ghost
Burn
Hunt (novella)

BOXED SETS

Order of the Blade (Books 1-4)
Protectors of the Heart (A Six-Book First-in-Series Collection)
Wyoming Rebels Boxed Set (Books 1-3)

For a complete list of Stephanie's books, click here.

COPYRIGHT

For all the women out there who need a little reminder that you're awesome, you matter, and you never, EVER need to apologize for who you are, what you want, or how you feel. Because you're amazing, exactly as you re.

Also dedicated to my mom, who is my Kitty: strong, bold, and empowering, who fills the world around her with massive amounts of love! I love you, Mom!

ACKNOWLEDGMENTS

Special thanks to my beta readers. You guys are the best!

There are so many to thank by name, more than I could count, but here are those who I want to called out specially for all they did to help this book come to life: Alyssa Bird, Anette Taylor, Ashlee Murphy, Brenda Wasnock, Bridget Koan, Britannia Hill, Carolena Emer, Cindy Abbott, Deb Julienne, Denise Fluhr, Diana Kassman, Dottie Jones, Elizabeth Barnes, Heidi Hoffman, Helen Loyal, Jackie Moore Kranz, Jeanne Stone, Jeanie Jackson, Jessica Hayden, Jodi Bobbett, Jodi Moore, Judi Pflughoeft, Kasey Richardson, Linda Rogers, Linda Watson, Nichole Reed, Regina Thomas, Summer Steelman, Suzanne Mayer, Shell Bryce, Susan Parker, and Trish Douglas. Special thanks to my family, who I love with every fiber of my heart and soul. And to AER, who is my world. Love you so much, baby girl! I am so proud of you! You're going to rock this world! And to Joe, who keeps me believing myself. I love you all!

ONE

There was a shirtless, muscled man in Piper Townsend's shower, and that was just not going to work for her today.

Or ever, quite honestly.

But especially today.

She put her hands on her hips as her landlord, Declan Jones, reared back with a freaking sledgehammer and aimed it at her still-intact shower wall. "Declan, don't—"

Her grumpy, ex-cop demolition squad slammed his sledgehammer into the tile, shattering the wall and eviscerating the last vestiges of composure she'd been clinging to when she'd walked in.

"Declan!" She strode into the bathroom and poked him in his shoulder.

He spun around so fast that he bumped into her, knocking her off balance. She tripped on his toolbox, and he grabbed her arm, swearing as he averted her certain death and hauled her upright again.

Of course he could toss her effortlessly to her feet. That was so irritatingly attractive in a man, and she didn't have time for irritatingly attractive men.

He removed his earbuds and scowled at her. "Don't sneak up on me when I have a sledgehammer. It's not safe."

"I shouted your name twice."

He frowned. "You did?"

She pointed to his earbuds. "Noise-cancelling?"

He looked down at his hand, then swore. "Sorry." He shoved the earbuds in his pocket. "You okay?"

Okay was such a vague term. "Technically, yes."

His brows went up. "You're not okay?"

"You didn't hurt me," she clarified, because did she want to have to explain to him what had happened to her in the last few days? No, she didn't. Home was her oasis, and Declan was probably the only human within a few hundred miles who didn't know what had happened.

Or maybe that was an exaggeration, but that's what it felt like, so she was going with it.

"All right." He picked up the sledgehammer. "What do you need?"

"My bathroom, but that feels like a reach right now." Normally, a glimpse of Declan's gorgeous shoulders was enough to boost Piper's mood in an art-appreciation kind of way, but today his royal hotness was simply a big mass of muscles and man in her path. She did not have time for her bathroom to be in a pile of rubble.

Declan glanced over at her with those bright blue eyes that always startled her with their intensity. "I told you I was starting the renovation today." He sounded cranky and tired.

Well, that was great for him that he was cranky and tired. So was she, and it was her bathroom that he'd just punctured a hole in. "Wednesday. You said you were starting Wednesday."

He frowned. "I said today."

"No, you said that you had to finish the molding in your kitchen, so you weren't going to start until Wednesday." It was currently Monday afternoon at five, which was not the time for Declan to be in her shower.

Well, in an alternate life, maybe any time would be the perfect time for Declan to be in her shower, but in this life? Never.

He narrowed his eyes, staring at her.

"Hello?"

"I think I did say Wednesday," he finally said.

Piper blinked. "I don't think I've ever heard you admit you were wrong about anything."

He flashed her a grin as he rested the sledgehammer against his leg. "I'm not that stubborn."

"You are, but I'm used to it." She waved her hand at her bathroom. "But about this—"

He'd offered to pay for a hotel while he redid her bathroom, but her little home was her oasis, and she'd needed the comfort of being there. She had a tiny powder room that had a toilet and a sink, and she could shower at her gym, so she'd decided it would work. "I didn't plan for this tonight. I need a shower."

And a miracle, but first things first.

Declan sighed and ran his hand over his short hair, his chiseled bicep flexing like God's gift to women. His hotness had never dawned on her prior to the last few weeks, but her trio of besties had recently been on a mission to get Piper back into the dating game, and they'd fixated on Declan as a good start.

She disagreed, but their constant harping on his physical attributes was working its way into her subconscious, which was incredibly distracting and annoying, especially when he was shirtless and sweaty.

Fortunately, she had a will of steel and enough relationship trauma to withstand any temptation, so it was all good.

"It was my mistake," Declan said, "so you can shower at my place."

"Your place?" Piper had never been in his gorgeous house that shared a gravel driveway with her little carriage house. She'd never even peeked through those beautiful French doors or tiptoed past his gorgeous, landscaped pool. Declan was private, closed-off. Almost a loner, from what she'd observed from her little vantage point in his guest house. He kept people away, except for the occasional visit by his mom and brother.

Whenever his mom, Kitty, couldn't find Declan, she always came to ask Piper where he was, if he was going on any dates, if he had gone out recently, if he had gone back to his job as a cop.

Kitty always looked upset when Piper hadn't been able to report any sexy shenanigans happening at Thirteen Hemlock Drive, but she'd always looked relieved when Piper hadn't had any police car sightings in his driveway. Kitty was sassy, chatty, unapologetically bold, and adorable.

Declan, in contrast, was a reclusive ex-cop who spent his life in jeans, boots, t-shirts, and a five-o'clock shadow. His sole existence appeared to be working on his house, playing ball with his dog, and bartending part-time at a neighborhood bar.

His mom and brother were well-dressed, sociable, and always looked like they knew what a shower was for. She had no idea how they were related.

"Yeah. Back door is unlocked." Declan looked at his watch. "I'll be working until six, so you'll have privacy. Use the guest bath to the left at the top of the stairs. It's the blue bathroom."

Piper stared at him. "You're inviting me unattended into your sanctuary?"

He cocked a brow. "Why? Should I not trust you?"

"No. I'm very trustworthy." Well, apparently she was also demon spawn cursed to destroy love and romance in all its earthly forms, but she doubted Declan would be worried about that apparent flaw in her character. He didn't seem the type.

He grinned. "I know you're trustworthy. I ran a background check on you before I rented you the carriage house. You have an hour. Once I'm finished in here for the night, I'm kicking you out, so make it quick."

A background check? Sudden alarm gripped her. Did he know about her past? He was an ex-cop. If he'd decided to dig deep, his tentacles would have gone far. "What did you check?"

His smile faded. "Credit. Prison record."

"That's it?"

He leaned on his sledgehammer, studying her with open curiosity now. "What else is there to find, Piper?"

"Nothing." She shook out her shoulders. If Declan had uncovered her past, he wouldn't have rented her the carriage house. It was fine. Her past was still hidden. No one except her friend Maddie Vale knew. *Relax, Piper.* She ducked past him and grabbed her shampoo and conditioner off the sink where he'd moved it. "I'll be on my way—"

"You're getting married?" he asked.

"What?" Alarm leapt through her, and she instinctively glanced at her left hand. Where there was no longer an engagement ring. Had he heard what happened?

He pointed. "The magazine."

She looked down and saw that her copy of the June issue of *Elite Bride* was facing him. Relief rushed through her. *He didn't know.* "No. I'm a wedding planner."

Or rather, a wedding killer, according to Kathryn Vespa, one of her bridal clients.

Kathryn had also called her cursed.

And bad luck.

And, most significantly, *fired.*

A second bride had also fired her today. And social media had embraced the new, viral hashtag #weddingkillerpiper. And then last night's fiasco…

And now, a third bride, the biggest client her firm had ever acquired, had left Piper three voicemails today, demanding that Piper call her back. She wasn't going to do that until she figured things out, since bride #3, April Hunsaker, was definitely going to fire her.

April was her last chance. If April fired her, Piper's career would be over.

Everything she'd worked for…destroyed.

Which meant she had to figure out how to regain April's trust tonight.

As in, within the next few hours.

Tomorrow, it would be too late.

Game over.

Piper had twelve hours left to fix the unfixable. Hence the need for a miracle.

She'd find a way, but right now, she had no idea what that path was. She was worried that there wasn't an out, and that scared her more than she wanted to admit.

"Wedding planner?" Declan looked amused. "That job title brings fear into every man's heart."

"What? Why? I make dreams come true. And very well, I might add." Well, except for the string of bad luck over the last ten months…beginning with her own. But that wasn't bad luck so much as a nightmare of her own creating. Either way, same result, though.

"The bride's dreams, maybe, but that poor groom?" Declan chuckled. "Now he's got two women to complicate his life. All he wants is to get married, and now he has to deal with things like tablecloths, seating charts, and table centerpieces."

Piper rolled her eyes. "That's so unromantic! Just wait until you fall in love. You'll realize that your greatest joy is seeing your bride's face light up as her dream day comes to life."

His amusement faded, and his jaw got hard. "No chance. No wedding in my future."

It was her turn to be curious. His reaction had been intense and unyielding, far beyond a typical marriage-averse manly-man reaction. "Really? Why not?"

Something flashed across Declan's face, an emotion so raw and ragged that she sucked in her breath. "Because it's not." He turned away, picked up his construction assault weapon, and slammed it into the wall of her shower again.

Piper didn't move for a moment, stunned by the expression she'd seen on his face. Declan was always so reserved, so controlled, so grumpy, but that had been pure, raw emotion raking across his face for that brief second.

Declan had secrets, she realized. Secrets that would probably rip him to shreds if he let them out.

Wow. Just...wow. She'd had no idea that her reserved, solitary landlord was a boiling cauldron of secrets.

He looked over his shoulder at her. "You're down to fifty-eight minutes."

"Right. I'm going." She grabbed the rest of her toiletries and bolted.

Declan had just gone from annoyingly attractive on a physical level to maddeningly intriguing on a human level.

Which didn't fit into her life.

At all.

Piper was standing on the ruins of a promise she'd made to her mother before she'd passed away. If she failed to fix things in the next twelve hours, the dream she and her mom had created together would be shattered.

She needed miracles right now, not mistakes.

And Declan would be a mistake.

A huge, irrecoverable mistake.

Which meant she was keeping her distance from him.

In every way.

Because she was a woman on a mission, and she wasn't going to mess it up with romantic dreams of knights in shining armor.

She'd done that already, and the scars still burned.

Never, ever again.

Declan could still smell the flowers.

Piper was gone, and yet, he could still smell the flowers. Was it her shampoo? Her soap? Some sort of body lotion?

The thought of body lotion put a visual in his head that made him swear.

He set his sledgehammer down and stepped back, trying to focus on the carnage around him. Demolition was always satisfying. He knew damn well that he'd told Piper he was starting on Wednesday, but a few hours ago, he'd run into someone he used to know, and his past had been triggered.

He'd had to do something to distract himself. From the memories. From the pain in his gut. From the truth that wouldn't stop haunting him.

As soon as he'd gotten home, Declan had grabbed his tools and almost sprinted to the guest house, ignoring the instability in his knee. That first swing of the sledgehammer had reverberated through his body, jerking him back from the grips of the past and returning him to the present.

Now? He felt back in control again, locked down, focused… except for the fact he could still smell the scent of flowers that seemed to follow Piper wherever she went.

He fucking loved how she smelled.

He was going to have to find a way to get over it.

Because he wasn't ready for a woman, and he never would be.

That part of his life was over, and he was never going back.

At that moment, his phone rang. He pulled it out and looked at the caller. When he saw who it was, he had to take a breath before answering it. "Declan here."

He listened for a moment, his gut tightening the longer they spoke. "Yeah, I can come in on Friday at eleven. Thanks."

He hung up and let his hand fall to his side, stunned.

He'd passed the physical to return to police work.

Interview on Friday.

After three years on the sidelines, fighting to get his body to work again, he'd done it.

It was all he'd been focused on. The only thing that mattered.

But now that he was going back there on Friday… *Fuck.*

It was only for an interview, but the nightmares were going to start again. He could already feel it.

He took a breath. Nightmares were fine. He was fine. He had a bathroom to destroy and that would get him right.

But as he picked up the sledgehammer, he caught a whiff of flowers again.

This time, he closed his eyes, paused, and inhaled, using that light, delicate scent to steady himself.

Piper was freaking sunshine, and she had no idea how she grounded him every time he saw her.

And she never would know, because he was never going there with her.

But would he take a minute to breathe in the flowers and let it settle him?

Yeah. He would.

Because he had only a few days to figure out how to make himself walk back into that station and return to the life that had nearly destroyed him.

TWO

Declan's house was gorgeous.

Truly breathtaking.

Piper couldn't help but pause to breathe in the magic of his home when she stepped into his family room through the patio doors. He was such a sweaty grump that she would have expected the house to be a sparsely decorated man cave.

But it was the exact opposite.

The kitchen was spacious and bright, with sky lights, huge windows, and granite counters. A huge, beautiful stone fireplace took up almost the entire end of the adjoining family room, which was filled with a cozy sectional couch big enough for a thousand dogs...but only one was on it.

A large, black, shaggy dog lifted her head to stare at Piper.

Piper paused. She'd met Angel a couple times when Declan had been walking her, but invading the rescue dog's home unescorted was different. With the exception of her friend Maddie's therapy dog, Violet, Piper wasn't a dog person. They didn't like her, and she had no idea how to interact with them.

So, yay for this moment of personal growth or death. "Hi, Angel," she said softly. "We met before, remember?"

Angel slowly rose to her feet, her fur up.

A low growl echoed from her throat.

Umm... "Angel," she said again. "I'm not the enemy. It's okay. Violet loves me, and Violet doesn't like most people."

Angel growled again, then lowered into a crouch position, as if she were preparing to launch.

"Angel," she said, taking on a firmer voice. "Sit."

Angel didn't move.

"Angel. *Sit.*"

Slowly, Angel lowered her butt to the couch. Piper almost started laughing at how slowly the dog sat. "I get it," she said. "Who likes authority? How about we be friends?"

The tip of Angel's tail wagged once, and Piper relaxed. She went down on one knee and held out her hand, palm up. "Friends, sweetheart. Girl power means we need to stick together."

Angel watched her for a moment, then eased off the couch, and slunk across the room toward Piper, almost crouching. Piper's heart turned over for the dog. She knew Declan had rescued her, but it was clear the pup still lived in the shadows of her past.

That was something she understood. "Come on, Angel," she said gently. "You're safe now. Declan will never let any harm come to you, and neither will I."

The dog reached her, and instead of pausing, she pushed right into Piper's chest, and buried her face against her.

Piper's heart softened, and she wrapped her arms around the dog. "I've got you," she whispered. "You're so beautiful, Angel." It felt so good to hug the dog. She felt settled, safe, for the first time since everything had fallen apart. Months. Maybe longer, because things had been falling apart long before the world found out.

For the first time, she fully understood why Maddie had her therapy pit bull, Violet. Hugging Angel felt like a part of her soul could breathe for the first time in months.

She took a moment to sit with Angel, to remember what it felt like not to have tension radiating through every muscle in her body. Maybe it would be okay. Maybe she had a chance. Maybe she would feel okay again someday.

Piper wanted to stay there forever, but she knew the clock was ticking on Declan's return. The last thing she needed was his royal moodiness invading this precarious moment of peace. She kissed Angel's head. "I gotta go shower." She stood up, patted Angel, and then headed for the stairs.

Angel trotted along beside her, so close that her fur was brushing against Piper's leg.

Piper knew what the dog was feeling. Safety was precious, and Angel didn't want to leave it. "I get that, honey. You can stay with me."

Angel followed her up the beautiful, curved front stairs and right into the most gorgeous bathroom Piper had ever been in. Angel curled up on the thick, blue bathmat as Piper shut the door.

The molding around the door was intricately carved, the tile-work detailed and artistic, and the shower appeared to have been hand-built, one flat stone at a time. "Did he do this himself?" she asked the dog as she set her supplies on the sink.

Declan had mentioned that he'd rehabbed the house himself, but this was truly extraordinary. "If he did this, he's an artistic genius." Piper couldn't wrap her head around her grumpy, reclusive landlord having the vision to create something so beautiful.

Maybe he hadn't. Maybe he'd hired someone. Or maybe he was so much more than she'd realized…

Not that it mattered who he might be. Their relationship wasn't personal and never would be. Which was fine. Right now, she had time for only one focus: finding her way past the catastrophic damage she'd done to her life and her career. She didn't have time for Declan or any other man. Not today, and quite frankly, ever.

She'd learned her lesson.

But she *would* thoroughly enjoy his shower, his dog, and his tilework, and then she'd get back to finding the elusive emergency solution that would fix her life.

Well, not her *life*. That was a big ask.

She'd go with fixing the situation with April as a start.

The world could be conquered one bride at a time, right?

Her phone rang as she turned on the shower. She looked down and saw it was her friend Tori Cardenas. She picked up, because she knew all her friends were worried about her after the fiasco of yesterday. "Hey, I'm getting in the shower—"

"How are you doing, sweetie?"

Sudden tears filled Piper's eyes at the sound of a friendly voice. "I got fired by two brides today."

"Crap. Don't let them get to you. You did the right thing yesterday."

"I know." Piper took a breath. Yesterday's wedding had been the biggest one of the year for the tiny firm she worked for, and she was the one who was being blamed for what had happened. "April Hunsaker has called me three times today. She's trying to fire me. I'm avoiding her, but I don't know how to fix it."

"April? She's here."

"Here? Where?"

"I'm meeting Maddie and Keira at the French Quarter Bar and Grill," Tori said. "April's here with her friends. You want me to kneecap her? I'll do it for you, but you need to promise to come visit me in prison."

Piper laughed through the tears. "You deserve better than prison."

"I know, but saving my bestie might be worth it. Might be. I can't promise."

"I appreciate that you're even considering it."

"Always, babe. Seriously, though. You want me to talk to her?"

"What would you say?"

Tori paused. "That you're freaking amazing, and she's lucky to have you at her back. You think that would work?"

Piper smiled. "You're not fancy enough to convince her. Maddie's fiancé might be. Is Lucas coming tonight?" Lucas Hart was a cowboy billionaire who'd fallen madly in love with one of their squad, Maddie Vale. He was a celebrity, but he was one of the nicest, most loyal humans Piper had ever met. The whole Hart family was, actually. She was glad Maddie had found a place with them.

"Lucas is in Oregon at the Hart Ranch," Tori said. "He left earlier today. Those private jets are so damned handy. I want one."

Piper laughed again, her heart lightening the longer she spoke to Tori. "Me, too. Let's steal one."

"Great. I'll meet you at the airport in twenty."

"Perfect." The idea of heading off in a private jet made Piper smile. It was the kind of banter her mom would have loved. Her mom also would have told her to stop running away from April and find a way to fix it. "Look, I'm going to take a quick shower and then head over there. If April starts to leave, maybe stall her?"

"I'm on it. I'll throw myself on the ground in front of her and block her exit."

Piper grinned. "Subtlety is overrated."

"Right? Oh, I see Maddie and Keira. We'll keep April here until you arrive. It should be fine. They haven't even ordered their dinner yet. You're amazing. You'll figure out the right thing to say. I have faith."

Piper sighed. "Thanks."

"See you soon." Tori hung up, and Piper's energy faded almost right away.

The weight of the last few days and last year settled back on her, pressing down relentlessly.

She leaned on the sink and stared at herself in the mirror. Around her neck was the necklace her mom had given her on her sixteenth birthday, just before she died. It was a tiny little diamond, barely even visible, but it had been her mom's only treasure in a life that had been a grueling disappointment.

Piper touched the necklace and took a breath. "Come on, Piper. You can fix this."

But the woman staring back at her didn't have any answers.

Yet.
She'd find them.
She had to.
She hadn't come this far only to fail now.

THREE

"Let's go, Angel," Piper said, as she gathered her toiletries a short time later, hurrying as fast as she could. Any other time, she'd have basked in the chance to indulge in the gorgeous shower and beautiful bathroom, but not today. "I have a date with a woman who believes I'm literally a curse on happiness. Don't want to miss out on that fun time."

Angel wagged her tail happily, making Piper grin. "I have joy envy, Angel. I think I need to come back as a dog."

With Angel at her heels, Piper jogged down the stairs, her hair wet, her feet bare, her toiletries in her arms, still trying to figure out how she was going to handle April.

Still not coming up with an approach she felt would work.

Come on, Piper. You can do this—

She ran around the corner, then screamed when Kitty stepped out in front of her. Angel yelped and jumped back beside her.

"Piper!" Declan's mom caught her arm as Piper stumbled backward. "Sorry! I didn't mean to scare you."

"No, it's fine." Piper took a breath. "Good to see you, Kitty." She instinctively reached down to pat Angel and make sure the dog wasn't scared. "It's okay, sweetie."

Kitty, as always, was dressed to stylish perfection. Her dark hair was short and fashionable, her white pants and high heels flawless, and her white leather jacket was fashion victory. Her artistically styled brows arched as she took in Piper's wet hair and bare feet. "You're sleeping with my son? When did that start? Why didn't I know about that?"

"Sleeping with Declan?" Embarrassment flooded Piper. "Oh, heavens no. I just used his shower. He's destroying mine."

"Is he?" Kitty's eyes sparkled with interest. "His dog loves you. She doesn't trust anyone. You must be around a lot for Angel to trust you."

"What? No. We just bonded tonight." Piper suddenly realized that, given Kitty's attire, she might travel in the same circles as the clientele Piper catered to as a wedding planner. There was a chance Kitty would link Piper to the rumors about the wedding planner with the same name, and Piper didn't want to deal with that. "I have to go. Declan gave me a time limit."

Kitty rolled her eyes. "And you're listening to it? That boy needs a woman to push back, not let him have his way."

"I'm not his woman. I'm his tenant. He tore apart my bathroom without warning, and I needed a shower."

Kitty narrowed her eyes, then sighed. "Dammit. Of course Declan's not sleeping with you. That wouldn't make any sense. A mom just doesn't like to give up, though."

Piper paused. "Why wouldn't it make any sense?"

Kitty shot her a look of surprise. "You don't know?"

Interest piqued through her. "Know what?"

Kitty sighed. "Oh, Piper, the man does like to keep a secret, doesn't he? And he thinks that makes it all go away? It doesn't, you know. It keeps eating away at you until you die from the inside out."

Piper blinked, startled by the sudden, dire turn of the conversation. "What?"

Kitty put her designer handbag on the counter, turned to face Piper, and folded her arms. "I want to hire you."

"For a wedding? You know someone getting married?" Piper

wanted to be excited, but she knew that unless she fixed things with April, whoever it was Kitty had in mind wouldn't hire Piper for any price.

She wasn't even sure fixing things with April would be enough, but without April, she had zero chance when her boss returned from her extended family emergency in the morning and walked into the crisis.

"A wedding?" Kitty looked confused. "Why would I hire you for a wedding?"

"I'm a wedding planner."

"Really? I didn't know that. But that's irrelevant." Kitty waved her hand dismissively. "I don't know anyone getting married. I want to hire you to date my son."

"What?" Piper stared at her.

"Date Declan for a month, then break up. What do you say?"

Piper started laughing. "Kitty, there's no chance. There's zero spark between us—"

"Create one. You're beautiful, vibrant, sassy. Yes, you're not his type, but you're good enough. I'm sure you can become what he needs. How much for a month?"

Not his type? What was his type? Not that it mattered. "Sorry, Kitty. I'm not dating him for money." For a thousand reasons, including the fact that she was done with dating anyone, even fake dating. Plus, dating for money made her an escort, and that…wow…just wow. "No."

"Ten thousand dollars. Would that do it?"

Piper stared at Kitty. "You want to pay me *ten thousand dollars* to date Declan for a month?"

Kitty nodded. "Plus expenses, of course. I know it'll be work to bring him around, so that includes a hardship fee—"

"No. God, no." She'd had a lot of strange conversations around romance during her years as a wedding planner, but this might be the weirdest. "I can't help you, Kitty."

"Twenty thousand dollars?"

This conversation was *staggering*.

"It's not about the money." Piper couldn't imagine toying with anyone's emotions like that. She could never do that, no matter how desperate she was. But she was kind of stunned Kitty lived in a world where she believed money could buy anything, including her son's dating life. Yes, all her clients traveled in those circles, but to experience that in her personal life was a little insane.

Especially because Declan walked around in jeans and t-shirts, most of them paint-splattered. He didn't act or look like money. And yet, his mom was offering twenty grand like it was nothing. Maybe Kitty was insane. Offering money she didn't have. Or maybe Declan was more complicated than Piper knew. Either way, she wasn't getting involved. "Look, Kitty, I need to go. It was great seeing you."

She gave Angel a quick pat, then hurried out the door over Kitty's protests.

Piper jogged across the beautiful grass, barely taking time to notice how soft it was under her feet, then ran down the cute stone stairs that led to the pathway to her house—

"Watch out!" Declan grabbed her arms, catching her a split second before she crashed into him.

Shock ran through Piper at the feel of his hands on her arms, and she jumped backward. Dammit. His grip felt nice, and that wasn't acceptable. What was wrong with her brain? "Sorry."

Declan was sweaty and dirty, and his t-shirt did little to hide his muscles. She stared at him, suddenly imagining what it would be like to date him. What it would take to get him to look at her like she was a woman and not simply a responsibility, like his yard or his truck? It would probably take a lot. A miracle even. The man didn't seem to have a romantic bone in his well-sculpted body.

He cocked an eyebrow. "What? Why are you looking at me like that?"

Oh, heavens. She cleared her throat. "Nothing. Your mom's

inside." Nothing like a guy's mom to wipe out any romantic moods, right?

He swore under his breath and looked past her toward his house. "What's her mood?"

Um… "Fine, I guess." There was no way she was going to get in the middle of his relationship with his mother.

He narrowed his eyes. "Was she rude to you?"

Other than treating her as an escort for hire? "Oh, no. Not at all."

"Then what happened?"

"Nothing." She could see from Declan's face that he was going to march in there and ask his mom what she'd said to Piper. Crap. He was in a grumpy mood, and she had a feeling that if he found out his mom had tried to pay Piper twenty grand to date him, it wouldn't go over well. She had to give him something else to focus on. "It was just a little awkward."

"What was awkward?"

Persistent much? Yeesh. "When I came downstairs and she realized I'd just gotten out of the shower, she thought that…" She paused, grimacing. She and Declan had *never* even hinted at anything romantic between them, and it felt weird to bring it up.

Understanding flooded his face. "She thought you and I were involved romantically?"

"Yes!" Yay for men who could pick up on subtleties. Well done, Declan.

He sighed. "Sorry about that. She's on a mission to get me to date someone. Anyone."

"Is she?" Piper asked brightly. "I had no idea. But it was fine. Just a moment of awkwardness, but it's all cleared up." She paused. "She was embarrassed by the mistake, so don't say anything to her. We worked it out. We're good."

Declan stared at her. "You're a terrible liar."

"I'm not lying." She tried to duck around him, but he stepped sideways to block her.

"You're my tenant," he said, "which makes you my responsibility. What did my mom say to you? Because clearly, it wasn't okay."

See? She was just like his car. A responsibility. Which was great, because he was just an annoying man who ruined her shower and took her money. Exactly as they both wanted it. "I feel like it's not something I should get involved in."

He didn't say anything. He simply waited.

She didn't have time to wear him down, even though she definitely could. She had a bride to reclaim. So, she gave up trying to spare his gentlemanly sensibilities and told him. "Fine. Your mom offered me money to date you for a month and then break up with you."

Declan got a pained look on his face, but didn't seem surprised. "How much did she offer you?"

"Her last offer was twenty thousand dollars, but I got the vibe I could have gotten more."

"Twenty grand?" He swore again and strode a few feet away, his hands clasped on his head. "Did you say yes?"

"God, no. You're my grumpy landlord." Had she been tempted? No. Had she started thinking of him in a way that she never wanted to again? Unequivocally yes. "Dating you would be like dating a plant."

His brows shot up. "A plant?"

"Yeah, like a rose bush. Really pretty to look at, but armed with thorns or hired bee assassins."

He put his hands on his hips. "You wouldn't date a plant for twenty grand?"

"No. I don't need the money that badly." She paused. "Actually, I'd probably date a plant for that much," she admitted. "I mean, how bad could it be?"

Declan grinned. "So, you'd date a plant, but not me?"

"That's correct. Yes. I am not interested in dating humans at this time, especially not ones where there is no romantic spark whatsoever. If we ever kissed, it would probably be like kissing a jellyfish, and who wants that?" It would definitely not be like

21

kissing a jellyfish, but she was going to set her boundaries nicely and give them lots of love.

"A jellyfish?" he echoed. "I'm very offended. I'm a great kisser."

Something flickered inside her at all the kissing talk. "I'm sure you're a great kisser. It's not your skill. It's the lack of chemistry between us. No amount of skill can overcome a complete lack of romantic attraction." Right? Of course, right.

He raised his brows. "Most women tell me I'm a good-looking guy."

Piper started laughing. "Oh, God, now you're just being annoying. You know what I meant! I'm sure you'd experience the jellyfish vibe if we kissed, and I'm also a great kisser. It is what it is. Can you deny it?"

He studied her. "I like how you smell."

She blinked. "What?"

"You smell like flowers. I like it. So maybe it wouldn't be like two jellyfish making out."

Again, a little flip of her belly. "It would definitely be jellyfish, and let's leave it at that. I don't want to date anyone, and I don't need you trying to mess with my mind." She gave him a little wave and ducked around him. "Bye."

She didn't turn around as she scooted back to her house, but she felt him watching her, all the way until she closed the door behind her.

The moment it was shut, she leaned back against it, closed her eyes, and let out her breath. After two years of jellyfish vibes, she was now thinking of Declan in a way she didn't want to deal with. Like a dateable, yummy dessert.

Damn Kitty and Declan. And her friends.

Between the lot of them, Piper suddenly couldn't stop thinking of what it would be like to kiss Declan…and it wouldn't be jellyfish. It would be hot, dangerous, and consuming.

Oy.

The last thing Piper needed was to think of him as a man. She was going to have to stop it immediately. Her life was just too complicated for dating, let alone dating the guy who held her home hostage in his callused, landlordy hands.

She needed to get the image of Declan's shirtless perfection out of her head before she found herself tempted to accept his mom's offer.

Before the offer, Declan had been no more than a grumpy landlord, but his mom's proposal had changed the vibe to visions of sweaty biceps and shared showers, and Piper didn't appreciate it one bit.

FOUR

J ellyfish.

Piper had actually said kissing him would be like kissing a jellyfish.

And dating him would be like dating a plant.

And Declan could tell she'd meant it.

It was pretty priceless, and he was glad for it.

It would have seriously messed with him if Piper had accepted his mom's offer and she'd started making moves on him—

Declan paused, his hand on the doorknob to the French doors. He could see his mom in the kitchen. She was on the phone, talking animatedly, and waving her hands with excitement.

He dropped his hand, watching her, his gut sinking.

Was his mom proposing her twenty-grand-dating-idea to someone else? Definitely. Now that she'd thought of it, his mother wouldn't stop until she found someone to accept the project. His mom was a savvy businesswoman who knew how to negotiate.

She'd find a way to get what she wanted.

He swore. How many women would turn it down the way Piper had?

He didn't want to deal with that. With a woman. With dating. With complications. With feeling anything for anyone ever again.

He could go in there and tell his mother to back off. She might agree, but he'd never know if she'd gone ahead with it anyway. He'd be second-guessing every woman who tried to talk to him, even Piper. How much would his mom raise the price to try to win Piper over? Everything was for sale at some price, and twenty thousand dollars was nothing to his mother.

Shit.

Declan stepped back, sinking into the shadows as he pulled out his phone. He called his brother, who answered on the first ring. "Declan," Eric said. "Everything okay? You all right?"

"I'm fine." He was tired of his family worrying about him. "Mom just offered my tenant twenty thousand dollars to date me and then dump me."

Eric let out a low whistle. "Damn, bro. She's been talking about that, but I thought I'd convinced her not to do it."

Declan paced across the grass beside the pool, flexing his stiffening knee. "Piper said no. What's your take on Mom? Is she going to keep going until she finds someone else to do it?"

Eric was quiet for a moment, then sighed. "Yeah, honestly, I believe she will. She's worried about you, Declan. We both are. You have to start living again, or you're going to start dying."

"I don't need to date anyone to be alive."

"No, but you're not okay. We see it. And honestly, I think Mom's not wrong. We've been waiting for you to pull yourself together on your own, but all you do is work on that damned house and pour drinks at your buddy's bar."

Declan swore. "I'm fine, Eric." Now was the moment to tell Eric that he had an interview to get back on the force, but he wasn't ready to say it. Besides, he was pretty certain his mom and Eric would consider a return to police work to be a bad move, not a good one.

"No. You're not fine. Stop lying to yourself, Declan. You'll never move forward unless you face the truth. And it's time."

Declan took a breath and stared up at the sky. Even if he told

Eric about the interview, it wasn't worth it. Eric would tell Kitty, and that would unleash holy hell.

Eric sighed. "How about we go hit some golf balls this weekend?"

And listen to more shit about how he needed to start dating? How he needed to forget? How he should find some fulfilling job to light up his soul? "No, thanks. I'm busy. I'll talk to you later." He paused. "But thanks for caring."

"Always, bro. *Always.* I'm here if you need me. Whatever you need."

"I know. Thanks."

Declan hung up the phone and pressed it to his forehead, thinking. Tension radiated through him, and he knew he couldn't go into his house. He couldn't sit there and listen to his mom's litany of worries about him.

He needed space to breathe, and his mom and Eric were giving him less, not more.

He could go for a run. Run hard. Run fast. Run until his muscles hurt so much that he couldn't remember what he'd been trying to forget. Except his knee wasn't up to that yet, even though he was pretending it was. Even though he needed it to be.

A light came on in the carriage house, drawing his attention to it. As he watched, Piper hurried out onto her patio to grab something off the table. She was still barefoot, but now she was wearing loose white pants and a black tank top that made her look sexy, adorable, and badass, all at the same time. Her hair was down, drying in loose waves around her shoulders.

He was surprised his mom had chosen to target Piper. She was nothing like the vision his mother had for who he should be with. And honestly, he was intrigued that Piper had said no. He respected that about her. A lot.

Declan narrowed his eyes as he studied her, as an idea came to his mind. A ridiculous, crazy idea that just might work.

Piper had just stepped back inside her kitchen when she heard Declan call her name.

Her heart leapt as he strode around the corner of the carriage house and onto her patio, looking much too sexy for anyone's good. "Hi." She ambled back onto the patio. "What's up?"

He strode right up. "I have a proposal."

He looked very intense and serious, which made her step back, away from that energy. "Okay," she said cautiously. "What's going on?"

"I want you to accept my mom's offer."

She blinked, staring at him. "What? Why?"

"Because she'll keep going until she finds someone who will say yes. And then I'll be stuck dealing with some woman trying to seduce me and earn her twenty thousand dollars. I don't want to manage that situation."

Piper had a sudden vision of some random, hired woman sitting in Declan's kitchen, laughing and flirting with him, and that vision didn't feel good. But... "I can't take twenty thousand dollars to date you. That makes me an escort."

He shook his head. "No, we won't really date. We'll just fake it for my mom. You'll get your money, and I won't have to deal with whatever scheme she concocts."

Piper sighed. "Look, Declan. I don't know what's going on with you and your mom, but I'm not lying to her and taking her money. It's just not right. Plus, I can't date you for money."

"Why not?"

She raised her brows. "Aside from the multitude of moral implications, what if it got out? My reputation is destroyed right now, and if people found out that I took twenty thousand dollars to fake-date you, my career would be over, even if it is with your consent. I'm not giving up on getting my career back, which means I'm not going to take a chance like that. What if your mom told someone? People talk, and I'm not having that said about me. I can't afford it."

He narrowed his eyes. "What happened to your reputation?"

Crap. She hadn't meant to let that slip out. "It's complicated," she said evasively.

"Let me guess," he said, watching her. "You were one of the top wedding planners for the rich sect. You did something that destroyed your reputation, so no one will hire you. You got fired. And can't get another job. Right?"

She bit her lip. "Basically." That made her sound like she'd embezzled funds or something, but the effect was the same.

"So, what you need is a rebuild of your reputation." He grinned. "Dating me would fix that."

Piper cocked her head. "You're a grubby landlord. Hot, but grubby. And you seem to be unemployed. No offense, but that doesn't really help me."

"A *hot* plant?" He looked amused. "My stock is rising."

"Not high enough to help me."

"Actually my stock is plenty high. My mom was a huge pop star in her twenties and thirties. We're rich. Celebrity rich. I'm part of that circle. I can get in at any club or any event I want."

Piper digested that little tidbit. "So, your mom really has twenty-grand to pay a woman to date you?"

He nodded. "It's pocket change for her. Look, you and I don't even need to date. Just tell her that you'll do it and take the money."

"No. I won't date you, or anyone, for money. I need my career fixed, not some extra cash in my bank account. I'm a long-term visionary, not a short-term dopamine addict, so, no thanks." She'd seen how the latter had ruined her family, and there was no chance she'd ever go there. She turned to head back into the kitchen. "I have twelve hours left to fix my reputation, and I need to focus."

Her deliciously hot and apparently insanely wealthy grump of a landlord followed her into the house, not bothering to wait for an invite. "I can help with your reputation. My mom can, as well. The Jones name is powerful around here."

Piper grabbed her coffee mug from the center island in the

kitchen. "Not if I'm dating you for money! That's not going to work—" She paused suddenly, as an idea came to her.

His eyebrows shot up. "What's that look for?"

"What if—" She cut herself off. "No. Never mind."

"What if, what?" He leaned on her kitchen counter, watching her intently. "What are you thinking?"

He was too close.

She pushed back from the island to give herself space from his intensity. "Did you mean it? That your family's reputation carries weight in the elite circles?" The elite circles Piper traveled in were small, but somehow Piper hadn't paid attention to Kitty Jones. Maybe because she focused on brides and their mothers, and Kitty was outside that life phase.

"Absolutely."

Piper chewed her lip. "What if I didn't take your mom's money? What if we just made a deal between us where we fake date? No one knows but us. Your mom already thought we were sleeping together, so that wouldn't be a stretch to convince her of that."

His gaze narrowed with suspicion. "If you're not doing it for money, then what do you get out of it?"

"A fake fiancé who adores me." She thought of April, and hope flittered faintly through her. Would Declan be enough to convince April that her wedding planner had created a happily ever after for herself? "You come to some events with me, look rich, gorgeous, and completely smitten with me."

He stepped back, his body suddenly tense. "*A fiancé?* You're serious?"

"Yes. A very public fiancé." The idea of being engaged again made Piper tense, but she reminded herself it would be fake. Not real. Not trapped.

"For how long?"

She shrugged. "Hopefully not long, but you'd have to stay flexible about it. You and I can show up at a couple of events. I get my reputation stabilized, hopefully, and you get your mom off your back."

Declan drummed his fingers on the counter. His body was coiled tightly, a reflection of the tension ramping up inside her. "You want me to go to events? Like fancy dinners and shit like that?"

"Yes."

He swore. "I've avoided those for years. I hate them."

Relief rushed through her. "Okay, then. Fine. That's fine. No worries." She waved him off, and shook out her shoulders, trying to relax them. "Probably for the best. Fake engagements can get complicated, right? Good luck with your mom." She turned and hurried toward the living room before he could respond.

The minute she was out of his sight, she stopped and braced her hands on the back of the couch. What the heck had she just proposed? The idea of being engaged made her whole body go into flight mode. Her heart was racing, and she felt panic clogging her throat.

She'd find another way—

Her phone rang, and she looked down. It was April again. *Shit.* She put the phone into voicemail and pressed her palms to her forehead. If April was still at the French Quarter, then she'd just tried to call Piper in front of her friends. It was great to know that April was crowd-sourcing her firing of Piper.

"Piper."

She whirled around to see Declan in the doorway, his shoulder propped against the frame. "What?"

"I'll do it."

She stared at him in surprise. "Really?"

"Yeah. I can't deal with my mom sending women after me. This deal with you gets me freedom without me having to actually date anyone."

Her heart started racing. Fear? Hope? Maybe some of both. "You're serious."

"I am. We both get something out of it. What do you think?"

She took a shaky breath. "Honestly, I have some issues when it comes to getting engaged. Dating. Anything that ties me down. People."

He grinned. "I do, too. Makes us a perfect match."

"I guess." She studied him, his strong jaw, his blue eyes, his muscled shoulders. He was such a compelling man. So attractive. He could have almost any woman he wanted, and yet, he was so unwilling to date that he wanted to get fake engaged to avoid it. "You might be more averse to dating than I am," she mused.

"Maybe," he said. "So, here's the deal. You need to rebuild your reputation, so I'll agree to playing the role of your fiancé in whatever way you need to achieve that. I need to get my mom off my back, so you agree to help me with that. Three weeks, and then we break up, in a way that's mutually beneficial to both of our goals. What do you say?"

"Why three weeks?"

He took a breath. "I'm probably going back to work at that time. I won't have time to go off and do parties."

Three weeks to rehab her reputation? She could handle being fake engaged for a few weeks, and then she'd be free again. "This is insane."

"But brilliant."

She couldn't help but grin. "It kind of is," she admitted. God, what if it worked? The first glimpse of hope she'd had in a long time glimmered in her heart. "It might work," she said softly.

"It will work," he said. "We'll make sure of it." He held out his hand. "Deal?"

Was she really doing this? She wanted to, she realized. She'd fought so hard to get where she was, and if she didn't take this deal, she'd lose everything she'd spent her life working toward, everything she'd done to make her mom's dreams come true. "Dating in name only. No actual emotional attachments. At any time, one of us can pull the plug, and it's over."

He nodded. "Deal. We both have a fast-exit option."

"And a gag order. No telling anyone. Ever."

"Absolutely."

They stared at each other, and then suddenly she let her breath out. "Okay. Let's do it." She stuck out her hand. "Deal."

He shook it, his larger, strong hand wrapping around hers like a great warmth. "Deal."

She let out her breath, excitement dancing inside her. "So, what's the first step?"

Wickedness flickered in his eyes. "We get caught in bed by my mom."

FIVE

Declan almost laughed at the look of alarm on Piper's face.

"What?" she asked. "Why? We can't just tell her?"

Declan hadn't felt this good in a long time. He felt so free, like he was taking control back from the life that had been wrenched away from him so brutally. "You already told my mom we weren't romantic, so for this to sound real and not just a knee-jerk defensive move after her offer, we need to get caught. Make it seem like we didn't plan to tell her."

Piper leaned against the back of the couch, bracing her hands. "I get that," she said slowly. "What do you propose?"

"She knows I'm at your place right now, working on your bathroom, right?"

Piper nodded.

"So, she's only going to wait so long until she decides to march over here and find me."

Her eyes widened. "Tonight? You want to get caught in bed *now?*"

"We only have three weeks. We need to get started." His mind was whirring as he strategized. "She wouldn't walk into your house if the door is closed, so we'll leave the front door open just enough that she invites herself in. And your bedroom door will have to be open as well, because she'll have to walk past it to get to the bathroom."

Piper took a breath. "Wow. Just wow. We haven't even kissed yet, and you want to get me in your bed."

He grinned at her sass. Her attitude was perfect. "No. I want to be in your bed." He stood up. "Let's do it. She won't wait much longer."

Piper let out a little groan. "I'm feeling very awkward about getting into bed with you."

"Pretend I'm a plant."

She laughed, a soft chuckle that made him smile. "A flowering cactus," she said as she stood up. "That sums you up."

"I'm not that bad."

She glanced at the clock on her wall. "I only have a few minutes. I need to get going."

"My mom won't wait long, trust me." Was he really agreeing to this insanity? Yes, he was. Apparently, he was officially desperate.

"Okay, then. I'll get the door." She jogged across the living room, as if she also felt the sudden tension between them.

"Great." He walked into the living room, suddenly noticing the gentle sway of her hips. The loose pants didn't hide the way she moved, sexy and natural, like she was a cat, lithe and agile.

Damn.

He'd never thought of Piper's walk before. He needed to stay focused. This would never work if he actually let himself be attracted to her. *Jellyfish. Jellyfish. Jellyfish.*

She opened the door and peered out, then jumped back. "She's on her way here!"

Adrenaline rushed through Declan, but he didn't move. He wouldn't push Piper, no matter how much he wanted to make this work. "Ready?"

She met his gaze, and he saw trust in those brown eyes. Real trust, which made him pull his shoulders back. He wouldn't let her down. "I'm ready," she said, her voice firm and committed.

He grinned. "Then lead the way."

They both heard the crunch of his mom's high heels on the walk outside. Piper burst out laughing, and then took off in a sprint up the stairs. Declan hustled after her, trying not to limp.

They ran into her bedroom, and Piper pointed to him. "Shirt and jeans off," she said. "Toss them on the floor by the door."

"Yes, ma'am." He turned his back on her while he ripped off his clothes. Downstairs, he heard his mom shout their names.

"Ready!" Piper whispered.

He turned and saw she was under the covers. The sheet was up to her armpits, but her shoulders were bare. Sudden awareness coiled in his gut. How naked was she beneath those blankets?

His mom called for them again, and then he heard her start to climb the stairs.

Piper flipped the comforter back, leaving the sheet across her body. He strode across the room. The moment he landed in the bed, Piper whipped the comforter over him. He rolled on top of her, leaving the sheet between them.

The heat from her body was intoxicating, and he had to steel himself from the feel of her body under his. It had been a long time since he'd been in bed with a woman, and his body responded fast and hot.

Piper wrapped her arms around his neck. "Kiss me like you can't live without me," she whispered.

"No jellyfish," he said.

She rolled her eyes. "Please, no jellyfish."

It felt like ages since Declan had kissed a woman. He knew this moment was for show only, but the feel of Piper's body beneath him made it very difficult to remember that. He had a sudden memory of the last woman he'd kissed, and a sudden chill consumed him. He swore. He couldn't do this. "Piper—"

She pulled him down and kissed him.

The moment her lips touched his, the cold vanished. Heat flooded Declan, awakening desire he hadn't allowed himself to feel in years. He growled low in his throat and angled his head, taking over the kiss. Piper locked her feet behind his lower back, drawing him against her pelvis. His cock got hard, but there was no time to think about baseball.

He tunneled his fingers though her hair and kissed her fiercely, basking in the feel of her lips against his. Warm. Soft. Inviting. Completely trusting him even though he was pretty sure the only thing she was wearing was her underwear. He could feel her breasts against his chest, and the thin sheet did little to mute the sensation.

Declan slid his arm around her shoulders, drawing her into the protection of his body even as he deepened the kiss. Their tongues brushed against each other, and he went with it. The kiss turned to fire, pouring through them both.

Piper let out a little noise of desire that went right to his gut, and he slid his left hand down her side to her hip, cradling her against him—

"Declan! Piper! What are you doing?"

They both froze, and it took Declan several seconds to pull his focus off the kiss and remember why they'd done it. He swore audibly and rolled off Piper, pulling the comforter up to her chin, but Piper yanked it right over her head, shrieking with muffled laughter.

"Mom! Don't you knock?" He tried to hit the right note of embarrassed, annoyed, and protective.

His mom was standing in the doorway, her mouth open in stunned shock. The look on her face was comical, and he had to bite his lower lip to keep from laughing. He could feel Piper shaking against him as she tried not to laugh, and her muffled giggles made it even harder to keep a straight face.

"Piper!" Kitty squawked in outrage. "You specifically said you were not sleeping with my son! I know you're under there!"

Piper stuck her hand out from under the comforter and fluttered her fingers. "Hi, Kitty! So good to see you again."

The absurdity of seeing Piper's hand waving like a surrenderer flag above her head when the rest of her was buried under the blankets was hilarious. "Mom! Privacy, please." Declan fought not to laugh, but it wasn't easy. Piper was cracking him up.

"I'm glad you guys think this is funny," his mom said. "I will be forever scarred. No mother needs to walk in on this."

Declan grinned. "Well, maybe next time knock. Just a thought."

"I would have knocked if I had any inclination this could be happening! But Piper lied to my face, and I believed her." She paused. "Well done, Piper. I had no idea."

"Thanks, Kitty," Piper poked her head out from under the covers. "You know, I've always strived to be a good liar. I appreciate the acknowledgment of my skills."

Kitty rolled her eyes in exasperation, her hands on her hips. "Are you guys coming out of there soon? I have questions. So many questions."

Of course she did. "The door, Mom."

"Trust me, I'm closing this door. See you downstairs. I'll give you five minutes." She pointed at both of them. "Three minutes. Got it?"

They both nodded.

"All right, then." Kitty finally backed out of the room and pulled the door shut.

Piper flopped the covers down and burst out laughing. "Oh, God. Her face! That was so funny—"

"I can hear you," Kitty yelled through the door. "I can never unsee that, so thank you very much for that."

Piper grinned. "You're welcome! Glad to be of service!"

"Go pour some wine, Mom," Declan called out. "We'll be down in a minute."

"Champagne. We need some champagne. Or tequila. I'll find some." Kitty's heels clicked down the hall.

Declan fell back against the pillow, his arms over his head. *Holy shit.* "Wow," he said. "That was actually incredibly awkward." He decided to blithely ignore how intense the kiss had gotten.

"It was hilarious." Piper propped herself up on her elbows. Her face was glowing, and she looked so amused. "I've never seen your mom speechless before. That was at least two, maybe three seconds of silence there. I feel so powerful."

Piper's hair was tousled, and her lips were pure temptation. Being propped up on her elbows had made the sheet slip down, revealing the swell of her breasts. Declan could see the outline of her nipples peeking out, and need surged through him. He immediately dropped his forearm over his eyes to block his view of her. "My mom's not going to leave until we go down there and answer all her questions about our romantic life."

"Right. I know. We need to go quick though, okay?"

"Sure." He was curious why she was in a hurry, but making a Kitty Interrogation short worked for him.

The bed moved as Piper got out. "Wasn't that great? We totally did it."

"We did," he agreed. "It was brilliant."

He could hear her getting her clothes on. "We're a great team," she said. "This just might work. Honestly, I wasn't sure if I could handle kissing you, but it was fine."

Fine? *Fine.* He grinned. It had been so much more than that. "No jellyfish?"

"Just a little, but I can steel myself to endure it. I'm ready. You can open your eyes."

He moved his arm, and he saw she'd put on a short black skirt, pale blue tank top with lace, and sandals that made her legs look sexy as hell.

He liked it. A lot.

Wow. Just...wow. Why had he never noticed how damned adorable she was? And why was he noticing now? Being attracted to her was not part of their deal, and he needed to stop that shit immediately.

He swung his legs over the edge of the bed and grabbed his jeans. He swore as he thought about going downstairs and facing the inquisition. "She'll be relentless."

"I know." Piper paced the room. "We don't have a story yet, so we'll answer questions one at a time and just make it up as we go along. We'll try to remember all the details. Cool?"

He pulled his shirt on. "Piper. We need to talk about something." Shit. Shit. *Shit.*

She paused to look at him, apparently hearing the edge to his voice that he'd tried to neutralize. "What's wrong?"

He sat on the edge of the bed, braced his forearms on his thighs, and took a breath. "My mom's going to assume you know about my past."

Piper turned to face him. "She did mention something earlier when she was trying to bribe me to date you."

He swore. "Yeah, if I don't tell you, she'll make sure you know. I want you to hear it from me." Fuck. He didn't want to do this. But he had to do it. He needed to control the narrative. To control his emotions. To prepare Piper.

Piper walked over and sat on the carpet in front of him. She folded her knees and wrapped her arms around them. "Okay."

She was so calm. So non-demanding. So practical. It took some of his tension away. He let out his breath. "I was married."

Her eyes widened slightly. "Really?"

"Yeah. She died a while ago." Piper's mouth dropped open, so he kept talking, not wanting to give her a chance to ask questions, to interrupt, to put emotions into his story. "That's why my mom wants me to date. She's worried about me. I'm fine. I just don't want to date anyone." He wasn't fine, but it was his problem to deal with, not his mom's.

Piper nodded slowly. "Okay."

He could tell she wanted to ask questions, but he didn't leave space for her. "As you know, I was a cop, but I was kicked off the force due to injury. My family is worried about me. That's why mom is trying to set me up. I'm fine, but they don't believe it." He paused. "That's it."

Piper stared at him. "That's a lot."

"It's not. It's just information for the role you're playing.

Okay?" His palms were sweating, but he forced himself to stay calm as he stood up. "Ready?"

She didn't move. "That's it? Just drop that and then walk away?"

"Yes."

Piper stared up at him, and he tensed, ready for her to protest, to hug him, to cry for him. The minute she did, he was pulling the plug on their deal. He didn't want to get personal. He didn't want to feel anything. That was the whole point of this arrangement.

But to his surprise, Piper stood up. "All right, then. As you wish. Let's go lie to your mom. After we satisfy her, though, we have to go see my client."

And just like that, Declan felt back in balance. Piper had given him the space he needed. He'd faced the worst, bringing up his past, and he'd survived it. "Tonight?"

"Tonight. And you better be convincing as the greatest fiancé that any woman has ever had. *Ever.* Hot. Wealthy. Sexy. And head over heels for me, in a sexy way, not a stalkerish way. Got it?"

"Adorable, not creepy." He couldn't believe Piper had let him simply move on from that bombshell he'd dropped, but he was incredibly grateful. "Got it."

"Great." Piper slanted a glance as she walked past him toward the door, and he felt the weight of emotion in her eyes. Even though she'd given him space, she was looking at him differently.

As everyone always did. "I'm not broken," he said as she reached the door.

"No, I can see that," she said. "Cactuses aren't broken. They're just cactuses."

"I'm not a fucking cactus."

"You are, and that's okay." Piper adjusted the strap on her right sandal, drawing his attention to her pink toenails, which were really freaking cute. "Just so you know, if you ever want to talk about your past, I'll listen. And I won't even make you date anyone."

And just like that, the rest of his tension vanished. "You can't make me date anyone. We're engaged. That would just be weird."

"Not my style, at least." She watched him as she said it.

"Not mine either," he assured her. "I'd never cheat, even in a fake relationship."

"Okay." Visible relief flashed across Piper's face, but she didn't give him time to ask any questions about her visceral response to the cheating question. "Is your mom going to ask us about our favorite sexual positions? Because if she does, I feel like I might have to bow out of the conversation."

Declan burst out laughing. "If she asks us about sex, I'm the one who's going to take off running."

"So she might ask us that?"

"It's my mom. Anything is possible."

"Wow. Okay. I'll just start asking her whether she thinks that I should put up with your grumpiness or try to change you. That'll distract her before she can get to the sex questions."

"I'm not grumpy."

Piper raised her brows.

"Am I?"

"Are you?"

He frowned. He was used to having his family call him on his moods, but he'd discounted them as overprotective. But Piper calling him on it gave it more validity. More truth. Maybe. "No. I'm not grumpy."

"All right then. I'm so glad we cleared that up. See you downstairs, poochikins." She blew him a kiss, then darted out the door and raced down the stairs.

Declan stood there for a moment as he heard Piper call a greeting to his mom.

He'd been prepared for Piper to get touchy-feely when he'd told her about Diana, and he'd steeled himself to be hard. To feel nothing. But she'd sassed him right out of his melancholy and guilt with stunning ease.

He laughed suddenly, a snort of laughter that felt awkward

and uncomfortable. He'd picked the right fiancée to keep him from dwelling on the fact that she was the first woman he'd kissed in a very long time, the first woman he'd *wanted* to kiss, the first woman who knew how to get under his skin in all the right ways.

Okay, yeah, he *had* noticed all those things were happening with Piper, but they weren't suffocating him, because Piper was… well…*Piper.*

He felt alive for the first time in a long time. Three years. Longer, if he factored in the way she made him laugh. Laughter had been a lot longer than three years.

But more importantly, Piper made him feel protective of her. She was sassy, funny, and determined, but the little she'd shared with him had gotten him fired up in a damned hurry.

Piper was a freaking blast of sunshine, and it was bullshit that people were trying to bring her down.

He didn't like it, and he was going to help her.

And it felt good as hell to care, to have a mission, to focus on her, instead of his own shit. She'd gotten him out of his shadows and focused on hers. It had been a long time since he'd felt like being the man his dad had trained him to be, but Piper had ignited something in him that he'd been missing.

This fake fiancée was going to be exactly what he needed.

For the first time in years, he had hope.

Hope that he wouldn't live in darkness forever.

SIX

Kitty was pouring tequila when Piper walked into the kitchen. "You little minx," Kitty said, pointing the neck of the bottle at Piper. "You looked me right in the eye and lied to me. And to think I liked you."

"You still like me, but now you respect me as well." Piper took a breath, trying to focus on the present, instead of the little moment she'd just had with Declan. He'd been married? His wife had died? Holy crap. That explained so much.

His pain had been raw, etched into every word he'd so carefully chosen, into every taut muscle in his body, and she'd had to summon every last bit of self-control to shift her energy into a teasing vibe, instead of trying to open the door he so clearly wanted closed.

She knew if she gave him any sympathy, he would have shut down right then and there. Maybe ended their deal. So she'd fought to be light-hearted. It had worked, but wow. She could feel the weight of his past in her own heart.

"Hellooooo, Piper." Kitty waved the bottle in front of her. "Earth to Piper."

Piper took a breath and then forced a smile at Kitty. "Right. Sorry. I was trying to decide how best to play this. Would you believe we weren't involved until five minutes ago, and I wasn't actually lying to you at the house?"

Kitty barked with laughter. "More lies. I detest lies." She set the tequila bottle down and held out a glass to Piper. "Drink up, my devious little wench. I'm going to grill you like you've never been grilled."

"Right. Okay." Piper took the glass as Declan walked into the room. They met gazes, and she flashed him a light smile. Nothing heavy. Just following the tone he'd set when he'd told her about his past.

Declan gave her an adoring smile that was absolutely heart-melting. Tender. Warm. As if she was the only thing in his world that mattered. *Holy cow.* He could melt her defenses in a heartbeat if he chose to. What the heck?

He walked right over to her, put his arm around her shoulders and pulled her against his side. He kissed her cheek, clearly staking his claim to her, then turned to his mom. "It was my idea," he said. "I wanted to keep our relationship a secret."

"Why on earth would you keep it a secret?" Kitty asked. "I can't even express how happy this makes me, even if the woman you've chosen is a liar." She winked at Piper when she said it, though, so it was all good.

"Because it's about me and Piper," Declan said. "Not you or Eric. It happened gradually and naturally, without any external pressure. I needed that. I needed the privacy."

Hurt flickered across Kitty's face. "You think we would have messed it up? Is that what you think of us? All we want is for you to be happy."

"I know, Mom," Declan said. "I just didn't know how it would play out with Piper. We needed space to experience it. Just us." He tightened his arm around Piper again. "Plus," he said, "I didn't want you to scare Piper off. She's a fragile little thing."

Piper and Kitty stared at each other, then they both burst out laughing. And just like that, the tension was broken.

"Piper is no fragile little thing," Kitty said with a snort. "If she was, there's no way she'd be able to put up with you. Am I right, Piper?"

"He's not so bad," Piper teased. "He's much less cranky than he used to be."

"Maybe because he's in love, eh?" Kitty asked, her eyes glittering.

Tension flickered through Piper. Love? They hadn't discussed love. Yes, of course, if they were engaged, then they would be in love, but that felt so personal. Love was such a trap.

"I'm less cranky because Piper likes my famous macaroni and cheese, so now I have an excuse to bake it," Declan said, sidestepping the topic.

"Is that so?" Kitty eyed them both speculatively, clearly trying to figure out exactly what their status was, and how serious they were. "So, how long has this been going on? Days? Weeks? Months? The whole two years Piper's been living here?"

"Long enough," Declan said, again staying away from the details.

Awesome. Her fiancé was a great liar. That was a trait every woman needed in a man.

Oh, wait. No, it wasn't. She knew *that* from past experience.

"Long enough to…what?" Kitty asked. "Fall in love? Give me my first grandkid? Dance naked under the full moon?"

Piper's cheeks heated up. "Dance naked?" she asked. "Really?"

Kitty grinned. "Just testing the waters, my dear."

Declan looked at Piper and raised his brows. "Should we tell her?"

Piper's heart started to pound. Tell Kitty they were engaged? Oh, Lordy. That felt like such a door to open. Suddenly, she doubted whether that was such a good idea. "Maybe not—"

"What?" Kitty slammed her palm on the table. "What in the devil's cocktail is happening? Tell me now!"

Declan raised his brows, then he took Piper's hand. "I asked Piper to marry me."

"What? When? What?"

The next few minutes were an interrogation and chaos of epic levels. Piper made up a story about how he'd proposed by taking her to a hilltop at sunrise. Declan said he wanted Piper to pick the ring she wanted, which was why they didn't have one yet. Kitty did *not* approve of the absence of a ring on any level. And there was a lot of outrage that they'd kept it a secret.

But eventually Kitty ran out of steam, and they were able to edge her toward the door. She held up her hands in defeat. "All right. I can take a hint. No more questions tonight, but what's your schedule? Dinner Wednesday night at the country club?"

Declan glanced at Piper and cocked his brow. She knew he was letting her decide. They'd fooled Kitty, which meant the rest of their arrangement had to serve Piper's needs. Her half was a public resurrection of her reputation. A country club dinner would be perfect. "Sure," she said. "That might be fun."

"Great. Seven o'clock. Don't be late." Kitty grabbed the door-knob. "I'll see you both then. I must be off. I have some calls to make!" Kitty giggled herself out the door and fluttered a good-bye at them through the window, before hurrying down the sidewalk, already pulling her phone out of her purse.

Declan dropped his arm from Piper's shoulder. "We have about thirty seconds to stop her. After that, there'll be no going back."

Piper took a breath. "No going back."

"All right then."

They both watched as Kitty dialed the phone, waited, and then started jabbering frantically.

The beast had been unleashed.

They were committed, for better or worse.

SEVEN

Declan waited for regret or guilt as his mom hurried to her car, but he felt none.

He'd lied to her, but all he felt was massive relief. The weight of her expectations and pressure was gone, and it felt incredible. "I feel like I'm free for the first time in a long time," he said.

And alive. He had a mission now, and that was about helping Piper. Protecting her. She was his now, and he wasn't walking away.

Piper grinned. "Awesome. Remember that feeling when I start using you for my own nefarious plans."

He turned toward her. "Whatever you need. I'm in." And then some. He hadn't realized how much his mom's worry about him had been weighing on him, until he'd seen her look at him with joy in her eyes, instead of fear. A gift to his mom. A gift to himself. He owed Piper, and he was going to make damn sure Piper got what she needed from him.

He wasn't going to think about how to handle it when they broke up. For now, he was riding the feel-good wave of lies, deception, and jellyfish kisses.

"I told you, I need a hot, adoring fiancé." Piper cocked her head, studying him thoughtfully. "I'm thinking grungy, regular guy with a really expensive watch so that she knows you have money. But women like the bad boys, and that fits your persona. Maybe jeans and a T-shirt."

"I have a couple watches like that. Plenty of jeans. No problem." He was glad she wanted him to wear jeans. He didn't even own a suit anymore. He could probably find a tie and a jacket for the dinner at the country club, but he wasn't positive.

Piper raised her brows. "You're such an oxymoron. A sweaty carpenter who works magic with his power tools, and yet also, country club wealthy."

"My family's rich. I live on a cop's salary."

"Except when you don't. Like the watches. Like your gorgeous house."

He shrugged. "Both my watches were gifts. I would never buy them. The house was a dump that I bought for nothing. I rehabbed the whole thing myself over the last three years."

Her eyes widened. "You really did that yourself?"

"Every last bit."

"It's breathtaking."

Satisfaction flooded him, and he grinned. "Thanks."

"You seriously have a gift. You could sell your house for a huge profit."

"I don't need money. I just want my house." He didn't want to keep going on this subject. It felt too prickly to him. "What's the plan tonight? The objective? Our target?"

Piper nodded and took his cue to change the subject. "Her name is April Hunsaker. She hired the firm I'm temping for to do her wedding, but I think she's trying to fire me, and the firm." Piper paused, and he could feel her hesitation.

He sat down at her kitchen counter. "Give me the facts. I'm a cop. That's how my brain operates. What happened with your reputation?"

She grimaced. "It's kind of a long story."

"Tell me what I need to know to do my job well tonight." As a cop, he was well-accustomed to focusing on the relevant facts and not wasting brainpower on the details that were just clutter.

"Okay." Piper paced across the kitchen and picked up Kitty's glass to wash it. "Last summer, I was the assistant planner for a wedding for a high-profile couple. His brother was interested in me." She put the glass under the faucet and turned it on. "It's against protocol for a wedding planner to date a client, but he was kind of relentless and we wound up dating."

A flicker of jealousy jabbed Declan's gut. "What happened?"

"It went fast." Piper rushed her words. "We got engaged. My firm agreed to let me keep my job as long as I hired them for the wedding, so I did. Eight hundred guests. He paid for it because I don't have the money for that kind of event. Bride and groom at the altar, mid-ceremony." She grimaced. "And then I left."

He leaned forward, warnings prickling at the back of his neck. "You *left?* As in you walked away right in the middle of your wedding?"

"Yep. In front of everyone, at one of the biggest social events of the season. I actually ran, because I didn't want to give anyone, especially him, a chance to stop me. I ran out the side entrance, grabbed our limo, and took off."

Damn. She was a runaway bride? "That takes guts. I'm impressed." And what the hell had happened to make her walk away in the middle of her wedding? Piper was smart and capable. What could be so bad as to make her walk away? Did he need to hunt this guy down?

She flashed him a grin. "Thanks. It wasn't great PR for the firm or for me, as you can imagine."

He nodded. "What happened after that?"

"I was fired and unemployable. Finally, a few months ago, a woman I knew from there, who had opened her own company, had an extended family emergency in California. She hired me as a temp to cover for her. She's the only one who would touch me, and basically told me not to screw up."

He leaned in. "What happened?"

She sighed. "Over the last few months, five weddings I was in charge of have had issues. Three were couples who got married and are now filing for divorce. Another bride walked out on her wedding last weekend after finding the groom cheating. She said she was inspired by what I'd done at my wedding, and then yesterday…" she sighed. "Five minutes before the ceremony, the bride pulled me aside and said she didn't want to get married. She asked me to tell the groom and cover for her."

Hell. He could imagine the stakes for Piper to make that wedding happen. "You didn't try to talk her out of it?"

"No." She sighed. "What if I talked her out of it, and she regretted it? My mom—" She paused.

Her mom? What about her mom? Piper had more and more secrets, and he wanted to know all of them. "What about your mom?"

"Nothing. But I couldn't ever try to talk anyone into getting married. I said fine, but when I told the groom and his mother, they, well, they were angry. Things spiraled fast, and now I'm the Wedding Killer."

He almost had to laugh at the absurdity of calling Piper the killer of anything. "No shit?"

"I'd never lie about weddings," she said as she put the glass on the counter and turned to face him. "Another bride went on a rant on social media this weekend. She said I was the Wedding Killer, and I'd cursed her wedding. She's the one who discovered that three other couples that I had done weddings for were already divorcing. She said I was bad luck and any bride who wants to actually get married and stay married needs to stay away from me."

He sat back. "Damn."

"Right? She fired me publicly on social media today, then another one called me an hour later to fire me as well. And then, April is our biggest client, and she's left me three messages today. My boss gets back in the morning. If I've lost three clients, I'm sunk. No one will hire me. Brides are superstitious." She leaned on the counter. "I've spent my entire life working toward this, and I'm going to lose it all if I lose April. I'm desperate, Declan. This is my only chance. I—" She cut herself off, and he knew there was more to the story, more that she wasn't willing to share.

He wanted to ask, but she'd respected his privacy, so he owed her the same.

He knew it didn't matter whether the bride could be held liable for her social media posts or not. The damage was done. Trust had been broken. "Your plan, then, is to show April that your wedding not happening was actually a good thing, because you wound up with an even better guy?"

She wrinkled her nose. "I know that sounds silly, but I think it will work. But you have to be so amazing that she falls a little in love with you tonight."

He rubbed his jaw. He was committed to helping her, but romance? "I'm not the most romantic guy," he admitted.

Piper snorted. "That doesn't surprise me, but women love unavailable men. So just be your grumpy self, plus in love with me."

In love with Piper. Those four words sat like a weight in his chest. For so many reasons. But he owed Piper. He could fake it. It was like going undercover, which he'd done on plenty of occasions. He could do this. "All right," he said. "Where are we going?"

"A local place that has an outdoor patio. It's called the French Quarter. My friends are there, and they saw her." Piper shook out her shoulders, and he could feel her tension. "Sound good?"

Piper's career was at stake tonight, and whatever else she hadn't been willing to talk about. Like why she'd left her fiancé at the altar. Had she just decided she didn't love him? Or had it been something else? Something more? The cop in him wanted answers, but he'd get them later.

Because he would get them, if for no other reason than to make sure she was not in danger. Or in trouble. Or in need of help that she wouldn't ask for. "I'm in," he said. "But we need to make a stop on the way."

She checked the clock on her phone. "Where? We don't have much time."

He grinned. "It won't take long. Do you trust me?"

"No. You're a great liar. I'd be an idiot to trust you."

He felt the truth of her words, even though her tone was teasing. Frowning, he leaned in. "Piper, I swear to you, I won't lie to you. I promise."

She searched his face, and slowly nodded. "All right. But you get only one chance, and then trust is broken."

He could tell she meant it, but that was fine. He was a lot of things, but a liar wasn't one of them. Well…fuck…he *was* a liar. He'd been lying to his family for more than three years about what had really happened the night Diana had died…and how badly he'd screwed up.

But he wouldn't lie to Piper.

Because with Piper, it was different.

It was the chance he'd blown before. And now he had an opportunity for a redo.

Fake or not, he was doing it right this time.

For himself.

And for Piper…because he could tell she needed it, too.

EIGHT

As Declan pulled into the parking lot of the French Quarter, the diamond on Piper's left hand caught the light.

He glanced at it again as he parked the truck, and he grinned. *Yes.*

Piper held up her hand. "You could have warned me that the detour you wanted to make was to get me a diamond the size of my entire torso." Her eyes were glinting with amusement, which he found immensely satisfying.

"Big enough?"

"Big enough?" She rolled her eyes. "The jeweler said it was four carats? Plus the small ones? Was that what he said?"

"Yeah, something like that." Declan hadn't used his family money on Diana's engagement ring. They'd both wanted to live on their cop salary, grinding away like they had a mission to prove. His mom had been horrified. His dad? Amused. Declan? A part of him had always regretted it.

So, now was his chance to ditch his moral high ground with money and give Piper what she deserved. He had to admit, it had been fun as hell ringing up his mom's jeweler and getting a private showing, playing the part that he'd refused to play his whole life.

Piper looked over at him. "You're positive this thing is insured?"

"Absolutely. And Neil takes back the stones if the engagement falls through. So just enjoy it."

"I'm going to wind up with a bigger biceps on my left arm, but I guess that's the price to pay, right?"

He grinned. "Money is heavy. You'll adjust. You see April's car here?"

Piper looked around, then pointed at a red Porsche convertible. "There." She took a breath. "It's showtime, right?"

Declan glanced across the parking lot to the patio on the side of the building. He could see diners out among the planters and under the string lights. "We're visible from there."

Piper followed his glance and grimaced. "Yes, we are. I don't see her, though. She's probably around the corner."

"But someone else who recognizes you might be watching us right now. Stay there." Declan got out of the truck, then walked around to Piper's side and opened her door. It had been a long time since he'd opened the door for a woman, and there was something so damned satisfying about doing it. About having the chance to treat a woman like a queen. He leaned on the door and studied Piper after he opened the door.

Piper was wearing a slinky black dress with a slit up the side. High heels. Just enough makeup to tease. She was pure sex and sin, and she was dressing to impress tonight. She was everything he'd rejected about his legacy with the way she was dressed for luxury, but instead of rebelling against it, his whole body thudded with recognition of the woman before him. Hot. Bold. Sexy. "Damn, you look good."

Piper flashed him a grin. "You're pure testosterone, the way you're leaning on that car door like that. She'll never notice you're a jellyfish."

"I'm not a jellyfish." He held out his hand. "Come on, my darling. Tonight is our night."

She took a breath, then stepped out of the car, moving with the grace of a woman who knew how to be pure class. *Shit.* He should not find her this attractive. What the hell?

He was glad he liked kissing her, though. She might be okay with kissing a jellyfish, but he'd prefer jellyfish stay in the ocean, and since they had to kiss for the sake of her career, it might as well be damned good.

He slipped his hand around her wrist, and tugged her toward him as she passed. "We're on public display here," he whispered, before he slid his hand around the nape of her neck.

Her eyes widened. "Oh."

"Right? It's jellyfish time, sweetheart." He angled his head and kissed her, a long, sensual kiss designed to make anyone watching feel nothing but pure envy for the heat between them. Piper leaned into him, and when her hand went to his biceps, he felt like she'd burned him with her touch.

The kiss was searing hot, and it rocked him to his core. He wanted more and more, and *more.*

Hell.

He broke the kiss, and for a long moment, they stared at each other.

"Jellyfish?" His voice was rougher than he'd intended. He knew there was no jellyfish in that kiss, but he was curious how long it would take her to admit what that kiss was. Pure heat.

Piper cleared her throat. "Totally, but I'm getting used to it."

Totally. He chuckled to himself. She was holding onto that illusion as hard as she could, which he understood. He wasn't here for anything real either, so he understood her walls. He was surprised, however, how much he was enjoying playing the part.

Maybe it was because they both knew it wasn't real, so it was easy to simply let himself enjoy it. No pressure, no future, no promises, other than to be the hero she needed.

Not that he was any kind of a hero, not by a long shot. But he was willing to play one to help her, and he was surprised at how damned good it felt.

Piper stepped back. "Shall we go?"

"Yeah." He took her hand, wrapping his fingers around hers, then tucked her hand in the crook of his elbow, tugging her close. He bent his head toward her as they walked, putting on the appearance of intimacy and connection.

"You're pure seduction," Piper said, sounding a little grumpy about it.

He chuckled. "Is that bad?"

"It's just…unexpected. I thought you only knew how to use hammers and saws. I didn't know you could…" She waved her hand at him. "This."

He grinned. "I made a deal, and I stick with my deals. You basically hired me to be your career bodyguard, and I'm a damned good bodyguard."

"Have you been a bodyguard before?" She looked intrigued, which made something coil in his gut.

He liked how she was looking at him. "Yeah. I've helped out a few times."

"Everyone still alive?"

"Hell, yeah." He reached the front door and pulled it open, holding it for her. "Let's go, my love."

Piper gave him a wary look as she squeezed past him. "I feel like an alien possessed my antisocial, sweaty landlord. It's kind of alarming."

He laughed out loud then. "I'm a scary guy. Just ask all the drug dealers. They run for cover when I show up."

"Do you kiss them into confessing all their crimes?"

"Something like that." He was still grinning as they reached the maître d's table. He'd called ahead for a reservation, and they were soon escorted outside to a corner table. He scanned the patrons as they walked in, and his gaze landed on a table of four twenty-something women at the table by the bar. They were wearing expensive jewelry, tailored clothes, and had that vibe he'd seen too many times at his mom's events growing up.

Not his kind of women.

It was the kind of woman that Piper was trying to be, but she didn't quite pull it off, he realized. That was why he wasn't bothered by her fancy-assed sass. Because she *wasn't* those women. She might be wearing the clothes, putting on the attitude, but she was nothing like them. Was it her irreverence? Her sass? Something in her past? He wasn't sure.

But he wanted to know.

Piper touched his arm. "Green dress," she whispered.

As Piper sat down, his gaze fell on the only brunette at the table, who was wearing an emerald-green dress. She was taller than the others, fit, and elegant. She held herself with a poise that said she knew what she wanted, deserved it, and would settle for nothing less.

He slid in beside Piper, taking his gaze off the women. He turned his back toward them to focus on Piper, who was facing them. "You don't need her," he said softly, as he bent in and began to nibble on her shoulder.

Shit. Her shoulder tasted amazing.

Piper sucked in her breath. "I do need her," she said.

"Forget her." He trailed his fingertips down Piper's bare arm. "And the others. Whatever the rumors are, whatever people are saying about you...forget it. They don't matter. They never do."

Piper put her hand on his cheek, her touch so soft and tender that it hit him right in the gut. "But they do matter," she said quietly. "April, her friends, and everyone like her, hold my future in their hands."

Declan met her gaze. "Don't let them."

Something flashed across her face, an emotion so raw and ragged that he sucked in his breath. "It's not that easy."

He immediately regretted pushing at her, realizing that he had no business challenging her when he had no idea what she was dealing with, what her stories were that she hadn't shared with him. "Yeah, I guess so. Never mind." He took a breath. "What now?"

"I don't know. I was thinking that she'd notice us and come

over." Her gaze flicked to the women. "But they seem completely absorbed."

"Want me to dance naked on the bar?"

She snorted. "No, please, I can't have my fiancé engaging in such behaviors."

He cocked his brow. "You spend a lot of effort trying to manage what people think of you."

"Because I'm in a career where it matters."

"Don't you get tired of it?"

She shrugged. "It doesn't matter if I do or not. It's how the game is played, and I'm going to get what I want."

He leaned in, fascinated by her letting him in. "And what is that? What do you want?"

"Eventually? I want to start my own firm." She grinned, her face lighting up. "I want to be the most sought-after wedding designer in the country. I'll probably have to move to New York to do it, so my next step is to get hired by Elizabeth Cortaine, who owns the top firm in New York."

He sat back, stunned by her vision. "Hell, that's impressive."

She grinned. "Thank you. I appreciate that. My mom used to tell me to dream big, but—" She stopped, and Declan knew it was the second time she'd cut herself off when talking about her mom. She shrugged. "Some people don't appreciate big dreams."

He wondered who she was talking about. There was an edge of pain to her voice that made him want to tell her to ignore whoever had tried to turn down her passion. "Piper—"

"What the heck is this?" Maddie Vale, one of Piper's friends, sat down at their table, her face sparking with interest. "I just saw you two kissing. What is happening?"

"Wait! I want to hear!" Another of Maddie's friends pulled a chair over and sat down. She had thick, dark hair streaked with blond, olive skin, and dark eyes that were both smiling and haunted at the same time. She waved at Declan. "I'm Tori Cardenas, and I need to know why you were chewing on Piper's shoulder like you wanted to eat her for dinner."

"Hey!" A third woman squeezed in. She had curly hair, brown skin, and sass in her eyes that reminded him of Piper. "Hi there, Piper's hot, moody landlord. I'm Keira Vogel. Why were you running your fingertips down Piper's arm like her skin was super soft velvet you couldn't get enough of? Last I heard, there was no spark at all between the two of you." She set her purse on the table. "Piper! What is going on?"

Declan sat back, amused by the sudden influx of estrogen. He'd seen Piper's friends around the carriage house from time to time, and he'd been in his backyard when they'd been out on her patio, roaring with laughter and wine. He knew the foursome was bold, loyal, and tight.

He would definitely be on the outside of this crew. But he was surprised that there was no hostility toward him making a move on their friend. Just open curiosity. And excitement. Did they want Piper to date as much as his mom wanted him to date?

Piper put her left hand under the table out of sight. "Guys! No one read the text I sent to our group chat?"

"Text?" Maddie rolled her eyes. "Why would we read a text when we have you here to grill?"

Piper rolled her eyes. "Because I have a plan. Read it."

"Tell us," Tori said. "So much gets lost in translation over text."

Declan was curious what Piper had told her friends. Would she trust them with the truth? That would be a hell of a statement about how close they were, given that her career was at stake.

"Read your texts."

Maddie rolled her eyes and pulled out her phone. She opened it and scanned the screen, while Tori and Keira read over her shoulder.

Declan leaned in so his mouth was next to Piper's ear. "How much of the truth do they know?" he whispered.

She looked over at him, then grinned. "Watch."

NINE

Maddie put down her phone, and the three women looked at each other, then back at Piper and Declan.

Declan waited, curiosity mounting. What were these women up to? He knew Maddie was a fighter because he'd helped her and her dad out with a situation recently, but the others?

Maddie suddenly broke into a big grin. "Well, it's about damned time you came clean. I've been sitting on this gossip for months!"

"Right?" Tori beamed at them. "I love it when great sex turns into true love."

"I know. Remember when we walked in on them in Piper's bedroom, and they told us they were cleaning mold?" Keira shook her head. "And it was sex all this time. Damn. I want to have hot, sweaty landlord sex. Then maybe I'll have a guy nibbling my arm in public—"

Piper held up her left hand, and all three women screamed.

"Holy shit!" Tori grabbed her wrist. "This is real? How is this real? What the heck, Declan!"

Keira shrieked and smacked Piper on the shoulder. "Get out. Get out! What is that?"

Maddie simply grinned at Declan. "Well done."

"Thanks." Declan wasn't quite sure what was happening. Did they think it was real, or had they jumped right into the façade seamlessly? He sat back, resting his arm on the back of Piper's chair, watching the women.

He'd spent a lot of time observing people as a cop, and yet, he couldn't quite figure out these four women.

Keira held her arms up in the victory sign. "I called this! I said Declan was too hot to handle and Piper knew it."

"You did," Tori agreed. "Piper said Declan was a grump and there was no chemistry."

"Little liar," Keira said. "You've had the hots for him all this time."

"I never had the hots for him," Piper said. "He's not hot. He was handy."

"Handy?" He grinned. "I'm *handy*? And grumpy?"

"You could have picked anyone, and you picked him?" Maddie was openly smiling now. "Lucas has a number of single brothers, who are freaking rich as hell. He would have set you up, but you picked your grumpy landlord?"

Piper's smile faded. "He was handy," she said again.

"He's less handy than Lucas's brothers," Maddie said. "It's not too late. You could upgrade to celebrity status."

Declan knew who they were talking about. Lucas Hart, Maddie's fiancé, was one of the Harts. They were a found family that had met as homeless kids, taken the same last name, and called themselves family. They were now billionaires, thanks to their software genius, and owners of a massive ranch in Oregon.

And Piper's friends were right. The Harts were reclusive celebrities that any woman would want.

He was a washed-up cop with an ex-pop star mom who had some well-loved songs.

All his energy dropped in a hurry. The thought of some other guy kissing Piper to save her career didn't sit well with him, but he'd already decided his job was to protect her, and if that meant handing her off to someone better, then that's what he had to do.

He ground his jaw and leaned forward. "Piper. Maddie's right. The Harts carry a hell of a lot more weight than I do."

All four women stared at him, and Tori hit his arm. "You don't want to help Piper out?"

"You're ditching her?" Keira asked.

"What? No. I just feel like a Hart can do a lot—" He stopped as Piper stared at him, an inscrutable look on her face. "What?"

She turned to face him, lifting her chin. "If you want out, that's fine. You have an exit at any time." Her voice was cool. Reserved.

He felt the weight of all the women staring at him. "I don't want out," he said carefully. "I want you to have what you need."

No one said anything. They just watched him. He could probably feel their disapproval.

Declan knew he was definitely screwing things up right now. "Look, Piper, I'm all in, but I do realize that a Hart could do more. I hadn't thought of Maddie and Lucas, but—"

Piper held up her hands. "Stop talking."

He swore. "Piper—"

Maddie interrupted. "Declan, Piper was well aware that the Harts exist, have two private jets, and consider all of us family now. And yet, she picked you. Sit on that for a second."

Piper looked away from him, watching the table with April. "You have about three seconds to take off before April notices us," she said. "I'll keep the ring for now until the Harts can get me one. Which Hart, Maddie?"

No one answered, but Declan felt Piper's three friends all glaring at him.

He thought about what Maddie had said. That Piper had chosen him. Why? He didn't know. But he knew Piper was dealing with a lot of shit that was weighing her down, and she'd picked him.

Was he going to let her down? Fuck no. He wasn't a Hart, but he'd once been damned good at making things happen. He put his arm around the back of her chair and leaned in. "Piper," he said quietly. "I'm going to say this only once, and I mean every word of it. Got it?"

Her gaze flicked briefly to his, and then returned to April. "Whatever."

"Kissing you was like waking up from a coma that's kept me trapped for years."

Her gaze shot to his face immediately.

"Kissing you is no fucking jellyfish, and we both know it." He took a breath, then continued. "You're damned sunshine, and helping you is a gift to my soul. I'm a fucked-up mess, and you don't want to see past the shiny exterior, which is fine, because I won't let you in there, but know that I fucking love being the one walking around with your hand in mine, and the last damn thing I want to do is have some Hart kissing you. If you want or need to get yourself fake-engaged to a Hart, go do it. You owe me nothing. But never make the mistake of thinking I want to be anywhere but right here, seeing this damned thing through to the end."

The table was silent. Everyone just stared at him.

Then Maddie spoke. "That was a lot of profanity packed in that little speech. Very heartfelt."

Keira nodded. "He's an ex-cop, a part-time bartender, and wields a sledgehammer. Profanity fits. Emotions equate with profanity for men like him."

Tori sat back. "I'm not going to lie. I've sworn off men and dating for at least a thousand years, but that little speech hit me right in the feels. He gets my vote."

Piper said nothing. She just stared at him.

Declan shifted restlessly, but he was done. He had nothing else to add. He actually wished he could take that whole speech right back, because he'd said a lot of things he hadn't ever planned to say, but it was out there, so yeah.

Piper finally spoke. "I'm sorry. I totally spaced out there for a minute. Can you repeat that?"

It was his turn to stare at her. "Seriously?"

She grinned. "No. Not seriously." She leaned in. "You're very intense sometimes, Mr. Jones. I can feel your earnestness, and I like it."

His tension faded. "You do, eh?"

"I do." She put her hand on his shoulder and faced the table. "I'm keeping him. I think he's going to be perfect."

He felt himself relax at her announcement, which almost made him laugh. He was being claimed by his fake fiancée, and he liked it. Liked it a hell of a lot, actually.

He was going to have to think about that later.

"Amen to that, sister," Tori said. "Declan's got that thing."

"He does," Maddie agreed.

"Absolutely," Keira said.

He looked around at the table. "What thing is that?"

"That undefinable, magical vibe that makes a man completely irresistible, even if he's a world-class jerk," Maddie said.

"Except to me, of course," Piper interjected. "Declan, just to be clear, you are completely resistible to me because I'm an iron wall of heartlessness, but April will fall hard for you."

He studied her thoughtfully. "I don't think there's a single damn bit of heartlessness in you. Toughness? Hell, yeah. But heartless? No."

Something flickered in her eyes. "I am tough," she agreed.

"With the biggest heart on the whole planet," Tori said.

Piper's glaze flicked to Tori, and Declan saw pain in Piper's eyes. Raw pain that said his fake fiancée was anything but heartless.

Maddie sat up. "April just saw you. She's talking with her friends and looking over here."

Declan's gaze slid over to April's table. She was talking animatedly with her friends, and she looked angry. He immediately slid his arm over Piper's shoulders and eased her against him.

"Do you want us to stay or go?" Tori said.

"Go," he said, before Piper could answer. "This show is about me and Piper right now."

Piper nodded. "If I put my phone on the table, it means I need help. Then you guys come over and rave about Declan."

"Rock on." Tori stood up, and the others followed. "We'll be watching." She blew Piper a kiss. "Congrats, my friend. You found a good one!"

"I'm a little jealous," Keira said.

"We'll have a party with the Harts," Maddie said.

Maddie's parting words got Declan thinking. The Harts did carry power, but he'd known the Harts for a long time. Were they his found family? No. But friends? Yeah, they were.

He saw April shoot to her feet, toss her hair back, and start striding toward them, her body language ready for a fight.

Yeah, she was definitely going to fire Piper.

The minute he thought it, protectiveness surged through Declan. Piper was under his protection, and it wasn't okay with him for anyone to go after her. Especially not a woman like April.

He bent over Piper, angling his head and his shoulders for privacy, making a private bubble for the two of them, turning his back on April. "I adore your friends," he said softly making his voice as intimate as he could. "But I'm damn glad they left."

Piper's gaze flicked behind him. "She's almost here—"

"I know." He then leaned in and kissed her, a kiss that was sensual and hot, a kiss that was the kind of kiss a man would give a woman if he couldn't last one more second without touching her, and he wanted her to know it.

It was no damned jellyfish kiss.

Piper tensed, and then relaxed into the kiss. She rested her hand on his biceps and kissed him back. The moment she did, everything in his body coiled into a tight web of anticipation and need.

Damn. He really loved kissing her.

TEN

"Piper!" April pulled out a chair and sat down as if it were her throne.

Declan swore under his breath as Piper jumped back. He was slower to let Piper go. He didn't lean away from her. Instead, he simply turned his head toward their new guest, giving her a slow once-over.

Nice engagement ring and several rows of diamond stud earrings. Extra bling around her neck. Clothes that looked a little uncomfortable, but that had all the right brand names. She was dressing to impress.

"I've been calling all day!" April was clearly irritated that Piper had ignored her calls, which made him lean forward to interject his presence.

"Hi," he said, his voice low. "I'm Declan Jones."

April glanced at him dismissively, then she saw his watch, and she paused to really look at him. "April Hunsaker." She held out her hand to him in that way women did when they wanted a man to kiss their hand.

He almost started laughing. He was so far from the kind of man who would kiss April's hand upon meeting her.

But since Piper had said women loved unavailable, rough

men, he did exactly what he wanted to do, which was to ignore her hand, lean back, and survey her.

April's eyes narrowed as she lowered her hand. She was pissed, and it made him want to grin. Who the hell went around expecting strangers to kiss their hands? It was such a strange world his mom lived in, and that Piper wanted to be a part of.

"April," Piper said, leaning forward, taking the conversation back. "We need to talk."

April's gaze swiveled back to Piper. "Yes, you're fi—" She paused when Piper scratched her nose with her left hand, and her massive diamond glinted. She grabbed Piper's hand and almost dragged Piper out of her seat to get a better look at her diamond ring. "What is this?"

Declan narrowed his eyes. Yeah, he knew the ring was something special, but it was also stunning to see how quickly a big ass diamond could distract someone like April. It reminded him of why he'd stayed away from these circles.

Piper's face lit up with what appeared to be absolute joy. "I'm engaged!"

"You're *engaged?*" April's shock was impressive.

"I am." Piper put her hand on Declan's shoulder. "I'd like you to meet my fiancé, Declan Jones. Declan, this is April."

He gave her a casual nod and slid his arm along the back of Piper's seat, trailing his thumb over her bare arm. "Hey."

"Hi," April said, barely giving him a glance before turning back to interrogate Piper. "When did this happen? You were engaged to Clark ten months ago!"

Clark. Now Declan had a first name. He wanted more information on this guy.

"I know." Piper leaned forward. "This is what I wanted to talk to you about. When I walked out on Clark, I didn't know why I was doing it."

Lie. She's just lied. Interest shot through Declan. Piper knew exactly why she'd walked out on her wedding. Why was she hiding that?

Piper continued with her story, not aware that she'd just revealed a secret. "All I knew was that as I stood there across from him, I couldn't do it. I imagined the next fifty years with him, and this voice inside me said 'No. Run.'"

That was the truth. Fight or flight. What kind of situation had she been in with Clark that her nervous system had put her in fight or flight mode?

"So you ran," April said.

"I did. And then, a month or so later, I was talking to Declan, something inside me came alive in a way I'd never been alive before."

April glanced at him, and Declan leaned forward, absorbed by Piper's story.

"We'd only been friends before that, but in that moment, some-thing shifted. For both of us. We went out on a date, and I realized that the man who'd been my friend all this time was actually the piece of my soul that I'd been missing."

Well, damn. That was impressive.

April's eyes widened, but before she could speak, Piper continued her story.

"I'm happier than I ever thought possible. I feel loved in a way I didn't know existed. Being with Declan makes me realize that the reason it didn't work with Clark was because I deserved more. He wasn't my one. And I'm so grateful beyond words to have found that out before I married Clark."

Declan decided it would be helpful to interject, so he put his arm around her shoulders and kissed her cheek. "I'm so grateful every day that Piper had the courage to walk away from what wasn't right. She's the most incredible woman I've ever met. She lights up my life and makes me a better man."

The words felt fake to him, but at the same time, they awoke something inside him. A yearning. A desire. A need for them to be real, to be a truth he was actually living. The yearning shocked him to his core. He'd thought he was done being in a relationship.

Over with love. With marriage. With wanting more. But the way those words resonated inside him felt absolutely compelling.

Fuck.

He was not happy with that little discovery.

Piper gave him a tender smile that strengthened the yearning inside him. "Bitsy's wedding got cancelled because her fiancé was cheating on her. She can definitely do better than that, right? Think how happy she'll be when she finds the man who treats her the way she deserves to be treated."

Bitsy. Who had a name like Bitsy? That was freaking hilarious.

April shrugged. "I mean, yeah, I guess."

"And Tricia? She realized she deserved more, just like I did. She'll find her Declan."

Declan lifted her left hand and pressed a kiss to her palm. "Piper isn't a wedding killer, April. If anything, she's a bride protector, keeping her from marrying the man who isn't right for her." Damn. That was good. He liked that.

April looked back and forth between them. "Bride protector?"

"Yeah," Declan said. "Piper casts her net of protection over all her brides. Most of the time, it means the perfect wedding. But sometimes, maybe she gives the bride the clarity to realize she's making a mistake, and a bigger diamond from a better guy is waiting for her."

He tossed out the ring thing because he had to. Because it was funny as hell.

April's gaze predictably went to Piper's ring, then she looked at Declan and Piper. They both beamed at her, and he suddenly wanted to laugh. The expression on April's face was as hilarious as the one on his mom's had been. Shock. Confusion.

Piper leaned forward. "I'm *good* luck, April, not bad luck. It's the loser dudes who are the ones being cranky because they're losing the women who are too good for them."

April started to smile. "That's true. I never liked Bitsy's fiancé."

"Right? And, I'll be honest, your Wendall is a treasure. You've got a wonderful man. My only job will be to make your wedding perfect, trust me."

April's smile widened. "He is great, isn't he?"

"Absolutely. You know I'm the best at what I do. All you have to do is enjoy the most special day of your life." Piper winked. "I'll even keep Wendall's mom off your back. She loves me."

April laughed. "She does. I don't know how you do it, but you're amazing with her."

"Because I'm great at what I do." Piper patted April's hand. "It's all good, honey. I'll see you tomorrow at Vale's Flowers. Sound good?"

April nodded. "Yes, okay." Then she glanced at Declan. "Can he come? I think my mom would like to meet him, to know that everything's okay."

Can he come? Like he was Piper's dog? But when Piper glanced at him with raised eyebrows, Declan knew he was in. Oh, boy. He gave April a lazy smile. "What time?"

"Eleven?"

"I can work that in and stop by for a few minutes," he said.

Relief flashed across April's face, making Declan wonder if it was actually her mom who had wanted to fire Piper, not April herself. He saw from Piper's frown that she had noticed the same thing. "I'll see you later," April said. "So glad I have a bride protector on my side! That's such a better job title than wedding planner!"

Piper grinned. "I'll add it to my business card."

"Perfect!" April gave them both a quick wave, then hopped to her feet and strode back over to her table. She hadn't even sat down before her friends were leaning in, looking at Declan, and asking questions excitedly.

Piper sat back, her shoulders slumping with relief. "We did it. I can't believe it."

"That was well done. Quite a story you fabricated." Declan continued to watch April's table, and the glances shooting their way. "I think we need to dance."

"What? Why?"

"Because we're being watched. We need to do a steamy dance that makes every one of those women jealous of us, and then we can jet." Oh, boy. A steamy dance. This night was becoming far more than he bargained for. "We need to get their discussion off you being a wedding killer and onto you being luckier than all of them combined."

Piper started laughing. "You're that great of a catch?"

"No, but I can make them think I am." He winked. "I did some undercover work in my day. I can lie with the best of them. Let's go get hot and steamy."

Piper's cheeks turned pink, and she grimaced. "I'm not really into PDA."

"Me either. We can be super awkward and uncomfortable together, but make it look like we're suave, polished, and completely comfortable making out in public. Duplicity at its best."

She laughed, as he'd hoped she would. "A perfect pair."

"Yep." He rose to his feet and held out his hand to her. "My darling, this is one of my favorite songs. Would you care to dance?"

"My little pumpkin latte, it would be my greatest joy."

He started laughing as he led her to the little dance floor. "Your pumpkin latte?" He pulled her against him, so her torso was against his, and clasped his hands behind her lower back.

She linked her hands behind his neck and gazed up at him with a deadpan expression. "No. You're not a latte. You're my Man O' War."

He grinned. "Your jellyfish?"

"Big, deadly, long-tentacled jellyfish," she said. "If there was such a thing as a hot, sexy jellyfish, it would definitely be the Man O' War."

"I'll take it as a compliment, then."

"As it was intended, of course."

He pulled her closer and brushed his lips over her neck. "They're still watching," he said.

"I know. Don't they have anything better to do than watch a grumpy old man and his hot, young fiancée?"

He swore. "I'm not old."

"Yes, but you're so grumpy that it's almost like you're an old man."

"I'm not grumpy either. At the moment."

Piper laughed, her eyes sparkling as she looked at him. "No, not at the moment, although I thought we were in for it when April first sat down. You really couldn't have kissed the back of her hand? Just a wee, little show of grace?"

"No. I couldn't have done that. It might have killed me." He swung her around, swaying to the music. "But it was fine. She was left yearning for my touch."

Piper laughed. "She's engaged. She better not be yearning for your touch."

"All women yearn for my touch. It's a burden I've learned to deal with." He pulled her close, tucking their joined hands against his chest, cradling her hand. "You'll probably need a bodyguard. Women all over the world are going to be coming for you, now that word is out that you got me."

She laughed. "I can handle it. Once you've been shot a couple times, not much can scare you."

He stiffened, and his laughter faded. "You've been *shot?*"

"Only twice, so it's fine."

His heart started pounding suddenly, and fear gripped him. *She'd been shot. Shot. Shot. Twice.*

Piper's arms tightened around him. "Declan? What's wrong? What's happening to you?"

He pressed his face to her neck, trying to ground himself in her presence. Piper was all right. She was alive. He felt her body against his. The heat. The warmth. Her curves.

"Declan?"

"Just give me a sec." He held her tightly, needing to feel her against him, forcing himself to move with the music. To his surprise, the panic attack, the terror, the memories receded before they took him. Somehow, being in Piper's arms had grounded him enough to keep ahead of his past.

Piper wrapped her arms around him and held him close. The strength of her embrace seemed to provide a shield against the memories, and his breath steadied. His heart rate slowed. His skin cooled, the beads of sweat settled on his skin.

For a long moment, they simply danced. She didn't ask again, didn't press him for details he couldn't articulate, and eventually his energy settled back into the moment, into Piper, into the present.

"That was a deep breath," Piper said. "You okay?"

"Yeah." He pulled back to look at her. "Sorry about that."

She smiled. "It's totally fine. Did I do something wrong?"

"No, hell no. It's not you." Movement behind him caught his eye, and he saw that all the women from April's table were still watching him. Shit. He'd forgotten his job. "I gotta kiss you."

Piper's eyes widened. "You don't have to do anything."

"I want to." The words slipped out before he realized he was thinking them. Piper's brow furrowed, and he swore. He didn't want to have to answer a question about what he'd meant by that, so he pulled her in, angled his head, and kissed her question away before she could get it out.

ELEVEN

Piper's lips were warm and receptive, and kissing her felt like the most natural thing in the world. Declan's connection with her was strong after she'd pulled him back from the edge with her touch, and he wanted more with her. He did want to kiss her. Deep. Intense. No holding back.

So he did, and she kissed him right back, with the same level of intensity that he offered.

They came together, their bodies tangled with each other, hands moving, trying to get closer, trying to touch more. The moment became about them, only them, about the way she felt in his arms. About how alive she made him feel. About how much he wanted all of her. To lose himself in her. To protect her. To make her laugh. Smile. To embrace the way she made him want to smile again.

Declan pressed his hands to Piper's lower back, and then slid them lower, over the curve of her ass. Part of the show, he lied to himself, knowing damn well that he just wanted to touch her. How was this happening? Piper had lived in his guest house for almost two years, and he'd never thought of her as anything but his tenant.

And now he was consumed by her kiss, by her energy, by his need to drag her into his arms, toss her onto a bed, and make love to her until neither of them could move, until she filled him so completely that all the pain sewn into his soul lost its grip and faded away into the unknown.

"Piper?"

A man's voice broke through Declan's haze. Piper stiffened instantly in his arms, and Declan pulled back, instinctively moving Piper slightly behind him so his body was between the intruder and Piper.

It was a man who looked like the male version of April. Tall. Fancy. Clean-shaven. Smelled of aftershave and money. Attractive. But there was a vibe about him that set Declan's radar on edge.

Piper stepped away from Declan, but he moved with her, refusing to let her move to where he couldn't protect her if the man pulled out a knife and moved fast. Not that he'd seen a knife, but his cop instincts were burning right now.

"Clark," she said stiffly.

Clark? Wasn't that her ex's name?

Her ex was *here?*

Hot damn. This was going to be fun.

Declan studied the man carefully. What the hell had Piper been doing with him? His energy was about as far from Piper's as it could be.

"Who are you?" Clark sounded stiff and annoyed as he stared at Declan.

Declan grinned. The fact that Piper had made the courageous-as-hell decision to leave this dude at the altar meant there was something about this guy that wasn't right, at least for Piper. And yet, he'd almost managed to convince her to marry him.

That meant he was a formidable opponent.

Declan put his arm around Piper's waist and pulled her against him. He stuck out his hand. "Declan Jones. Cop. Piper's fiancé. Who are you?" He threw in the cop thing intentionally, wanting this guy to know not to fuck with him or Piper.

Clark's eyes narrowed. "Clark Houston. Piper's fiancé until recently." He didn't shake Declan's hand, which made Declan chuckle. Definitely trying to posture. He narrowed his gaze. "You move fast, Piper."

Before Declan could step in to defend her, Piper pushed away from Declan and put her hands on her hips. "What I do is not your problem," she said, her voice firm and confident.

Nice. Declan liked her vibe. She wasn't backing down.

Clark ground his jaw. "That's right," he said. "You aren't my problem anymore." He shot a look at Declan. "Good luck. You'll need it." Then he turned and strode away to the bar, where he wound himself around to a woman who was tall, curvy, and in a slinky blue dress.

"Let's go," Piper said. "I'm done here."

"No. Not yet." Declan took her hand and coaxed her to turn toward him. "If you let him drive you out of here, then you give him power over you. Take a breath, dance with me, and find your equilibrium." He knew that, because he hadn't taken the time to face his demons, so he'd never been able to get free.

Piper glanced at him, tension etched in her brown eyes. "I just want to leave."

"No." He tugged her hand gently, guiding her into his arms. "You want to be away from the energy that he created in you. You need to show yourself that you can be yourself in his presence. Come on." He pressed a kiss to her forearm. "I'll be your shield. Just focus on me."

She dragged her gaze off the bar and looked at Declan. Her shoulders were tense, and he could feel her shaking. What the hell had happened with them? Now wasn't the time to ask, but he was definitely going to look the guy up when he got home. "Piper," he said. "Did I mention you look gorgeous tonight?"

A little smile curved the corners of her mouth. "No, you didn't.

But you don't have to pretend. I know you don't look at me like that."

"Tonight I did. Tonight I am."

She stared at him, and he knew she'd heard the truth in his voice. "Don't do that. It's not our deal."

"I know." He gently spun her around, so she was facing the opposite direction of Clark, and he began to dance them to the far end of the dance floor. "I didn't expect to notice how sexy you look in that dress."

"Well, stop noticing."

He raised his brows. "Stop noticing you look great?"

"Yes. Now." She was still stiff and tense, even though she wasn't looking at Clark anymore. "This thing between you and me is an arrangement. Nothing real. If you can't do that, then we'll call it off—"

"I can do it," he cut her off immediately. He wasn't going to let her send him packing. He wasn't ready to go yet. Yeah, he liked kissing her. Yeah, he was more intrigued by the minute. But he was disciplined. He could keep it impersonal. "Jellyfish all the way. You're my squishy, slimy, tentacled fake fiancée. Who could possibly want to cross a line with that?"

A tiny giggle escaped her. "You're so weird."

"I know. You're welcome." He could feel her relaxing. "And I'm a cactus. A cactus engaged to a jellyfish. Now that's the stuff of fairytales right there."

"You're the jellyfish."

"I'm not. I'm a cactus." Declan kept going with the banter, noting her relaxing into it. Piper had some significant walls, and despite his proclaimed willingness to keep it fishy between them, he had no interest in backing off.

The woman was riveting, and more importantly, she made him feel alive for the first time in a long time, and he couldn't walk away from that.

"You're both," she said. "I'm just a gorgeous, charming, fantastic wedding planner with an amazing career."

"Engaged to a fishy cactus."

She laughed. "Exactly."

Ah, that laugh. He fucking loved it.

The moment he thought it, his amusement faded.

He was falling for this woman, he realized. Despite the fact he'd sworn never to fall again…he was.

What was he going to do about it?

TWELVE

Declan managed to get Piper home without making an ass of himself.

He didn't tell her she was getting under his skin.

He didn't invite himself to sleep in her bed to keep her safe.

He didn't even kiss her good night.

He congratulated her on April, promised to be at Maddie's flower store at eleven, and hauled his sore knee over to his house to take Angel for a walk.

But all the dog kisses didn't get Piper out of his mind. So, as soon as Angel was on the couch and napping, Declan surrendered to his old cop instincts, and he got involved.

It took him about thirty seconds to find a long list of articles on Piper's wedding, and her ex-fiancé.

Clark Houston was the president of Gold Leader Investments, a successful investment firm his dad had founded. New generation wealth, and a lot of it.

There were plenty of photos of Piper, smiling into the camera, leaning on the arm of her fiancé. Piper's engagement photo: stylish, beautiful, and fitting in with the most elite. Her smile was electric, and she had a vibrancy that transcended the camera lens.

He leaned in, studying the photo closely, looking for some

indication that she wasn't happy in that photo, but he couldn't see it. He'd lay bets that on the day that photo was taken, Piper was in love with her fiancé and believed all was well.

And yes, the idea of her being in love with Clark prickled him a little bit, which he decided to ignore.

Their engagement had happened quickly, and the wedding had been scheduled fast. Clark moved swiftly, which made Declan think that he'd tried to reel her in before she had time to think about what she was doing.

The wedding.

Every article reported that she'd walked out mid-ceremony, leaving everyone stunned.

Clark and his family had lambasted her in the press, doing interview after interview, shredding her reputation, her morals, and her values. They claimed she'd never meant to marry Clark, saying that she'd become engaged to him solely to help her career, to use his family's name and prestige for her own benefit.

The press had shredded her...but as far as Declan could find, Piper had never uttered even one word in her defense, no explanation, nothing.

She simply let Clark and his family try to ruin her.

Declan sat back, considering that. Piper was strong, bold, and resilient. Why wouldn't she have defended herself, especially when her dream was at stake?

It didn't make sense...which meant he didn't have all the information.

But the same need to protect arose the more Declan read. No one had protected Piper.

Until now.

She had him now, and he was born to be a protector.

Declan clasped his hands on his head, thinking.

It didn't take a cop to realize something was very off about what had happened.

Blackmail? Had Clark's family bought her off? Or maybe Piper had simply changed her mind and had no "acceptable" reason that the press would deem worthy? Maybe she'd decided to rise above the crap and not engage.

Or maybe something else.

Declan scrolled back through some photos of Piper and Clark together, checking body language and eye contact between them. In all the photos, they'd been leaning in toward each other, touching, smiling, looking happy and relaxed. He couldn't see any tension between them, anything to indicate that things weren't going well, or that Clark was coercing or threatening Piper in some way.

Maybe she had simply left. No drama. No big story to tell. She just hadn't loved him, and she'd been willing to risk her career to follow her heart.

He drummed his fingers on his desk, thinking.

But what if he was wrong? What if there was something else at play? If Piper was going to insert herself back into those circles, he needed to know if she was going to stir up something that would endanger her.

He picked up his phone and opened it. He scrolled to a name he hadn't reached out to in five years. Ryan Bradford. Declan's thumb swayed over the name, but he didn't press it. Did he really want to open that door again?

Hell, no. He didn't.

He looked again at the paparazzi picture of Piper fleeing out the side door of the church again. No one had protected her. No one had defended her.

Not that she necessarily needed it, but she deserved it.

It had been a long time since Declan had had a cause. A person who made him want to get off his dark bench and engage on their behalf. But Piper did.

He hit the send button and put the phone on speaker.

Ryan answered after several rings. "Declan?" He was clearly stunned.

Declan's body kicked into sudden alertness at the voice he hadn't heard in so long. "Yeah, it's me." He hadn't expected such a strong reaction to the sound of Ryan's voice. Ryan was a former cop who'd consulted with Declan on many investigations. He'd been there the night everything had gone to shit.

"Damn, it's good to hear from you," Ryan said. "What's going on? You back?"

The idea of going back to being a cop made Declan recoil, but he nodded. He had to do it. "Soon."

Ryan let out a whoop. "Hell, yeah. About damned time. So glad to hear that. What's going on?"

"I need a favor."

"Anything. Name it."

"I need you to run a name for me."

"What's the name?"

"Clark Houston. He's the president of Gold Leader Investments."

"Got it. Why?"

"A hunch."

"Still have hunches? Your instincts were always the best I ever saw. I'll run it as soon as I'm back at the office." Ryan paused. "What have you been doing? You vanished."

Declan shrugged. "Rebuilding a house I bought. Doing some bartending."

"Bartending? Seriously? Where?"

"A place near my house. A neighborhood joint. I owed a favor to the owner to help out a couple times, and I kept going back."

"You were going to be the best the department ever had," Ryan said. "Everyone had you tagged as the next great—"

"I know. Things change." He cleared his throat. "I gotta go make some other calls."

"Wait. Let's meet for a drink."

Declan felt his body tighten. "No."

"It's been years, Declan," Ryan said. "Time to stop running."

"I'm not running."

"Then what are you doing? Living?"

"I gotta go. Text me when you have info. And thanks." Declan hung up before Ryan could protest, then shoved his chair back and got up, pacing away from the desk. He felt restless and edgy. Just that brief conversation had brought his past back full force. Hearing Ryan's voice had been...jarring.

Ryan had been there that night. Talking to Ryan made the night come back. The humid heat. The starless sky. The whisper that split second before all hell had broken loose. The guns. The bullets.

His wife's face the moment she'd been hit.

The raw terror that had hit him when she'd grabbed her neck, and he'd realized that the bullet had missed her vest. The roar ripping from his throat as he'd run to her.

He didn't remember getting hit in the leg by the bullet that had taken him down when he'd broken cover to get to her, but the scar still reminded him of that night, of that aching loss that never left him, no matter how much time went by.

He braced his hands on the couch, sweat beading on his shoulders as he fought off the sounds of gunfire. Of shouts. Of that gasp, that last gasp that Diana had managed before she'd died—

Of Piper. Who had been shot twice. *Twice.*

Fuck.

He couldn't do this.

He couldn't fake an engagement. Not with Piper. Not with anyone.

He was calling it off.

It was over before it was even going to begin.

THIRTEEN

Piper leaned back from the computer, unable to stop thinking about the kiss with Declan earlier.

The many kisses. The dance. Declan's smile. His protectiveness when they'd run into Clark.

Declan made her feel again. He made her want again. He made her soft.

She didn't want to be soft.

She had a goal. A goal she'd fought her entire life for. A goal that kept her mother's dream alive, which made her feel close to her. And now, she was on the verge of losing it forever. She had to stay focused. Not trapped. Not derailed. Not distracted by a man.

But the way he kissed…

The way he made her feel…

No.

It had all been for show anyway. There were no feelings involved. Just acting.

So, she had nothing to worry about, and she needed to focus.

Piper cleared her throat, sat back up, and refreshed the society page in the local paper again, looking to see who was dating, who had recently become engaged, who she might be able to secure as a client for her firm.

But she couldn't focus.

Dammit.

She shoved back from the desk and stood up. She was freaking out, and she didn't have time for that. She needed to calm down. Her yoga mat was upstairs, and she was afraid if she went up there, she'd just crawl into her bed.

She didn't have time to crawl into her bed and hide from life. She'd allow five minutes of meditation on the kitchen floor, which was just uncomfortable enough that she wouldn't fall asleep for hours and wake up at four in the morning, stiff, cranky, and unproductive.

Yes, she'd done that. Many times. Meditation was helpful, but it led to a long nap more often than she liked, so she'd learned to manage her meditation challenges.

She grabbed a dishtowel as a pillow for her head, stretched out on the unforgiving, hard floor, and closed her eyes.

The tile was cool, but the night was warm enough that it felt good.

She took a deep breath, then wiggled herself more comfortably onto the tile.

Breathe in.

Breathe out.

She focused on her breath, and her hands fell to her side limply. Her belly began to loosen, and she pictured herself sinking into the tile, her body so relaxed—

The front door slammed open, and she bolted upright as Declan came racing in, panic in his face. "Piper!" he shouted.

"What? Holy crap! What?" She jumped to her feet, grabbed a wooden spoon, and held it up, ready to fight. "What's going on? Who's after us? Serial killer? What?"

Declan skidded to a stop, staring at her as his breath heaved in his chest. "What the fuck?"

"What? What is it?" She spun around, her heart hammering. "Watch out!" she shouted to the unseen danger. "I'm armed!"

Declan put his hands on his knees, staring at her, disbelief on his face.

She was starting to freak out. "What is it!" She grabbed the electric can opener from the counter and held it up. "I swear, Declan, if you don't tell me—"

"I thought you were dead."

"What?" The can opener still above her shoulder, she stared at him. "Who was dead?"

"You!" He started laughing. "Hell, Piper. Why were you lying on the floor like that?"

"I was meditating." She lowered the can opener. "Wait a sec. Nothing's wrong?"

"No. Because you're not dead. Hell. Don't do that again."

"Lie on my own floor?" She was still trying to recover from the panic he'd thrust her into. "Why were you spying on me?"

"I wasn't spying." He sat down on a bar stool, still laughing. Or crying. It was unclear through her subsiding freak-out. "I came over to talk to you, and then I saw your feet sticking out from behind the island. I thought you were dead. Fucking meditation? Hell, Piper, on the tile floor? You haven't heard of a yoga mat?"

She set down the can opener. "I have my reasons." She held up her hands, which were now shaking. "I was meditating to relieve stress, and you just sent it through the roof."

"Well, you freaked me out, so we're even."

"Even? How are we even? I was minding my own business in my own home, and you broke in, shouting like a wild man, scaring the piccalilli out of me!"

"Piccalilli?"

"Yes!" She pointed the spoon at him. "Go away. You are not wanted."

He didn't move. "I was protecting you."

"I don't need protection." She held up the can opener. "Obviously."

He cocked an eyebrow. "What were you going to do with that?"

"Throw it."

A smile quirked the corner of his mouth. "Really?"

She narrowed her eyes. "The level to which I abhor your skepticism is immeasurable. Follow me." She headed for the back patio, not even waiting to see if he was coming.

He did. Because he was a man, and men couldn't deal with being wrong.

She got to the patio. "Pick a target."

He raised his brows. "All right, I recant my skepticism with the can opener. You don't need to—"

"Pick one."

He sighed and pointed to the lamppost about ten feet away, about four inches wide. "That."

"You'll buy me a new can opener and fix the lamppost when I hit it?" She knew she could be overreacting, but stress did that to her. He'd terrified her, and then had made her want to feel all warm and snuggly when he'd said he was protecting her.

She loved that he was protecting her. Absolutely freaking loved it. Which is why she had to end that nonsense now. Because she was also pissed that he'd run into her home, uninvited, and scared the daylights out of her.

Declan grinned. "Sure. I'll take care of it all."

Oh...that arrogant, attractive man. He didn't believe she could do it. "Okay." She turned toward the lamppost, hefted the can opener, took aim, and then hurled it.

It smashed into the lamppost and exploded into itty bitty can opener parts all over the patio with an extremely satisfying crash. Wow. What a brilliant throw. She was so impressed with herself. That could easily have ended in a complete miss, but she'd nailed it.

Yay for Piper.

Declan stared at the carnage. "Damn."

Exactly. "Yes. If an intruder ever shows up, he'll be the one who needs protecting." She glared at him. "Now go away." She turned and headed back inside.

"Where did you learn to do that?"

"Softball. And brothers." She walked inside and shut the door.

He opened it and followed her in. "You threw can openers at your brothers? Are they all dead now?"

She tossed him a grin over her shoulder. "It was impressive, wasn't it?" Honestly, it had been a bit of a crap shoot about whether she would actually hit the lamppost. It had been a while since she'd used that particular skill. Plus, can openers were tricky little things, and the lamppost had been pretty narrow. If she'd missed, Declan would have gotten to run home feeling all smug in his manly superiority.

But she'd been mad, the can opener had been handy, and she'd aced it.

"How'd you get shot? Your brothers?"

She laid back down on the floor and closed her eyes. "I'm meditating."

He crouched next to her. "I need to know why you got shot."

"I'm sorry. Did I not tell you that I'm meditating now? That means I'm not available for talking."

He sat down. "Piper. I *need* to know why you got shot."

Something about his tone caught her attention, and she opened one eye. He was leaning back against a cabinet, his arms draped over his knees, his gazed hooded and tense. "What's wrong with you?"

He rubbed his jaw. "My wife Diana was a cop. She was undercover. We raided the place. She got shot. Died in my arms."

Holy crap. Piper sat up quickly. "I'm so sorry, Declan."

He waved off her sympathy. "I'm edgy when it comes to people getting shot now. Especially women I'm engaged to."

"If it helps, we're not actually engaged."

The corner of his mouth quirked into the tiniest little smile. "It doesn't appear to help. I nearly lost my mind when I thought you were dead."

"Did you? I didn't notice."

His smile widened. "I haven't kissed anyone since Diana.

Haven't held a woman since Diana. I know our intimacy is fake, but it's still a real event. It's stirring up a little PTSD for me that I didn't expect."

Guilt flashed through Piper. "No problem. We'll call it off. I'll tell April that you got called away on business—"

"No."

"I think that's a good idea. We can't have you bursting in here and losing your mind every time I engage in self-care." Even as she said it, regret gnawed away at her. She didn't want to call it off. At all. Because of her career. Not because she wanted to hug this man who was baring his soul to her, then drag him into her bed to make them both forget about past relationships that still haunted them. Definitely not that.

"I've been hiding for three years. You make me not want to hide anymore."

"Oh." Was that a good thing? She kinda thought it was. "You're welcome?"

He laughed softly. "I'm not going to lie. Even if we called it off, I'd probably still come barging in here if I think you're in danger or dead, but it's okay. You can throw the can opener at me."

"If you're dead, then I have no fiancé, so throwing can openers at you won't work for me." She was so happy he didn't want to call it off. Too happy. Dammit. She needed some perspective. "I'll see you at Maddie's store tomorrow morning then?" She closed her eyes again, but all she could see in her mind was him holding his dead wife.

Dammit. That was heavy stuff. She felt terrible for him.

"Why were you shot?"

She understood now why he was asking, but that didn't make her any more willing to tell him the truth. If her past got out, it would destroy everything she'd worked for. Even the best strategy, connections, and hard work couldn't overcome some things, and that included her past. Even Clark hadn't known about her past. And with Declan being a cop? No way. "Skeet shooting accident," she lied.

He raised his brows. "Skeet shooting?"

"Yep. Want to see the scars?"

"Yeah."

She pulled up her shirt and pointed to her hip. The bullet hole was white and puckered, an old scar that had healed. He frowned and ran his hand over it. "Skeet, you say?"

"Yep." Um, hello? His hand on her hip was too intoxicating. She batted his hand away and glared at him.

"Where's the other one?"

She pulled the collar of her shirt to the more recent scar on her shoulder, the one that had galvanized her to finally take action. He touched that one, again sending electrical bolts of Hallelujah through her. "Those aren't from skeet shooting. Different bullet."

Wow, she definitely should have predicted that. The man was a cop, after all. He'd know his ammo. So much for deflecting his attention from her past. "Skeet shooting," she repeated firmly. "Bye."

She closed her eyes and laid back down again.

He didn't move.

Finally, she spoke. "I'm sorry about your wife, Declan. I can't imagine how terrible that was." Just talking about it made her throat tighten. She wanted to cry for him. With him. To rip the pain out of his heart, to give him back the life that was snatched from him.

"Thanks." He was quiet for a minute. "I do need to worry about you, don't I?"

"What's the point of worry? It gets you nowhere. You have to set your goals and keep moving." She wiggled to get more comfortable, trying to inject a lighter tone into the moment, but she couldn't drag her heart away from his pain, and his past.

"I guess." He still didn't move.

She finally opened her eyes. "What?"

"I came over here to call off our deal. I didn't think I could take it. Too much PTSD having a woman to kiss and think about, even if the engagement isn't real. But then you yelled at me and threw the can opener, and things felt okay again." He looked at her thoughtfully. "You may be what I need."

Her heart turned over. If she could help him heal, that would be such a gift to her. She felt like she was always sprinting on a treadmill, trying to get over the next hurdle, never really mattering to anyone. To make a difference to him would be... amazing. "I do think that sometimes people are put in your way for a reason," she said. "But I'll warn you. I'm feeling very emotional and touchy-feely right now, but that's most likely temporary. I'll probably yell at you again."

He grinned. "It was the yelling and the destruction that pulled me out of my funk. I've had enough sympathy. I don't want it anymore."

She let out a breath. "All right. We might be okay, then."

"Yeah." He *still* didn't get up, so she did.

"All right. I'll see you tomorrow," she said pointedly.

He grinned and rose to his feet. "Trying to get rid of me?"

"Yes, I still have work to do." She shooed at him. "Go away—"

He caught her wrist.

She met his gaze, and before she could decide to yell at him, he gave a gentle tug, pulling her off balance. She tumbled forward, and he caught her against him, his body warm and hard against hers.

"Oh, man..." she muttered.

Not giving her a chance to decide how to proceed, he kissed her.

A kiss that would break her heart wide open if she let it.

She had to stop. Kissing in private put a whole different spin on their relationship.

Then he angled his head to deepen the kiss, and she forgot about everything but the man whose arms were wrapped around her, and his decadent, deviously, oh-so-tempting mouth.

FOURTEEN

Declan hadn't meant to kiss Piper. But when she'd looked at him, with that sparkle in her eyes mixed with the pain she was feeling for him, he couldn't resist. She was just so damn vibrant.

She'd come willingly, immediately, with no hesitation.

And now…hell…kissing her was amazing. He loved the taste of her lips, the feel of them beneath his. Her body was warm and soft against his, melting into his chest as if she were born to be a part of him.

She was brilliant, and a complete liar. Skeet shooting? All those articles about her and Clark had been utterly devoid of a single glimpse into her past. Did no one care where this woman came from? They'd all been so consumed with her engagement, her wedding, her bolting from it that not a single question had been asked.

He had questions. For later.

He angled his head, kissing her more deeply, pouring years of isolation into the moment. With each kiss, he felt the shadows dissolving from his soul, replaced by a faint pulse of light, of energy, of *life*.

Piper sighed and slid her arms around his neck, and suddenly the kiss turned from fantastic to searing. Desire unleashed its fiery heat in his gut, winding its way through his body, cell by cell, gaining momentum, gaining power, gaining boldness.

She pressed closer against him, and he could feel her breasts against his chest.

Suddenly, the shadows of his past were gone, and all he was aware of was the woman in his arms. Piper. Only Piper.

He slipped his hands under her shirt, spanning his palms across the bare skin of her lower back. They both sucked in their breath at the same time, and they laughed. "Wow," she said. "That got my attention."

"You have a great back." He bent his head to graze his teeth over the side of her neck, still palming her lower back. He loved feeling her skin beneath his hand. There was something so intimate about skin-to-skin. An intimacy that made his awareness slow down and become fully immersed in the experience.

Piper let out a little groan. "Dear heavens, this is just ridiculous. How can one kiss feel this amazing?"

"Chicks dig guys in uniform," he said as he nibbled his way across her collarbone.

"You're not in uniform."

"I have one, though. Several, actually. That's all it takes. It's a vibe." He kissed her again, deeper, more personal, asking, taking, wanting more. Needing more.

When she sighed and leaned into him, gripping his biceps, he knew he was lost. He wanted it all with her. "I want you naked and wrapped around me," he whispered.

"Oh, God. That's a visual." She pulled back, staring at him with wide eyes. "You're so terrible. We're platonic. Jellyfish friends."

"There's no jellyfish anywhere in sight, and you know it."

"Don't destroy my illusions. That's just rude." She was breathing heavily from their kiss, and he could see the desire etched on her face. "Damn you, Declan. You're literally pure temptation. That's so rude to be that compelling on so many levels."

He grinned. "Back at ya, sweetheart."

"Really?" She brightened. "You're nearly desperate to rip my clothes off and lose yourself in all the glorious curves of my body?"

"Yeah. That."

"Well, level playing fields are always good."

The tension was coiling tighter and tighter between them. Desire was strung between them like a spring, dragging them closer and closer. All it would take was one of them to break the impasse, and they'd be naked within seconds.

He couldn't make that move.

The deal had been platonic. He wasn't going to be that guy who broke her trust.

She had to make the move.

Was she going to lean in? She might…she might…

A sharp bark sounded behind him, and before he could turn, Angel launched herself past him at Piper, taking a flying leap. Piper's eyes widened, but she managed to brace herself before seventy pounds of dog landed in her arms. She caught the dog, laughing as Angel started showering her face with kisses. "Oh, baby, your timing is perfect."

"Is it?" But he was grinning, too. "Angel's afraid of everyone except me and my family. But I've never seen her leap into anyone's arms except mine."

Piper backed up and sat on the couch. "I'm special like that." She laughed and hugged the dog. "We became friends when I was at your place showering. We have a bond."

"I can see that." He wasn't sure if he was relieved or frustrated by the interruption, but he knew damn well the joy it gave him to see his dog happy. It gave him an idea, a solution to the problem that had been gnawing at him. "Hey, when I go back to work, I'm going to have some long days. Any chance I could pay you to take care of her while I'm at work?"

Piper raised her brows. "I have long days too."

"Yeah, but maybe not on the same days I do." He nodded at

the dog. "She's had a rough time. I'd rather her be with someone she trusts."

Piper looked at the dog. "Do you want to hang with me while your papa is off shooting bad guys?"

Angel wagged and yelped.

"Great. We're in."

"Great." The worry that had been gripping him eased off. "I should go."

He wanted Piper to protest, to tell him to toss her over his shoulder, and race to her bedroom.

But she didn't. She simply patted the dog and stood up. "Yeah. And next time I'm on the floor, don't assume I'm dead."

"Meditating. Right. Got it." He snapped his fingers, and Angel came over and leaned against his leg. "Maddie's store at eleven?"

She nodded.

"Any instructions?"

Piper cocked her head and studied him. "Maybe a dress shirt and a tie? Make it look like you're a successful businessman?"

He stiffened. "I'm not."

"I know, but April's mom would like that. April would go for hot, rough Declan. Her mom's different."

He ground his jaw. "I'd rather not."

Piper sighed. "Okay, fine. Do what you want. I'll be fine. Thanks for coming." She gave him a little wave, then picked up her computer, put her feet on the ottoman, and started working.

He stood there for a long minute watching her type. She looked so comfortable, snuggled on the couch with her feet up. He had a sudden desire to sit down next to her, pull out a book, and just absorb the experience of casual intimacy with her. No sex. No talking. Just sharing space and being together.

Shit.

He'd missed those moments. Longed for them with an ache that had hurt like hell. So he'd stopped thinking about them. Moved on. Gotten a dog. And now, suddenly, he was thinking of those moments again.

And he was thinking of having those moments with Piper.

What the hell? They weren't even dating.

But she still felt right.

What was going on?

She looked up then, her brow puckering when she noticed him watching her. "You're like glue. What now? Why are you still here?"

He grinned. "Is glue bad?"

"Always." But there was a hitch in her voice that said she was lying, and suddenly he realized that she was facing the same struggle as he was. The bond between them was unexpected, intense, and neither of them had agreed to it.

Yeah, he got that.

But he was also starting to think that maybe it wasn't such a bad thing. Piper, on the other hand, he suspected was still a hard stop, which meant he wasn't going to cross that line and risk breaking his promise to her.

She'd have to come to him.

He had to get out of there, because if he didn't, she'd probably start calling him worse than glue. "I'll see you later. I'm going to take Angel for a walk." He snapped his fingers. "Come on, sweetie. Good night."

Piper watched him and Angel leave. "Good night."

Declan headed toward the front door, then swore when he saw the broken door frame, shattered from when he'd kicked it in earlier. "Shit." He tried to get the door to shut, but he'd broken it. He closed his eyes, swearing under his breath. "You can't stay here tonight."

Piper glanced at the door. "You broke it?"

"Yeah."

She started laughing. "You're such an overdose of testosterone."

He felt like an idiot. His life wasn't a drug bust. Breaking down doors wasn't life. "Shit. I guess I'm getting back into cop mode. A little on edge."

"Nice way to live, is it? Constantly on edge?"

He narrowed his eyes. "I make a difference."

"I know." She grimaced. "Sorry. Just tense. I'll be fine."

"Sleep in my guest bedroom."

Her eyes widened. "Absolutely not."

"I'll sleep in yours."

She started laughing. "Look, Mr. Jellyfish, I like my personal space. I'm also very capable of taking care of myself. No one is going to break in."

He shifted restlessly. "I can't let you stay here if it's not safe."

Her smile faded. "You don't get to tell me what to do. I pay rent on this place."

"I don't care—"

"Declan." Piper's voice was softer now. "You can't keep people you care about locked in prisons to keep them safe. You have to let go."

His eyes narrowed. "My wife died because I couldn't protect her."

"She died because she was a cop who made a choice to live. Would she have wanted you to lock her in a little safe room so she couldn't get hurt, but also couldn't go out and do what she loved?"

Declan stared at her. "You don't know anything about Diana."

"I don't. It was just a question. You know the answer, not me."

Tension coiled through him. "Fine. Stay here."

Her eyes were understanding. "I still have a toaster," she said. "I'll sleep with it under my pillow."

He wanted to laugh, but he couldn't find the laughter. "It's not a joke."

Piper set the computer aside, rose to her feet, and walked over. She opened her front door and leaned against it. "Good night, Declan. Sleep well."

He didn't move. "Piper—"

"Good night," she said firmly.

He swore under his breath, but finally turned and walked out.

She shut the door behind him, then started laughing when it swung back open again. He looked back and stopped.

"I'll be fine." Would she? Now that she realized the door wouldn't even stay closed, she sounded a little more unsure, but now it was too late for her to back down. She grabbed a sweatshirt, tied it around the knob, then pulled the door shut. She then tied the other end of the sweatshirt around a table leg.

Door shut.

Declan stood outside, watching her through the window. "That's not secure."

She looked over at him, then walked over and opened the window, grinning at him. "I'll put everything important in my bedroom and lock the door."

"I would like to sleep on your couch until it's fixed."

Her face softened, and she leaned toward him, resting her forehead against the screen. "Your alpha male need to protect me is very sweet, but I don't want it. I don't want a man who will break open my front door."

"Even if he thinks you're dead?"

She paused, then sighed. "Declan, my number one priority is standing on my own. I've made too many bad choices in life because I didn't feel like I could handle my life by myself. You're a man who wants to protect his woman, which is a very attractive trait in a man. But I need to stand on my own." She pointed back and forth between them. "This won't work with us. It can't."

He ground his jaw. She wasn't wrong about him. He was a protector, which was why he'd become a cop. Then his old instincts had died, leaving him a walking shell. Piper had woken that back up in him. She made him feel alive, like he had a purpose.

And she wanted nothing to do with that.

She smiled. "I appreciate you, Declan, but I need to get back to work. See you at Maddie's store at eleven." She paused. "You all right?"

He almost laughed at her question. She didn't want him

protecting her, but she was checking in on him? She wanted her space, but at the same time, her warmth and kindness were building a bridge between them.

Damn. She was complicated.

And he loved it.

"Yeah," he said. "I'll be there at eleven to win over the bride's mother."

Piper grinned, a heartfelt, relieved smile that made him feel like a hero. "I was afraid you were going to back out."

"Never. You can count on me."

Something flickered in her eyes. "Thanks. Declan. I appreciate it." She paused as if she were going to say something else, then she closed the window and pulled down the shade.

Declan shoved his hands in his pockets and stood there for a second. "Angel," he said softly. "I think I'm in over my head. What do you think?"

His dog whined and wagged her tail.

He looked down at her. "I didn't want to feel like this again."

Angel wagged her tail.

"If I stay in this, she's either going to ruin me, or save me."

Angel barked and continued to wag her tail.

"You think I should bail? Or man up and see where it goes?" He wasn't a man who'd ever let fear stop him, but Piper scared him shitless, as the broken doorframe proved. Did he want to open this door again? Did he want to feel? To care? To risk?

Twenty-four hours ago, he would have said "hell, no."

But now?

Ninety-nine percent "hell, no." One percent "hell, yeah."

But it was a hell of a one percent.

Angel barked again, then trotted off down the path, clearly tired of waiting for him to decide.

He took one last look at Piper's cottage, then turned to follow his dog. "Yeah, Angel. I agree."

FIFTEEN

Monday morning at eight, Piper was ready.

She sat at her desk in her temporary office and waited.

She heard her boss walk in, and she winced as she waited for Irina Williams to check her messages.

Surprisingly, it took less than three minutes for Irina to burst out in curses, yank her door open, and stride into Piper's office. She walked in, tan and fit, blue eyes blazing. "What the hell, Piper?"

Irina was almost six feet tall, broad shoulders, perfect posture, blond hair bleached almost white. She walked like a model, carried herself like a CEO. She could nurture a crying bride like the kindest mom on the planet, and then turn around and rip through a staff of sub-performing caterers like the worst demon-possessed villain. And she was a beast with design and organization. The best in the area, and Piper's last chance to get back in the business. "Wedding Killer? My firm has a *wedding killer* on staff?"

Piper took a deep breath and went to work. "I met with April last night. We're still with her, and I made some good progress helping her reframe what happened. I think we're in better shape than before." She'd spent last night and this morning canvassing the internet and social media to find new brides to win over. "I have meetings scheduled with four possible new clients this week. Here's the list." She slid the list of high-profile names across her desk.

Irina didn't look at them.

She just flattened both palms on the desktop and leaned in, tapping into her favorite power stance. "You lost two clients over the weekend, and a third cancelled her wedding, citing you as the reason. Tell me I'm wrong. Tell me I have the facts wrong. Tell me that while I was out fighting for my family, you didn't totally screw up my business. Tell me that, Piper. Tell it to me."

Shit. "April now considers me the Bride Protector, not the Wedding Killer. Trust me, that gives us a unique spin that no one else has."

"Us? There is no us. You were a temporary hire, and your season is over." Irina shook her head in visible disappointment and disbelief. "I believed in you, Piper. I gave you a chance, and you..." She held out her hands. "Wedding killer? Really? How did you even manage to do that?"

Piper managed not to grimace. Instead, she lifted her chin and met Irina's gaze. "It's a good thing," she announced with absolute confidence...that was a complete façade.

"Really?" Irina sat down. "Tell me how it's a good thing that I lost three clients in one weekend. I'm listening."

"I'm the bride protector, Irina. It means I protect the brides on their big day."

"Protect them from *what?"*

"Anything. Mother-in-law nightmares. Chaos. Or a man who is cheating on her who she'll regret marrying her whole life." Piper leaned in. "We're the company who the brides can count on to put their best interests first, and not simply use them to make money."

Irina crossed her legs and bounced her foot. "We do use them to make money."

"Everyone uses these women to make money," Piper said. "Literally everyone in their lives. If there is one person in the world they can trust to look out for them, like *really* look out for them, then they will trust us in a way they can't trust anyone else."

Irina didn't speak for a moment, then suddenly stopped bouncing her foot. "I'm almost certain this is asinine, but you have one minute to convince me otherwise. Start."

Piper quickly filled her in on the conversation she and Declan had had the previous evening with April. "She loved it," Piper finished. "And then she went back and told her friends."

Irina drummed her fingers on the arm of the chair. "How attractive is your fiancé?"

"Very attractive."

"Rich?"

Piper pressed her lips together. She didn't like Declan being reduced to money and looks.

"Rich?" Irina repeated.

Reluctantly, Piper nodded.

Irina thought about that. "All right. I'm willing to run with this. If you can land four new clients this week to replace the three we lost, then you can come to work on Monday. I'm not promising you anything long term, but you at least have earned yourself another chance. You have until Sunday at eight. Use this Declan of yours. He sounds helpful."

Relief rushed through Piper. "I won't let you down. I promise."

Irina leaned forward, and her face softened. "Piper, I know you're excellent at your job. But in this business, it's not simply about the execution. We create magic for brides, and you've managed to coat yourself in grime. No bride wants a fairytale covered in grime and doubt."

Piper's stomach tightened. Grime? She was *grime*? "I know, but—"

"The only reason I'm giving you a chance to turn this around is because it's a mess that you made that I don't want to take the time to clean up. Plus, you're hungry, and that makes a woman be the best she can be. Be better, Piper. Because this is the end of the line for you, and we both know it."

And with that, Irina stood up and strode out of the office, leaving behind her the scent of power and mercilessness.

Piper leaned back in her seat, fighting back the sudden tears. Everything about that conversation felt terrible. She was grime. She was prostituting Declan. Her job with brides was to take their money. And even if she achieved the impossible this week, all it got her was Monday morning at the office.

No promises beyond that.

Piper touched her necklace. "Mom," she whispered. "I'm trying. But I'm failing so badly."

How many hours had she and her mom spent dreaming of the life Piper was fighting for? Of the career she'd blown? Of becoming an independent woman who would never need to rely on a man for anything?

Her mom would be crushed if she saw how badly Piper was failing.

Not because she would be disappointed in Piper, but because this had been Piper's dream, and her last words had been to tell Piper to go for it, to get out of the life that had trapped her, to run like hell and make it.

Piper loved planning weddings. She loved creating magic, joy, and perfection for this important day in their lives. She wanted to be the romance and happily ever after specialist.

And she wanted to do it at this level. The top. The best. Like she and her mom had planned.

"Sunday at eight," Irina shouted from her office. "But I'm going to post your job now, just in case. I can't afford to be without an assistant, so if I fire you Sunday, I need to hire someone two minutes later. It's fine to feel threatened by my actions, by the way. Fear is a strong motivator."

Crap. Piper's heart started to race. The normal acquisition rate of new clients was one out of every six meetings, which was a pretty high rate. And this week, she needed to be four for three? That was impossible.

She touched the tiny diamond one more time. "I'm not giving up, Mom. I'm going to make it."

She needed a plan.

And fast.

The moment Declan pulled up to the florist and parked his truck, he had a flashback to when Diana had dragged him to the florist to choose flowers for their wedding.

He remembered his crankiness, and her happiness. He recalled her trying to coax him out of his bad mood, trying to convince him to care about the flowers, but all he'd wanted to do was get back to work on a case that had been pressing at him.

He sat back in his seat, suddenly remembering with vivid clarity the interaction they'd had, and what an ass he'd been. Damn.

He'd expected to feel sadness or PTSD upon showing up at the florist to look at wedding flowers, but he hadn't. He'd just felt this sudden sense of clarity about what a freaking jerk he'd been.

Shit. He almost started laughing. He'd remembered so much about his time with Diana, but this was the first time he'd seen it from the point of view of him being a jerk. It was Piper's fault, the way she called him out on being a grumpy cactus.

He let out a breath. Yeah, his first instinct had been right. As difficult as it was at times to fake this engagement with Piper, she was what he needed. He'd never met a woman who pushed at him so relentlessly, completely uncowed by his moods or his attitude.

Piper was fucking sunshine in a bottle, and he owed her better.

He hadn't been able to man up for Diana at the florist, but he could step up for Piper right now. He could almost feel Diana laughing, delighted that Piper was making him be the man he hadn't been able to be for Diana. "You sent her to me, didn't you?" he asked aloud as he got out of his truck.

There was no answer, but he felt the truth of his words. He was supposed to move forward. He was supposed to follow this path, no matter how fucking hard it was.

He shut the door and faced the florist. It was a different one than he and Diana had used, obviously. They hadn't had a five-star wedding, like the ones Piper planned.

But this was the world he'd grown up in. He could walk in these circles even if he didn't want to. "Right. Let's go."

He squared his shoulders, headed across the parking lot, and stepped inside.

Piper, April, and a woman he assumed was April's mom were gathered around a table filled with flowers in vases. Maddie was laughing with delight, beaming at the trio as if there was nothing more fantastic in the entire world than to be helping a bride select her flowers, which he was pretty sure was the truth.

Her smile was radiant, and her laughter was infectious, as high energy as Piper.

He was willing to bet that Piper had directed April to Maddie's store. Bride Protector indeed. Positive energy all around. Maddie glanced his way, and her smile widened. "Well, hello, Declan."

All three women turned, but Declan only had eyes for Piper. Her eyes widened when she saw him, and then relief filled her face. He was instantly glad he'd come.

"Declan!" Piper said. "This is my fiancé, Declan Jones. Come on over."

Declan strode across the room, summoning the power and authority that his money afforded him. His parents had both grown up poor, and they'd fought hard to get over their sense of not being good enough for these people. They'd taught their kids to present as if they belonged, no matter what they felt like.

So, Declan turned it on, and he saw April's mom stand a little taller, watching him with great interest.

He hadn't bothered with the jacket and tie, but he'd worn the watch. He walked straight over to Piper, slid one arm around her waist, and moved his body at an angle that was pure possession and protection. "I missed you," he whispered softly, just loud enough that the others would think they were overhearing a private moment. "Morning, love."

Piper's eyes widened, and then he kissed her, short and proper, but lingering with a promise of so much more. He flashed her a grin, then turned to April and her mom. "April," he said. "Good to see you again."

Her cheeks were flushed, and he had to keep himself from grinning. Yeah, he knew how to turn it on. He had to admit, it was kind of fun. "And you must be April's sister?" he said to her mom. Oldest damn trick in the book, but when in Rome, right?

April's mom gave him a look like she knew what he was doing, but she loved it anyway. "Any relation to Kitty Jones?"

He flashed her a grin. "Her favorite son."

She smiled then and held out her hand. "Lisbeth Hunsaker. Lovely to meet you."

He shot a glance at Piper, wiggled his brows, then took Lisbeth's hand and gave it a proper honoring worthy of the most well-bred country club sort.

Piper had to turn her head away to hide her smile, but April and Lisbeth both beamed at him. It was absurd the games that they played, how easy it was to make them fall for him. Money, connections, and obsequiousness. No wonder he'd walked away. No wonder his dad had declined to join his mom most of the time for her social outings.

"How did we get the honor of your presence, Mr. Jones?" Lisbeth asked.

"Declan. Call me Declan. I was in the area and wanted to stop in and say hello." He turned to Piper. "Piper—"

"What were you doing in the area?" Lisbeth asked, with a pointed glance at his jeans and work boots.

He turned back to her. "I was buying paint."

Piper gave him a look, and he swore. He probably should have said he was buying a new Rolex or making money doing something.

"For what?"

"My house. I'm redoing it."

Lisbeth's mouth pursed. "You're a laborer?"

"He's a genius," Piper interrupted. "Show her pictures."

Declan didn't give a shit what Lisbeth thought of him, but he knew Piper needed a win here, so he pulled out his phone. He flipped to a few before and after pictures of his house and handed his phone to Lisbeth.

She and April leaned in, scrolled through the photos.

To his surprise, he tensed, waiting for their response. He'd done the house for himself, but he loved it. He suddenly deeply regretted allowing anyone to see or judge what he'd created.

Then April looked up. "You designed and built this?"

"Yeah."

"It's gorgeous."

He couldn't help but grin. "Thanks."

"Will you build our house?" April said. "Wendall hired a contractor, but your work is so much better."

"Do your house?" Declan was startled by the offer. "I'm not for hire. It's not my job. I just do it for fun."

"How much would it take to make it your job?" Lisbeth asked.

"No price. I'm not for sale." He took his phone back and shoved it in his pocket. "I gotta go. Piper?"

She was watching him with a thoughtful look, and laughter chased away his crankiness. His little fake fiancée was planning something, and he knew he wouldn't like it. "No," he said.

She grinned. "You don't even know what I was thinking."

"It doesn't matter. You have that look in your eye." On a whim, he leaned in and kissed her, a little longer and less proper this time. Not for show, but because he needed to connect with her authenticity. Piper might play in this world, but she was nothing like it. He broke the kiss. "See you at home, my love."

She grinned. "You bet."

He nodded his farewell at the others, then headed toward the door. Just as he reached the door, however, it swung open and a man in a custom suit strode in. He glanced dismissively through Declan, then focused on the women. "April. My darling. So sorry I'm late."

Wendall?

Curious now, Declan turned to watch as Wendall strode up to the trio, then Declan saw Wendall's gaze sweep down Piper's body with an entitlement that made Declan's alarms go off.

"Piper, so great to see you." Wendall kissed the back of Piper's hand, lingering ever so slightly before turning back to his bride.

Son of a bitch. Declan would wager a month's salary that Wendall was cheating on April.

He'd been around enough scumbags in his life that he knew the details to look for, the giveaways they couldn't hide.

Declan ground his jaw. What the fuck? Piper needed this wedding to work. But if this guy was a jerk, April needed to know.

Declan's gaze shot back to Piper. She was fully immersed in the moment, laughing and coaxing smiles out of her clients. She was electric with her energy, he could practically feel them falling under her spell.

No wonder brides wanted to hire her. Piper's passion and zeal were infectious, and she was so capable that she dissolved tension and difficulty before it could even take root, navigating disagreements between the bride and the others with practiced ease.

Piper cared, he realized. She truly cared about what she did. It wasn't simply about the money or the fashion. Her heart was all in. She literally created joy. That was her job.

It was perfect for her.

Then Wendall laughed, a grating, annoying, much-too-bold laugh, drawing Declan's attention back to him. Declan didn't want to be right about him. Maybe Declan was just too damned cynical about this high-class world. Maybe he was looking for trouble.

Just because he didn't like the guy didn't mean he was cheating on April.

His gaze went back to Piper. Maybe he was simply jealous that another man had touched her.

Oh...*hell.*

Was that it?

It might be.

SIXTEEN

"You having second thoughts?"

Declan didn't look over at Aiden Black, the owner of the Night Owl Pub, as he executed a perfect pour of a local beer. "About what?"

"Going back to being a cop. About your interview on Friday. I know you've been trying to pass that physical for a long time, but you're not dancing around here with joy like I thought you'd be. So, yeah, second thoughts?"

Declan set the beer on the bar and took the credit card from the customer. "No."

"Then what's the mood for? I haven't seen you this tense since you first walked in three years ago wanting enough alcohol to kill yourself."

Declan turned to face his boss. Aiden was only a few years older than he was, but had just as much crap in his past as Declan did. Different crap, but still a lot. That's why they got along. Because they both knew how to keep going when they had to. "I didn't want to kill myself."

"I know. But you were in bad shape."

The bar was quiet, as it often was on Monday nights. A few folks were playing darts. One of the pool tables had a game. And there were about five tables that had ordered some appetizers with their drinks. Not much, which was too bad, because Declan wanted to be distracted tonight. "I'm not in that kind of shape."

Aiden leaned on the bar and folded his arms across his chest. Aiden had been a boxer for a brief time in his youth, and he still had the muscles from it. He didn't employ bouncers, because he could take care of anyone who caused trouble. "You're off your game tonight. What's going on?"

Declan ran his hand through his hair. "I made a deal with the woman who lives in my guest house. She's driving me a little nuts."

Aiden's brows went up. "A *little?* A lot, you mean. What kind of deal?"

"Fake engagement."

Aiden stared at him in surprise, and then burst out laughing. "You're kidding, right?"

"No." Declan grabbed a cloth and started wiping down the bar. "I wanted to get my mom off my back, and she needed a fiancé for work purposes."

"This is the woman who came in here that time because she locked herself out, and she needed a key from you?"

Declan nodded. He'd forgotten about the time Piper had tracked him down. She'd swept into his bar in her business suit, heels, and tight bun, in total control of herself. Cool. Collected. On a mission.

She was so much more than that. He'd had no idea at the time.

"She running you ragged? A control freak? Too much woman for you?"

"She's not a control freak," he shot back. "She's smart, determined, and kind as hell."

Aiden raised his brows, looking surprised. "Is she?"

"Yeah. And she's passionate about her job." Declan paused. "It's inspiring."

Aiden studied him. "Because you used to feel that way, and now you don't? I haven't seen that passion in a long time."

His friend wasn't wrong, but that didn't matter. Declan shrugged. "It's time. I can feel it."

"You feel it, eh?" Aiden hefted a tray of glasses from under the bar and set them on the counter. "Maybe you're just getting old, and you're feeling arthritis, not a siren call to go back to a job you don't actually want to do."

"I'm not old."

Aiden barked a laugh. "You're limping around here like an old man."

"My knee's getting better." But the minute Declan thought of it, the ache pulsed at him. *Shit.*

"If it's not the job that's getting to you, and I'm not convinced that it's not, then it's the woman," Aiden said. "Why is she driving you nuts? Because I *did* notice how quickly you jumped to her defense when I called her a control freak."

Declan glanced at Aiden, who was leaning against the bar as if he was settling in for a long girl talk. "Don't you have work to do?"

"I own the bar. I don't have to work. I just employ scrubs like you to amuse myself. What's going on with the future wife?"

Declan grimaced. "I like kissing her."

Aiden grinned. "That's fantastic. It's been a long time, eh?"

"Yeah." Declan tossed the towel down. "It wasn't supposed to be complicated, but it is."

"Because you like kissing her."

"Yeah."

Aiden paused, watching Declan too carefully. "And you like *her*?"

Declan shot a look at Aiden and shrugged. He didn't want to put it into words, but understanding settled on Aiden's face. "If you're interested in her," Aiden said softly, "it means you're ready."

"I'm not interested in anything."

"Until you're ready."

"It's not a matter of being ready. I just don't want to go there."

Aiden folded his arms over his chest. "I've known you a long time, Declan. You can be a stubborn ass. But sometimes you're also stupid."

Declan said nothing as he began unloading the glasses from the tray Aiden had pulled out from under the counter.

"It sounds to me like she might be exactly what you need. Stop fighting it. Jump in. See what happens. What's the worst that can happen?"

"That I fall in love with her, and she gets shot and dies in my arms." The words fell out before he realized he was saying them, but once they were out, it was too late.

They hung in the air, weighty and thick, taking up the oxygen like a thief.

"Hiding from possible loss isn't living," Aiden said finally. "And it's an insult to those who don't get to live. If you're interested in Piper, then you need to honor that. Don't kick yourself in the ass or try to crush the light that's trying to come back to life. Go with it. You owe yourself that. Just allow yourself to live your truth."

Declan braced his hands on the counter and let out his breath. "I don't want to."

"Yes, you do, or you wouldn't be having the response to her that you're having—" Aiden laughed softly. "Speak of the devil. Blue dress and everything."

Declan looked sharply to the door, and sucked in his breath when he saw Piper walking into the bar. She was wearing a blue dress that fit her like it was best friends with every curve on her. But in a fashion statement that was adorable, she was wearing sneakers and carrying a gray hooded sweatshirt on her arm.

She scanned the bar, and when her gaze fell on him, relief flashed across her face.

Something was wrong. He knew it.

SEVENTEEN

Declan instantly stood taller, and waved Piper over.

Aiden nudged him on the shoulder. "Go on break. I got this covered."

"Yeah, great." Declan didn't hesitate for a second. He just stepped around the bar and met her halfway. "You okay?"

She looked at him with her gorgeous blue eyes. "Do you have a second to talk? I need advice."

"Yeah, you bet." He took her arm and guided her to a table in the corner. "You want something to drink?"

"No, I'm good." She sat down and faced him.

"What's up?"

She grimaced and leaned in. "I think Wendall made a pass at me today. But it was subtle. I'm not sure. I might be imagining it. I'm imagining it, right? You met him. What did you think?"

Oh, fuck. He owed her the truth. "I noticed he was staring at your body today," he said. "I didn't like his vibe."

"Dammit." She leaned back in her seat. "I've felt something was off for a while, but I figured it wasn't my job to interfere. But now with this whole Bride Protector craziness that's going on, I'm thinking differently."

Declan leaned forward. "Because you're a good person. You care about people, not just making a deal. It's okay to be like that."

"Is it?" She drummed her fingers on the table. "I can't say anything to April. I don't have any concrete evidence. It's just a feeling. I can't say anything based on a feeling."

"No, you can't." He paused. "I have contacts who could trail him."

She rolled her eyes. "Oh, God. Can you imagine how that would go over? Hire me for your wedding, and I'll hire a private investigator to trail your fiancé to catch him cheating? I can't do that."

Declan chuckled. "Yeah, that's a whole new level of bride protector."

"Right?" She sat back. "So, what do I do?"

"Do nothing," he said.

"Nothing? Really?" She frowned. "That doesn't feel right."

"Has he actually done anything?"

"No, but—"

"Then do nothing. Just keep moving forward, and keep an eye out. If something actually happens, then reevaluate. If not, then you can't interfere. April may know exactly what is going on and not care."

"And if she doesn't know?"

"You don't know anything for sure either."

She let out her breath. "So, I just do my job as usual?"

"Yeah. Until and unless you witness something concrete enough that you need to take it to her. Other than that, you have to stay out of it. If he's cheating on her, it'll come out."

"Before the wedding?"

He shrugged. "Let's take it one day at a time." He paused, thinking. "I could help. I'll bond with him as a guy and see what I can get out of him."

Her face brightened. "You will?"

"Yeah. I can interfere without it affecting my career. You can't.

Find out where he'll be, and I'll show up. See what the male bond can uncover."

She beamed at him. "Thank you. You're amazing."

He felt like his whole soul lit up when she smiled at him like that. "No problem. It's what a good fiancé does, right?"

"I don't know. I've never had a good fiancé."

He wasn't sure he'd ever been one.

She touched his shoulder. "Thanks for your help. I'm going to head out."

He narrowed his eyes, studying her. She looked tired. Worn out. "You all right?"

Tears suddenly filled her eyes, startling him. "I'm great. Thanks. Just a long day."

Protectiveness surged through Declan, and he leaned forward. She might not want his protection, but that didn't mean he could turn it off. "Talk to me."

She raised her brows. "I'm fine."

He could feel the weight in her words. She wasn't fine. "I did mention to you that I'm a human lie detector, right? You know, ex-cop and stuff?"

The corner of her mouth curved up. "You're very irritating."

"I know." He paused, trying to think. He knew the stress she was under, and he also knew that mistakes happened when under stress. "All right. I'll make a deal."

She folded her arms over her chest. "What's that?"

"I'll stop asking about your emotional state if you play a game of darts with me."

"Darts?" Her gaze shot to the dart board near her, and interest flickered in her eyes. "I love darts."

Well, damn. How many wedding planners in his mom's circles know how to play darts? He wanted to ask why she was a darts girl, but he wasn't ready to push her away. "I'm excellent at darts. Better than you, I suspect."

Her brows went up. "You saw me with the can opener. You really want to challenge me to darts?"

Ah...she had a competitive streak. He loved that. "I do," he said. "I definitely want to challenge you. Throwing a dart is nothing like throwing a can opener. There's a lot more finesse involved."

Challenge flashed in her eyes. "I'll destroy your fragile male ego if we play."

"My ego isn't frail. It's rock solid."

"Is it?"

"Like a boulder." He turned toward the bar. "Aiden! You need me anymore tonight?"

Aiden shook his head. "The place is dead. I got it covered. Hey, Piper. Congrats on the engagement. Declan's a great guy."

She waved back. "Thanks," she said, before turning back to Declan. "He knows it's not real?"

"Yeah. He's a good friend. I trust him." He paused. "How could you tell?"

"Because he's a terrible actor." She raised her voice. "Aiden. Who would your money be on if Declan and I played a game of darts?"

"Declan," Aiden said without hesitation. "He's spent a lot of time in dive bars."

"And you assume that because I'm a woman I haven't?"

He grinned. "You don't look like someone who has spent a lot of time in dive bars playing darts, regardless of gender."

She stood up. "A free girls' night for me and my friends if I beat him? We get drinks and food."

Aiden grinned. "You're on. Declan, don't let me down."

"Never. I am not a gentleman when it comes to darts." He jogged over to the bar, grabbed a box of darts from under the counter, then came back. "You ready to lose?"

She snorted. "I might lose at being a wedding planner, but not darts. Never darts."

He set the darts in her hand. "Best two out of three?"

"One game, winner takes all, and then I have to go back to work."

Two hours later, Piper was laughing so hard she had to sit down on the floor. After five games of darts, Aiden had kicked them out, and they'd retired to Declan's house to play ping pong in his basement, which had been one of the best decisions she'd ever made.

She hadn't laughed that hard in a very long time. "You're the worst ping pong player I've ever seen."

Declan grinned, amusement dancing across his face as he dropped to his belly to fish a ball out from under his couch. "I'm definitely not the worst, because you're worse than I am."

She leaned against the wall, laughing as he wormed himself along the floor, trying to get the ball. "But I crushed you at darts."

"You did. That was impressive as hell. Unexpected. Aiden's going to put the girls' night on my tab."

She laughed. "Good. You deserve it for losing."

"I didn't lose. I was destroyed. I'm still bleeding from my soul...but not my ego. That's still intact." He wiggled back out, hopped to his feet, and held up the ping pong ball. "We both have won seven games in ping pong. Call it a tie or go for the title of grand champion?"

She looked around. "Are there any other games here? Maybe some air hockey?"

"Damn. I love air hockey. I'll get us a table for next time."

"Oh, heavens no. Don't buy an air hockey table for me. Who knows when we'll play again?"

He crouched in front of her, balancing on the balls of his feet. "You're scared of losing, aren't you? That I'll be the grand champion, and you'll be sad."

She pushed him off balance, and he fell over. "We can always do a tiebreaker of hurling can openers at posts."

"Hell, no. I concede defeat on that one. That's a special kind of talent." He rolled onto his side and propped himself on his elbow. "Where'd you learn to play darts like that?"

"Kindergarten. I was five. I owned recess."

He grinned. "The woman with no past."

Her smile faded. "What?"

"You have no past. I looked up Clark to see what he was about, and there's not a single hint of where you came from before you landed in the wedding planner arena. No hometown. No college. Nothing."

Okay, that was the end of the night. She faked a yawn. "I have a potential client meeting at eight tomorrow morning. I need to hit the hay. Tonight was fun. Thanks."

He rose to his feet at the same time she did. "Why do you hide your past?"

She raised her brows. "Because it's a thing."

He grinned. "A thing? What does that mean?"

"Exactly." She gave him a little wave, then patted Angel who had woken up from her couch nap and trotted over. "See you tomorrow at the country club. I'll meet you there at seven? I'll be coming from a meeting."

Declan followed her as she headed up the basement stairs. "You deserve not to hide."

She glanced over her shoulder. "I'm not hiding."

"When you carry secrets, they eat away at you," he said. "Whatever is in your past doesn't matter. It takes a lot of effort to hide things. I don't care what it is."

She turned to face him. "You're a cop."

"So?"

"What if I told you that I'd killed someone and there was a warrant out for my arrest? Still don't care?"

He grinned. "A fugitive on the run? That does complicate things."

"Right? So I can't tell you. One never knows what will trigger someone else."

"Try me."

"Can't. Not while I need you to be my adoring fiancé. And

then, I can't tell you because you'll be bitter and heartbroken when we break up and you might use the information against me." She patted his chest as she reached the top basement stair. "You're just going to have to see me for who I am today and go with it. It's really the best way to be. People aren't their pasts unless they choose to be. And I choose not to be."

He whistled. "That's a great life lesson right there."

"Right? I've practiced it a lot. Glad I got the chance to use it." She headed for the back door, but just as she reached for the handle, she turned back to him. "If you call upon one of the private investigators you mentioned earlier tonight, and you send him after my secrets, I'm going to tell your mom that you lied to her to get her off your back. Trust will be broken, and she'll pay thousands of women to stalk you."

He raised his brows. "The idea terrifies me." He held up his pinkie. "Pinkie promise to leave your past where it is unless you choose to tell me."

She locked pinkies with him. "Good boy. He knows when he is beaten."

"Do I?" He grinned wickedly. "Or am I just very clever and I have you exactly where I want you? All my nefarious goals are within reach."

"Nefarious is fun. Go for them and don't let anyone stop you." She pulled her hand free, despite the temptation to tug Declan right over to her. Seeing his fun, goofy side tonight had added to his charm, and she needed to be a smart girl and not play in his sandbox anymore tonight. "See ya."

He leaned on the doorframe, his athletic, muscular body like pure temptation as he watched her go. "Have a good night."

"Thanks. You, too." She took a breath, having to steel herself from throwing herself at his chest and letting things play out as they would. "You need to put yourself back in your dark, isolated corner."

His smile became more wicked. "Do I?"

"Yes." She waved her hand up and down his body. "This

muscley-thing combined with that smile and wit is just too much for anyone's good."

"I'll take that into account as I ponder my life tonight."

She couldn't help but laugh. "You're dangerous. Go away."

"Can't. We're engaged. You're stuck with me. Wait until you see me at a country club event. You won't find me so attractive. It sucks my soul dry, and I'll be a shriveled corpse of my former self by the end of the evening."

She paused, sensing an element of truth to his words. "Really?"

"Yeah. But I'll do it for love. And remember, I have nothing against sleepovers with my fiancée, so anytime you want to start those, you just invite yourself right in."

She burst out laughing. "And now you're a flirt? Seriously? You need to stop being so freaking adorable."

He grinned. "You bring out this witty, playful side of me I've never had before. I might keep it. It's fun."

"It is fun," she agreed, "but disconcerting. I like things to be predictable and orderly."

"I always did as well. Maybe this new attitude is temporary for me."

"I hope so." She stepped back, somewhat appalled by how big she was smiling and how much laughter was bubbling through her. "See you tomorrow."

"You got it, my darling." He waved her off. "I'm just going to stand here and admire your ass as you walk back to your place."

Heat radiated through her cheeks. "Go inside."

"Can't. I just noticed your ass tonight. Two years you've been living there, and I never noticed. I need to make up for lost time. It's my duty as your fiancé to help you feel gorgeous and secure all the time. So, great ass. I love it."

She stood there, staring at him, all sorts of emotions simmering inside her. She knew he was being silly, but she loved this side of him. And she absolutely loved the fact he liked her butt. She wanted him to check her out, which made her equally determined not to let it happen. "You're my fiancé only when we're around other people."

"Doesn't work like that. Any great actor knows that you need to become the part to make it real. Just doing my best for you."

She put her hand on her hips and glared at him.

He grinned. "I can literally hear you giggling right now."

"Oh, shut up." She threw up her hands in mock despair. "Good night, Declan. See you tomorrow." She turned and headed back to her cottage.

As she walked, she could feel the heat from his gaze on her. For a moment, she was tempted to tie her sweatshirt around her waist to block his view, but the minute she thought it, she dismissed the idea.

Instead, she threw back her shoulders and walked like she was the siren put on this earth to awaken the man who'd been hiding in darkness for so long.

The night was quiet as she walked, no sound but her sneakers on the stones.

When she reached her door, she turned and looked over her shoulder as she opened her door, which he had fixed for her at some point during the day.

He hadn't moved from the door, but his smile was gone. On his face was an expression of pure wanting, of desire, of *heat*.

Answering heat flooded her right back. *Oh, Lordy.*

Declan met her gaze, and for a moment, they just looked at each other.

She realized he wasn't going to go inside.

He was going to wait in his open doorway until she decided which door she was going to walk through. His offer was real. He wanted her, and he would welcome her if she invited herself into his house.

The realization struck heat in her belly, and suddenly, she couldn't breathe.

Declan, the man who had held himself in the shadows for

years, wanted *her*. He'd come out of his darkness because of *her*. Tonight, he'd laughed with *her*.

Wow.

Just...

She turned and bolted inside before she could make a choice she'd regret.

But the minute she shut the door behind her, she wondered if she'd already made that choice...the one she would always regret.

EIGHTEEN

K itty had won.

She'd played dirty, and she'd won.

And Declan hadn't seen it coming.

Was he really fit to be a cop if his own mother could successfully lie to him, and he didn't notice?

He was going to have to up his game.

He was pissed, but also impressed. *Go, Mom.*

Because dinner at the club with his mom had been a farce.

It was a damned fundraiser that had three hundred guests, a live band, and money dripping off every word uttered by the attendees.

Declan stood inside the ballroom doors, tension growing fast and dark inside him as he digested the event that his mother had tricked him into attending. He'd been actually looking forward to dinner tonight. Ready to laugh and feel a lightness in his heart that had come to life last night with Piper.

But when he'd said his soul would be a shriveled corpse by the end of the night, he'd vastly overestimated how long that process would take. In reality, the deed had been accomplished in about three seconds after walking in.

If it weren't for Piper, he would turn around and leave.

If she didn't show up soon, he might have to anyway.

Kitty trotted up, beaming at him. "Declan, my darling! You look so dashing! I have so many people who are dying to meet my reclusive son—"

"Dinner. That's what tonight was."

She beamed at him unapologetically. "We are eating dinner."

He shifted restlessly. "You didn't say it was a fundraiser."

"You didn't ask, did you?" She was clearly feeling sassy and unrepentant, and he wasn't in the mood for it.

"You knew I wouldn't come," he said.

"How would I know that? You haven't been here in years and suddenly you come for Piper. How do you expect me to know the rules about what you will and won't attend?"

He took a breath, trying to remain calm. "Mom. I can't stay."

"Declan!" Piper's hand slid into his, and he closed his eyes, breathing in the relief that her touch gave him. "I'm so sorry I'm late." She squeezed his hand, her thumb rubbing over his palm. "Hi, Kitty."

His mom beamed at her. "Piper! So delighted you're here. I think Declan was about to hightail it out of here!"

He opened his eyes and looked over at Piper. She was leaning into his shoulder, her blue eyes looking up at him with concern. His breath caught when he saw her. Her hair was falling in adorable curls over her shoulders, and her eyes were luminous with her makeup. He generally wasn't into women who wore a lot of makeup, but the way Piper was wearing it was stunning. "Shit, you're beautiful."

She beamed at him. "You're very handsome as well. I didn't think your body knew how to wear a tie."

"It doesn't."

She patted the tie, which meant her hand settled on his chest, easing the tension gripping him so tightly. "It's okay. I'll protect you from the tie."

He was surprised to feel himself smile. "Appreciate that."

"No problem. I got your back, big guy."

"Thanks." His equilibrium back on track, he looked over at his mom, who was watching them intently. "What time is dinner?"

"Seven thirty. We're at table three, down in front." She turned to Piper. "I have some folks I'd like you both to meet. Shall we?"

Piper smiled at his mom before he could answer. "We'll catch up with you in a few minutes, Kitty. I need to run a few things by Declan first."

Kitty frowned. "But—"

"We'll be right back!" Piper pushed Declan to the side, and waved at Kitty. "Promise!"

Declan let out his breath as Piper headed to the bar, her grip tight on his hand. She didn't slow down until she found them two seats at the end of the bar. "Sit."

He sat.

She sat next to him, spinning the bar stool so she was facing him. She leaned in, took his hands, and smiled, using her body language to send the message to the room that it was an intimate moment not to be disturbed.

He was impressed.

"You looked like you were about to drop dead on the spot when I walked up." she said. "What's going on?"

He shook his head. "Nothing. It's fine."

"Now, you're the bad liar. I need to know what's going on with you. There are a lot of people around here who are going to start talking to us really soon, and if you're about to crack, I need to be prepared. Do you need to leave?"

"No. Shit. No."

"What is it?"

He swore, his gaze going around the room, at all the fancy dress and artificial conversations he'd left behind. "I haven't been here since my dad died."

Piper blinked. "You miss your dad?"

"Yeah, well, I mean." *Shit.* "I don't want to talk about this."

"Doesn't matter. You're on a job with me, and I need the info required to get through tonight. What's going on?"

Declan ground his jaw, and suddenly the story started tumbling out, words he'd never spoken in his life. "My dad was a cop. My mom was a pop star. They met when he did security for her at a concert in town. They fell hard for each other and got married."

Surprise flickered in Piper's eyes. "That's so romantic."

"It is, yeah. But she wanted him to quit being a cop and go on tour with her. To be her arm candy. He refused. He didn't like this world. This superficiality. He never fit in, but she immersed herself in it as her career exploded."

Piper chewed her lower lip and nodded, listening.

Declan continued, surprised how good it felt to talk about it. "Eventually, my mom filed for divorce, because she felt like he didn't support her. Broke both their hearts because they really loved each other. After a couple years of separation, my mom quit touring and came home here to stay. They got back together, but my dad never came to these things unless he had to, and even then, he hated being here. Then my dad got sick. He died a few years later."

Empathy softened Piper's face. "Oh. I'm so sorry."

"Thanks." Declan became aware of how tightly he was holding her hand, but he didn't loosen his grip. He needed to touch her. "Before he died, he told me to be true to who I was. To not get caught up in the fact I was a trust-fund baby. He told me I still needed to be someone, do something, make a difference."

Piper nodded. "Sounds like a great man."

"He was. He left behind a lot of cases unsolved, so I became a cop. My brother is in my mom's world, but I felt like someone needed to keep my dad's legacy alive. So, that's what I did." He didn't tell her what else his dad had told his kids: to embrace love when you were lucky enough to find it. Never to prioritize ego or career or anything over love.

His dad had always mourned the time he'd lost with his wife, especially when he died so soon after they'd reconciled. "He told us not to waste a moment of our lives. To live the best we could, love the most we could, and to never betray the gifts we were given."

"By gifts, he meant who you are as a person, right?"

Declan grinned. Piper got it. "Yeah."

"And for you, that's being a cop."

"Yeah." Wasn't it? He leaned in, rubbing his thumbs over Piper's palms. "I believe that my dad died of a broken heart. The years he lost with my mom almost killed him, and when they got back together, it was too late. She'd rejected him for his lack of commitment to her money and fame, and he was never able to fully recover from that."

Understanding filled Piper's face. "You resent her for that? And you resent the money because of the tragedy it brought to your dad?"

Declan nodded. "I try not to. He forgave her. I love her, and I accept her, but sometimes, I see that same edge to her that drove him away." He waved his hand around the room. "This world haunts me."

Piper squeezed his hands. "We don't need to stay," she said softly. "I'll tell your mom I'm not feeling well—"

"No." Declan cut her off. "My dad lost the woman he loved because he refused to accept part of who she was. This world is important to you. You need to be here. And I'm here for you."

Piper smiled softly and brushed her finger along his jaw. "We're not married, Declan. You don't need to suffer for me."

"I think…" He paused to kiss the palm of her hand. "No. I believe that you are in my life because I need you to get out of my darkness, and that includes this. You give me reason to walk into this life again, the life my dad rejected, and I rejected as well. My mom and brother live here, and if I can't be in it, then I can't be with them."

Her gaze was kind as she looked at him. "But it's hard."

"It's easier with you." He grinned. "Don't get me wrong. I'm not going to start going to charity events every weekend, but a family dinner here and there? Might be worth it."

Piper smiled. "It might be. Kitty isn't that bad. I'd take her as my mom."

Declan was feeling so much clearer now. Sharing all that with Piper had lightened a weight that had been clamped down on his shoulders for years. He hadn't even understood what he'd just told her, until the words had come out of his mouth. "What about your mom? She good?"

Piper's smile flickered, just a little bit, but enough that he noticed. "Naughty boy. Trying to start another conversation so we never leave the bar? I see right through those manipulations."

What was she hiding? What was in Piper's story that she was so worried about keeping hidden, even from him?

Her gaze slipped past him, and she sat up. "There's a bride I'm meeting with tomorrow. Can we go dance next to her?"

"Yeah, sure." He couldn't hide his disappointment that she hadn't met him halfway, after he'd laid it out for her. He'd known he had emotional walls, but Piper's were even stronger than his.

But there was something there, deep beneath the surface with Piper, and he wanted to know what it was. He wanted her to trust him enough to tell him. He wanted her all the way.

NINETEEN

An hour later, Declan was restless.

Better than being in a high state of stress, but still antsy.

Piper was in deep conversation with a potential bride. His mom was off somewhere making the rounds. And he had no interest in wandering around chatting with strangers about things he didn't care about.

He knew the people at the fundraiser wouldn't appreciate it if he walked up to them and started talking about crime scenes or how to cut tile so it fit perfectly even at an angle.

He'd tried tonight to play the game. And he'd managed to be here. But he still felt no fire, no purpose. The only time he'd felt alive tonight was when he was with Piper or watching her. She was electric here. This was her world, and he marveled at how she seemed to light up anyone she spoke to, no matter who it was. People *wanted* to talk to her, and she wanted to talk to them.

And all he wanted was to lean on the bar and watch her until she needed him.

"Declan."

He turned his head at the familiar voice and saw Dylan Hart standing next to him. "Hey," he said, surprised. And relieved. The

Harts were wealthy as shit, but they were regular people, like him, and he liked them. "What are you doing here?"

Dylan was part of the Hart family from Oregon, nine siblings who had been homeless kids, and then come together as family when they were teenagers living under a bridge. They'd taken the last name Hart, and then made billions with the security technology they'd originally created to break into school and city systems to protect themselves from being dragged back into the foster system.

Although they were primarily ranchers, each Hart had their own business that they did because it moved them. Dylan had a detective agency, and he often worked with an attorney named Eliana Tiernan, who helped women and their kids escape abusive situations. She gave them a new identity, a life, and made sure that no one found them.

Dylan had recruited Declan's off-the-books assistance a couple times in the past when there had been a situation in the local area, but now that Lucas was engaged to Piper's friend, Maddie, the Harts were around more.

The Harts showed up at fundraisers from time to time. They had a ton of money, but they mostly created their own foundations.

"I'm working," Dylan said.

Declan's attention sharpened. "The kind of work I helped you with?"

"Yep."

"Here? Now?"

"Yep." Dylan picked up a beer and turned his back on the room. He leaned on the bar, and watched the room in the mirror above the back of the bar. "There's a woman in a yellow dress by the fireplace. Call her Jane."

Declan found Jane immediately. She was tall and curvy, dressed to perfection. She was smiling and charming, but his trained eye saw the tension in her shoulders. And, most importantly, Declan saw the way the man standing next to her had a tight grip on her elbow, a grip that Declan was pretty sure was leaving marks. "Her husband?"

"Yep. Name's Dick."

Dick was very tall, broad shoulders, and had a hard, cold gaze. "Status?"

"Dick was supposed to be in Paris at a meeting, but he showed up tonight. The kids were with a babysitter Eliana provided, so Eliana has the kids in a car outside. My jet is waiting. But we can't get Jane away from him. We need time for her to get on board before he notices she's gone. He's connected and can mobilize help fast if he knows she's on the run. We need to move fast, because it looks like he's planning to make her leave the party soon." Dylan's voice was low and casual, friendly. Anyone listening wouldn't be paying any attention to their discussion, because his tone was so neutral.

Shit. "You want help."

"Yep."

"What can I do?"

"We need a distraction so I can get Jane out to the car."

Declan studied Dick for a moment, assessing the situation. Dick's attention was laser-focused on Jane. There wasn't much that Declan would be able to say that would get his attention long enough for Jane to slip out, short of assaulting him.

If he wanted his job back, he couldn't assault a civilian.

Dick glanced at his watch, and Declan swore.

"We're running out of time," Dylan said.

"I know." Declan's adrenaline was firing now, all senses on high alert. "I have a secret weapon tonight." He gestured at Piper.

She caught his movement, and paused her conversation.

He gestured a second time and nodded.

Piper, as he knew she would, immediately ended the conversation and hurried over. She glanced at Dylan, then frowned. "Hi Dylan. What's going on?"

Declan didn't waste time. "There's a woman here who needs an extraction."

She blinked. "What?"

Dylan turned to face her. "My team was hired to help a woman and her kids disappear, but her husband showed up. We need a distraction. Yellow dress."

Piper stared at them for a split second, and Declan could see her processing what Dylan had told her. Now that Maddie was engaged to Dylan's brother, he suspected that Piper knew a little bit about the relationship the Harts had with Eliana and her business helping women escape from bad relationships.

As he expected, Piper pulled her shoulders back and set her jaw. Ready to help. "What's her name?"

"Jane. Her husband is Dick."

"Her real name."

Dylan hesitated, then answered. "Jessie McWilliams."

"Okay. I'll get her away, and then Declan, you need to talk to him and distract him."

Declan nodded. "Give me a topic," he said to Dylan. "What would get his interest?"

"Guns. He's carrying concealed. Notice it and talk guns."

Hell. The guy was carrying? This was a fucking situation. "Okay."

Piper glanced at Dylan, but didn't hesitate with the new information. "Okay, let's go." She strode across the room, waving her hand. "Jessie! Jessie! Yoohoo, Jessie!"

Dylan swore under his breath. "Are you fucking kidding me?"

Declan grinned. "Trust her. I do." He jumped into action, heading across the room after Piper, staying close enough to protect her if things went south.

Because there was no damned way he was letting another woman he loved get in the way of a bullet.

Shit. Love? Had he just put Piper on the list of women he loved?

He had no time to deal with that thought, because Dick and Jane had already turned toward Piper as she charged over to them.

TWENTY

Piper's heart was racing, and her adrenaline spiked as she waved and called Jessie's name again. She hadn't even thought before acting. The minute she'd understood what was happening, she knew she needed to help, and she knew what she was good at.

Jessie's gaze shot to her, her face confused, while her husband looked over at Piper, his eyes narrowed.

"Jessie!" Piper gave her a big hug, using her body to break Dick's grip on Jessie's elbow. "So sorry it's taken me this long to get over to you. I had a bunch of clients to meet with here. This is my busy season for events!"

Jessie stared at her. "Um, that's okay—"

"Thank you for your understanding!" Piper beamed at the circle standing around Jessie. "I need to steal her. I'll have her back in a few."

Dick opened his mouth to protest, and Piper waved him off, turning her attention to Jessie, speaking loudly enough to be heard over the music. "The planning for your husband's surprise party is going great! I'm so glad he's not here tonight so we can finalize the details."

Dick stared at them, and then she saw a smug smile on his face, his ego clearly jumping to the forefront of his perception of the situation.

Jessie still looked confused. "Um—"

"I was thinking about the musical guest. I checked with all the names you gave me, and I can get any of them, so we need to decide who is his ultimate dream band, and I'll book them."

Dick's smile widened, an indulgent smile as if he were humoring his wife by letting her dote on him.

Jessie glanced over her shoulder at Dick, but he was grinning. He waved her off, his chest practically puffing out at the idea of Jessie planning a party for him, at besting a party planner too stupid to know that the husband was right there.

Men with egos were astonishingly easy to manipulate, especially those who underestimated women.

Piper tucked her arm around Jessie's. "I'm with Eliana," she whispered.

Understanding dawned on Jessie's face, and she pivoted instantly. "My husband's here. He was next to me. Do you think he heard you?" She also said it loud enough for him to hear.

Piper looked back over her shoulder, and Dick immediately turned to the person next to him to chat. "No, I think we're good. But let's talk in the conference room so he doesn't overhear. I have so much good stuff to show you!"

"Awesome! I can't wait to see his face!" Piper hurried away from Dick, guiding Jessie through the crowded room.

As she moved, Declan walked past her, headed toward Dick. He winked at her, then continued on, moving into the little group to talk.

Piper got Jessie out into the hallway, where Dylan was leaning against a wall, scrolling on his phone. "Okay," Piper said to Jessie. "Tell me you need to run to the bathroom, and then you'll meet me in the conference room."

Jessie saw Dylan, and she nodded. "I have to run to the bathroom," she said loudly as she stepped away. "I'll meet you in the conference room."

Piper put her hands on her hips. "But we have so much to talk about." A couple nearby looked over, and a few others glanced their way. "This is my window!"

"I'll be right back," Jessie said. "I promise!" She turned and strode down the hall, and around the corner. Dylan levered himself off the wall and ambled after her, his body relaxed, giving off a chill vibe that didn't begin to explain what he was up to.

He nodded at Piper, then disappeared around the corner after Jessie.

Holy crap! Piper's hands started shaking, and she broke into a sweat. What had she just done? No, she wasn't finished yet. She needed to complete this, to give herself an alibi and Jessie more time.

She looked around, and saw Kitty walking by. "Kitty!"

Her future mother-in-law spun around. "Piper! There you are. I have someone I need you to meet."

"Come with me." She grabbed Kitty's arm and dragged her down the hall until she found an empty conference room. "Come sit."

Kitty grinned at her. "I sense drama. What's going on?"

Piper pulled out a couple chairs and sat them both down. "A woman named Jessie has been sitting with us going over plans for her husband's surprise party. She just stepped out to go to the bathroom, and she'll be right back. Got it?"

Kitty's smile faded. "Oh, bloody hell. I recognize cop stuff when I see it. What is Declan up to?"

"Her life depends on this, and so does my reputation."

Kitty folded her arms across her chest. "It's always someone's life at stake," she said. "It never stops. It just sucks you in deeper and deeper. Don't let my son endanger you."

Piper blinked. "He's not. I wanted to help—"

Kitty snapped her fingers. "So it *is* cop business. Dammit. Is he back at work? Did he lie to me?" She shoved to her feet. "He knows how I feel about him being a cop. Do you know that his wife was killed in the line of duty? I don't want to lose my son. Or you—"

At that moment, Dick walked into the room. "Where is she?" His energy was cold, hard, and coiled.

Piper's heart started to pound. He felt like a threat. Dangerous. Where was Declan?

Kitty whirled around. As soon as she saw Dick, her entire demeanor changed. Her irritation vanished, and she gave a twittery laugh. "Well, hello." She walked up and held out her hand. "My name is Kitty Jones. I'm a benefactor for this event. How is your evening?"

He didn't even seem to notice her. He just kept his gaze on Piper. "Where is she?"

Piper leaned back in her chair. "Who?"

"Jessie."

"Jessie? She ran to the bathroom."

"Which one?"

Piper raised her brows. "I'm not paid to keep track of my clients' bathroom habits. She'll be back in a minute. Can I give her a message?"

He glared at her, then spun around and stalked out of the room.

Kitty frowned. "Is that who is after that woman?"

Piper put her finger to her lips and nodded.

"He feels like a monster. I get that." Kitty took a deep breath and turned to Piper. "When I see a man with that kind of energy, I get it. I do. But here's the thing. The list of men like that is endless. It'll never stop until it sucks you dry or kills you."

Piper inclined her head. "I wasn't in danger. And neither is Declan. We're just helping out—"

"No." Kitty held out her hands and made a wiping motion. "Stop!"

"But—"

"Don't let Declan drag you into that world, Piper. I like you.

Being in love with a cop will destroy you. As much as I want my son to find happiness, I can't in good conscience stand by and watch you fall into a trap that will wreck you. I thought he was done being a cop, but he isn't, is he? He'll never stop." Tears filled her eyes. "Dammit!"

Kitty's anguish was visceral. Piper knew how much Kitty wanted Declan to have a relationship, but in her mind, she would rather warn a woman off from him than let him find happiness, because being in a relationship with a cop was that bad, in her mind. "Kitty," she said softly. "Help me understand."

"Understand?" Kitty pressed her hand to her forehead. "There's so much, Piper. Wondering every single day if it's the last day you'll ever see him. The obsession with the job, never able to stop thinking about it. People's lives depend on them, so a good cop like Declan or his dad can never step back from it. If they take a break, or miss a clue, people will die. It's what they live for, and anyone else in their lives are secondary."

Piper's heart ached for Kitty's pain. "Kitty—"

"And what if you want kids? You'll give them a dad who won't be there for them? Who might die at any moment?" Kitty stared at her. "When Diana died, I was so grateful that they hadn't had kids who would now grow up without a mom. I quit touring when my kids reached school age and couldn't come with me. They deserved a mother who wasn't on the road ten months a year. I never regretted it. But their dad couldn't even make it home for dinner most nights. We were all secondary, and we knew it."

"I'm so sorry," Piper said gently. She didn't know what else to say.

Kitty sank down onto the chair across from Piper. "I see how you and Declan are together. I see how much you love each other. Talk to Declan. Make him walk away. It's the only way it will work." She paused. "I can't go to bed every night, wondering if I'm going to get a call that he got shot. Like Diana. Like Hank."

"Hank?"

"My husband. That's why he quit the force." She paused.

"Declan didn't tell you? He was shot in the back and almost died. It took a year of rehab to even walk again. He was never the same, losing his mobility and the job he loved. His work stole everything from us. If you love Declan, if you love yourself, if you love the kids you might have some day, talk him out of being a cop before it's too late."

Kitty's pain was real. Born from a place of unconditional love. But the impact was too much. "I can't steal his purpose in life, Kitty. I can't steal his joy."

"Then you'll let him steal yours." She stood up. "I'm going home. I didn't need this tonight." Then she turned and strode out of the room.

Piper leaned back in her seat and clasped her hands behind her head, breathing in through Kitty's pain. Her heart broke for Kitty, but at the same time, now she better understood the complexity of Declan's relationship with his mom.

She understood it, because it was the same that she'd had with her family. They hadn't understood what she'd needed to do. Why she'd needed to leave. Why she couldn't keep living the life she'd been born to.

With the exception of Piper's mom, they'd never understood. Never supported her. They'd never understood or supported her mom, either, which was why Piper had had to get out. She'd had to live the life her mom hadn't been able to get.

But in Piper's family, the ones she'd left behind were the ones with the high likelihood of death, not her, but still. She understood the conflict.

Dick walked back in the room. "Is she back yet?" His jaw was hard, and anger radiated off him.

"No." Fear rippled through Piper. Not fear for herself, but fear for the woman who was racing toward a billionaire's private jet to keep herself and her kids safe. Piper was suddenly intensely, gloriously grateful for people like Dylan Hart who were out there helping women. Making a difference.

And she was exhilarated by the role she'd had in it.

Kitty might not understand what drove Declan, but Piper did. Because she felt the same need to make a difference. By bringing joy with her weddings, but also, surprisingly to discover, by helping women walk away from men like Dick.

He swore. "When she comes back, make her wait for me."

She raised her brows. "And you are…"

"Her husband."

"What?" Piper bolted upright, feigning surprise. "Oh…hello."

"I know about the party. I'm not an idiot."

Piper grimaced. "Don't tell her you know. She was so excited to surprise you. We've been working on this for weeks."

He flexed his jaw, and Piper could see him warring with distrust and delight. "What are your plans?"

Piper shook her head. "No way. There has to be some element of surprise. But trust me, I'm excellent at what I do. It's going to be fantastic."

"When is it?"

She grinned, forcing herself to act as if she were speaking to a normal husband, not one who was so bad that his wife had needed to hire Eliana and Dylan to help her escape. "Ah…you don't know, do you? Perfect. There will be an element of surprise."

He walked over to her. "Tell me when the party is." His voice was low, full of threat, and warning prickled down Piper's arms.

Instincts made her want to bolt to her feet and face him down, but she knew her job right now was to play party planner. When it came out that Jessie had gone missing, Piper needed to be sure her alibi as an innocent party planner was intact. "You know, I totally get that," she said easily. "You're super busy, and I'm sure you want to make sure you're available." She cocked her head, giving him a flirty smile. "You won't tell her, will you? Just between you and me."

He narrowed his eyes, and his gaze went to her chest, then back to her face. "All right."

"Wonderful." She beamed at him, even as she fantasized about taking the electric pencil sharpener and whipping it at his well-coiffed head. "It's three weeks from tonight."

"Where?"

Crap. That was something he could confirm. "Your house, of course. That's part of the plan. How we're going to get you away from the house all day so we can set up. It's going to be fantastic, but you need to go with it when you get an invite that gets you out of the house all day. Okay?"

A small smile finally played at the corner of his mouth. "What's the invite going to be?"

"I don't know yet. Any suggestions?"

"Golf."

"Great. Golf it is. Then what? That won't take you all day."

He paused for a moment, rubbing his jaw. Now that his anger was subsiding, she could see that some people would find him handsome. He had that air about him that would draw people into his web with ease, like a spider who would then take them prisoner and destroy them whenever he felt ready to do so. "Breakfast at the club in the morning. Then golf. Then..." He paused. "Call Jack Schott. Tell him that you need me out of the house all day. He'll know what to do."

"Jack Schott. Got it." She pulled out her phone. "What's his number?"

Dick rattled it off, and Piper put it in her phone. "Fantastic." She stood up. "I need to go meet with another client. When you find Jessie, tell her I had to run. I'll give her a call tomorrow to reschedule." She poked his chest as she walked past. "But make sure to ask her who I am, because you need to pretend you don't know about the party!"

He nodded, his eyes far too interested in her for her own comfort. "Will do."

"Great!" She couldn't believe she'd managed to get out of there without him asking what her name was, but she knew he'd notice soon that he hadn't asked, hadn't figured out a way to track her down. "Have a good night."

As he nodded, she stepped around him and then strode out into the hall, her heart racing. She saw Declan walk out into the hall, and she shot him a look to follow her.

His gaze went behind her, and she knew he'd seen Dick walk out of the room she'd just exited. Since he'd jumped in to distract Dick when Piper had spirited his wife away, they couldn't be seen together.

She walked past Declan, not even looking at him. "Going to my car," she muttered under her breath. "See you at home."

"Meet you there." He kept walking the other way, calling a greeting to Dick as he passed him.

She glanced back as she rounded the corner, relieved to see that Declan had managed to stall Dick long enough for her to slip out of sight without him following her. Relief rushed through her, and she hurried down the hall, cutting back through the kitchen toward the front entrance. She waved at a few of the staff, who she knew from the weddings she'd put on there, then emerged in a back hall.

She bolted down the empty corridor and then slipped out a side entrance.

The parking lot was eerily empty, and as she raced across it, she thought about Jessie and her kids, racing along the highway toward Dylan's jet. She knew they would make it, because they had a head start, but it was still nerve-wracking.

She couldn't imagine needing to run away from her life so completely that the only option was to disappear. Because that was what Eliana did. New identities, new lives, never to be found.

Piper's car was where she'd left it, and there was no sign of Dick, so she ran over, got in, locked it, and started the engine. She pulled out quickly, and didn't relax until she was on the road and there were no headlights behind her.

As the night settled around her, she thought about Jessie. Did she have parents she was leaving behind? Did she have to go into hiding forever? Would she lose every bit of her life forever, just because she'd married the wrong man?

Suddenly, Piper's throat became tight at the idea of never seeing her family again. She'd left them behind, worked hard to disassociate herself with them, but in her heart, she always knew they were there.

She stopped at an intersection, then looked down at her phone. It had been so long since she'd spoken to anyone from her family. She didn't want them back in her life.

But she suddenly needed to know they were all right.

"Hey, Siri. Call Roman." She hit the gas and eased through the intersection as the phone rang. Would he even answer? It had been so long.

It kept ringing, and sadness crept into her heart. What if something had happened to them? She'd changed her phone number so they couldn't find her. What if she couldn't find them either?

Finally, a familiar voice answered. "Roman here."

Her throat tightened at the sound of her older brother's voice. "It's me."

There was a long pause, then he said, incredulously. "Piper?"

"Yes. Hi." She suddenly didn't know what to say.

"Where the hell have you been? Shit! We've all been so worried! You just disappeared."

Tears filled her eyes. "I'm sorry. I had to go."

"You didn't have to go like that. No one knew what happened to you. Fuck. I thought that someone had—" He stopped, but she knew what he'd been about to say. He'd been worried that one of his business associates had killed her.

"I had to get out, Roman. I did it the only way I knew how."

"I thought you were *dead*, Piper."

"I know. I'm so sorry."

"It's been seven years. *Seven* years since anyone has heard from you. What the hell?"

Piper pulled into her driveway and parked the car. "Roman," she said, trying to hold her emotions together. "I'm sorry I worried you and the others. I just...I was going to die if I stayed there, and

I knew it. If I told you, I never would have gone. You wouldn't have let me go. None of you would have."

"You underestimate us," he said. "Is that really what you think of us?"

"Well, I don't mean you would have chained me to my bed. I just meant that you would have talked me out of it." Dragged her down, just like he was doing right now. Making her feel guilty for taking care of herself, and doing what she needed to survive.

"You so sure about that? Or do you think that it's possible we would have been glad that you made it out? That you had a chance to be more? Did that occur to you?"

She closed her eyes. "No."

"Maybe it should have." There was so much anger in his voice, so much blame. Which was why it had been seven years since she'd talked to him, or the others.

"Roman. I need to go, but I called tonight to tell you that I love you. And the others. You'll always be my family, and I will always hold you in my heart." She almost added that she would always be there to help them out if they needed it, but she didn't.

Because she knew what kind of help her family would want from her, and she wouldn't give it to them.

There was a long silence.

"Roman?"

"You coming home soon?"

"No."

"Ever?"

She couldn't make herself say "no," even though that felt like the truth. "I don't know."

He was silent again.

"This is my cell," she said finally. "Call me if you need to."

He was still silent.

"Okay, um, so that's it, then." She paused. "Tell the others I love them."

More silence.

Should she just hang up? Roman was the one she was closest

to, the one she really missed, but also the one who was the most dangerous to her because of that very reason. "Hello?"

"I missed the hell out of you," he finally said. "You always have a home here, little sis." He paused. "I'm sorry I drove you away. I love you."

Tears filled her eyes. "Roman—"

He hung up before she could say more.

TWENTY-ONE

Declan got a text from Dylan as he got out of his truck at his house. *We're clear. Thx.*

Triumph pulsed through Declan as he slammed his door shut. Hell, yeah. They'd gotten away from the club safely. *Anytime. Just let me know.*

Will do.

Declan put his phone in his pocket as he strode down the stone walkway to Piper's cottage, whistling cheerfully. It felt so good to make a difference like that. It took so little effort to help someone. Granted, when he'd seen Dick walk out of the room Piper had just been in, he'd had a moment of absolute panic that Dick had hurt her.

But Piper had flashed him that smile, and he'd relaxed.

She was fine.

It had been easy enough to stall Dick long enough for Piper to get to her car, and then he'd followed her home. What a damned night. His mind was still reeling. Starting off from hell, walking into the world he didn't fit. Ending on a high note.

He saw Piper's taillights were still on, so he jogged up to her car and knocked on the window. "Hey!"

She looked over at him, and he saw tears on her cheeks.

Alarm shot through him, and he yanked the door open. "What's wrong?"

She pulled her emotions in and smiled. "It's all good. Did they get away?"

"Yep. They're on their way to the airport." He frowned as he stepped back to let her get out of the car.

Her head was down, her shoulders hunched. "Great. That was fun tonight. I liked helping." She gave him a smile that was a little more real, then turned away. "I'm tired. I'm going to bed."

"No." Declan fell in beside her as she walked toward her house. "What's going on?"

"Nothing! Can't a woman just cry and have it not mean anything at all? I'm happy! I got some good headway on clients. I helped a woman and her kids escape a sociopath." She held up her hand. "I have an amazing ring. Why would anything be wrong? Nothing's wrong!" She flung the front door open and stalked inside, leaving the door open.

There had been a time in his life when Declan would have taken her response as an excuse to walk away and not engage. Many times, actually.

But with Piper, he didn't want to. He wanted to be better.

So, he followed her inside and closed the door behind him, pausing to assess as she paced into the kitchen and grabbed a bottle of water. Her hands were shaking, and her cheeks were streaked with tears.

She sat down on the bar stool and hit her fist on the counter in visible frustration.

He said nothing as he helped himself to water, and then sat down on the bar stool beside her. He faced forward, not looking at her, and drank his water.

She didn't tell him to leave or go away, so he kept sitting there.

Silence sat between them for a while, and it took all his willpower not to start talking at her, demanding she tell him what was wrong, and offering solutions.

But he did it.

She started peeling the label off the bottle.

"I'm installing the new filtering system on Friday," he said casually. "You'll be able to drink the tap water after that. It'll taste good."

She looked over at him. "Why don't you build houses for your job instead of being a police officer?"

He blinked and managed not to react at the edge in her voice. "What?"

"April asked you to build her house. You're amazing at it, and you love it. Why don't you do that?"

Um… He knew that wasn't what was on Piper's mind, but she was talking now, so he went with it. "I never thought about it. I'm not licensed or anything like that. I just do it because I enjoy it."

"Why wouldn't you want to do for a job the thing that you do for fun? Then you have fun all day and get paid?"

Interesting philosophical question. "I'm not a builder."

"You are a builder! Look around you! You're incredibly talented."

She sounded like she was about to cry, and he had a pretty good idea it wasn't because she was heartbroken that the world wasn't going to get a chance to have homes designed by Declan Jones. "Thank you. I like what I built here," he said easily. "Never considered doing it for a living, but I'll think about it."

"Oh, my God! You're patronizing me! Why are you patronizing me? It's a valid question. I've spent my life trying to build a career I love, one that gives me joy. Why would you go back to being a cop when you love building?"

He ground his jaw, reminding himself that whatever was bugging her wasn't his choice of work. He used to let Diana get a rise out of him, but with Piper, it was different.

He wanted to be that guy she could vent to. "I do like being a cop. It's not what I do. It's who I am."

"Then who have you been for the last few years when you weren't a cop?"

He tapped his fingers on the table, trying to figure out how to refocus the conversation into something productive, not something that set his teeth on edge. "Healing."

She blinked and looked over at him. "What?"

"Healing in body and soul. I got shot in the leg. I was in no shape to carry a gun and run after bad guys. So, I built things, and I healed."

She stared at him, and then new tears filled her eyes. "I'm such a bitch. I'm sorry."

"Shit, no. I didn't mean it like that." He put his hand on the back of her bar stool and leaned in. "What's going on, Piper? It's not about me being a cop."

"Your mom freaked out on me tonight when she realized we were helping that woman. She said I shouldn't let myself get sucked into your cop world, and she was so mad that you were being a cop again. She said that your dad being a cop killed their marriage and that I would die a lonely death if I married you and you were a cop."

He closed his eyes. *Shit.* He did not want to unpack that right now. "You're crying because my mom got upset at you?"

"No." She put her water down. "I'm crying because you losing your dad and your wife made me miss my family, so I called my older brother tonight and it was...it just..." She stared at him. "I walked out on my family. I can't be with them. They're not good for me. But how can I walk away from them when you don't even have your family anymore? And he was mad. God, Declan, hearing Roman's voice...he'd thought I was dead. And he asked me if I was ever coming home, and I didn't know."

She was letting him in. Declan had to fight to keep his face calm. After hiding everything about her past, Piper was finally lowering her walls that had kept him, and everyone else, out. He wanted to give her what she needed, to build a connection of trust between them, so he weighed his response very carefully.

"How long has it been since you left?" he asked, trying for the bridge between support and neutrality, not wanting to push her back into her cave, doing his best not to ask a question that would feel threatening, that she wouldn't want to answer.

"Seven years."

He wanted to ask why she left, why they were bad for her, but he knew he was standing in the middle of her darkest secrets, and he had to tread gently. "Family isn't always good for us," he said softly. "And if we need distance from them, that's okay."

She looked over at him. "You didn't walk out on your family."

"No, but my mom walked out on my dad. She couldn't handle who he was, and she still can't."

Piper sat back to look at him. "Did you forgive her? Did he?"

"He stayed married to her, so yes."

"Did you?"

Declan shook his head. "No, I didn't marry her. I felt like that would be weird."

Piper stared at him, and then she snickered. "You're such a dork."

Relief rushed through him. His attempt to release a little of her tension had worked. "Yeah, but if I'd married her, then it would be worse than being a dork."

She rolled her eyes and pushed at his shoulder. "Did you forgive your mom, you toad?"

"I am still working through my issues with her, as you know," he said. "It's not about forgiveness. It's about that she sees my dad in me, and she doesn't like it."

"And you see your dad in you, and you embrace it."

He shrugged. "My dad was a good man and a great cop. I'm proud to be like him."

She cocked her head. "But…"

He smiled. "You weren't supposed to notice the 'but.'"

"I'm a wedding planner. I have supersonic empathy skills. What's your but?"

He took a breath. "I don't want to go back to work," he admitted. "I don't know what's holding me back, but it's like this vise that's been around my chest for years. It's my world. My life.

What I love. But I don't want to put on the badge again, and I don't know why." He was absolutely fucking *lost,* and this was the first time he'd admitted it aloud. "I thought I would be ready when it was time, but I'm going in on Friday, and I don't fucking want to."

He felt raw and restless, but he didn't want to go for a run or sweat it out. He wanted to sit there with Piper, not hide in sweat and physical stress anymore.

"Oh…" She sat back. "That's not good to carry a gun and a badge if your heart's not in it."

"Nope. People die."

She cleared her throat. "So, maybe build stuff, then."

"I can't."

"Why?"

"Then my mom would win. I can't let her win. It's a pride thing. I do my best to make all my major life decisions based on ego."

Piper looked at him sharply, and then started laughing. "You know, I did have you pegged for an ego guy."

"No other way to live."

"Exactly." She put her water bottle on its side and rolled it toward him. "I don't talk about my family," she said. "Ever."

He caught the bottle and rolled it back to her. "I don't talk about my feelings, so I get it."

She put her hand on the bottle, and then pushed it back toward him. "It felt good to have you here when I was upset," she said. "Thanks."

He caught the bottle and flung it a little harder toward her, a little game that was a good distraction for both of them. "You're welcome. I'm still undecided how I feel about the fact I told you I don't want to go back to work. If I decide I'm good with it, then I'll circle back and thank you for drawing that out of my reluctant man-cave of emotional isolation. If not, then I'll probably pretend it never happened."

She burst out laughing and caught the water bottle. "Either

way is fine." She shoved the water bottle at him, and it skidded off the counter.

They both lunged for it, and their heads cracked against each other.

"Ow!" Piper tumbled off the stool, and Declan grabbed her.

He caught her arm, slowing her before she hit the floor, but lost his balance in the process. He landed on the tile beside her, grunting at the impact of his knee on the tile.

Piper rolled onto her back, laughing as she held her forehead. "Your skull is a deadly weapon," she groaned. "Holy crap. That hurt so much."

His head was throbbing too, but he ignored it. "Sorry." He grimaced as he propped himself up on his elbow. "Let me check. I'm a certified EMT. I can stitch it up for you."

"Yes, please. Without numbing it." She moved her hand out of the way. "Am I going to die?"

He leaned over, peering at the red mark on her forehead. "Not from that."

"Stitches?"

He ran his finger over the mark. "There's no cut, but I could put stitches in anyway. Just for fun."

"Oh, yes, please, do. That would be great."

"You bet." He paused. "The proper treatment might be a kiss. It's a proven effective treatment for booboos."

And with that, the heat between them suddenly came on like a furnace. She glanced at him. "Yes, please. Fix it."

"You bet." He leaned over and pressed a kiss to the mark on her forehead.

"Oh." She winced and started laughing. "That actually hurt."

"Shit. And to think I was trying to seduce you with that kiss. I'm not into seduction with pain. Not my thing."

She raised her brows. "What are you into, then?"

He paused, then brushed his lips very gently over her brow. "Today? Now?"

"Yep. Right now." She closed her eyes, going still as he trailed kisses across her forehead, carefully skipping the red mark.

"Right now," he said, his voice low and intimate, "I'm thinking about long, tantalizing kisses."

"Can you give an example? Just for clarity."

"Yeah. Sure." He leaned over and kissed her. Slow, leisurely, and tempting. He added in some kisses on her throat, along the corners of her mouth, and finished with a precisely orchestrated kiss of pure ingenuity and well-planned tongue seduction.

A damned good kiss. He may have intended to seduce her, but it had worked its magic on him as well. Desire was coiled tight in his belly, and he pulled back, anticipation coursing through him.

Piper didn't move. Her eyes were closed, and her lips were parted, as if she were waiting for more.

"How was that?" he asked.

"What?" She opened her eyes. "Did you kiss me? Sorry. I was thinking about your house-building skills. Do it again. I'll pay attention this time."

He burst out laughing. "It's a good thing I have a strong ego."

"You literally just said you live by the ego, so I was helping you strengthen it."

"So, you did notice I kissed you."

"Did you really kiss me?" She propped herself up on her elbows, giving him a wide-eyed, innocent look. "I thought you were kidding. How did I not notice?"

He growled playfully and pulled her into his arms. He kissed her again. This time, it was a kiss of pure heat. No more seduction. Straight into the fire. He threw his leg over her hip, locking her against him as he deepened the kiss. He kept it up, not giving her a moment to breathe, until she finally surrendered to the kiss.

He knew the moment she gave up the pretense. Her arms slid around his neck, her body melted into his, and she began kissing him back just as fiercely as he was kissing her. The heat that had been building between them since their first faked kiss in her bed came to life with a roar.

Memories and emotions from his past tried to grab him and drag him under, but he shut them out. Instead, he focused completely on every sensation of having Piper in his arms. The feel of her body against his. The taste of her lips. The adorable way she held onto him, as if she were afraid he was going to pull away. The way she smelled, that flowery scent that he'd always noticed about her, which was now wrapped around him, delving into his skin and his clothes.

He wanted more.

He wanted it all, with Piper, right now.

The thought was stunning. He'd been dead to romance for so long. His need for Piper, his response to Piper was so unexpected…and it felt so right.

But did he dare cross that line with her? They'd made a deal, and getting naked wasn't part of it. He swore and broke contact, rolling onto his back. He draped his arm over his forehead and took a breath, trying to ease the raw need for her.

Piper didn't move. She just stayed on her back on the tile floor, also breathing hard. "What was that?" she asked.

"Sorry. That got away from me."

"What are you sorry about?"

He closed his eyes. "Breaking our deal."

"Okay."

He kept his eyes closed. "Okay, what?" The woman was so damned elusive sometimes. She kept him guessing and he loved that.

"Okay, that's what you were sorry about."

"What else would I be sorry about?"

"Kissing me like you wanted to throw me over your shoulder, cart me upstairs, and have your shirtless, sweaty carpenter way with me."

This conversation was not helping him get his libido under control. "Is that how I kissed you?"

"It is. That's not what you meant to do?"

"I didn't have a clear plan."

"If you had one now, how would you kiss me?"

He caught his breath. "Same way."

"Okay."

He smiled to himself. "Okay, what?" He loved that she was such an enigma.

"Okay, you can kiss me like that again, but only on one condition."

He still had his arm over his face, but anticipation rippled through him. "What's that?"

"You don't break your promise."

"To not get naked with you?"

"No. The implied promise that you're going to cart me off to the bedroom and have your shirtless, sweaty carpenter way with me."

He swore under his breath, then sat up and leaned over her. She opened her eyes to look at him, her blue eyes wide and clear. "What?" she asked.

"I would love to take you upstairs and get naked with you."

She smiled. "That's such a nice thing to say to a woman. You're definitely a dangerous charmer."

"What about our deal?"

"We're still fake engaged."

He hesitated. "Piper—"

"Shut up and kiss me, you silly man."

He grinned. "Well, when you put it that way—" He got up, held out his hand to her, then pulled her to her feet and into his arms.

He took a moment to kiss her thoroughly, then he picked her up, not over his shoulder, but against his chest, so her legs were around his hips, and he was holding her ass. She put her arms around his neck and kissed him as he set off toward the stairs.

She was a hell of a lot lighter than most of the construction crap he hauled around, and so much more fun, and they were both laughing as he headed up the stairs, carefully balancing so as to protect his knee.

They hit the second floor, and then they made it to her bedroom, still kissing. By the time they collapsed on the bed, their clothes had already come off in a desperate frenzy. They were both naked before the mattress had finished sinking beneath them, but the moment he felt her body against his, he had to pause to experience it. "God, this is amazing," he whispered, bending his head to trail a row of kisses along her collarbone. "Your skin is incredible."

She smiled, her lids at half-mast. "My skin likes your lips."

He laughed as he ran his hand down her hip, and along her thigh. "You're so weird."

"Right? You're welcome. It's a gift to be with someone like me."

"Nope. Not someone like you. It's a gift to be with you, specifically." He kissed her before she could respond, saving himself the awkwardness of having to backtrack on it.

She locked her arms around his neck and kissed him back. The kisses were electric and intense, and he knew she wasn't holding back any more than he was. They'd crossed that line, and neither of them wanted to go back.

With heat and need driving him, he explored her body with his hands and mouth, tracking her responses to figure out what she liked the most, what took her to the edge, and then brought her back every time before she went over. It was heady and electric to have her respond to him so completely, with full trust and surrender. She let herself fully embrace the moment, which was such a massive turn on that it was all he could do to keep himself from going all the way.

But he wanted it to last. He wanted to bring her to the precipice so she had no control, nothing left but complete surrender to what was happening between them. He hadn't wasted time with women who didn't matter, so his list of past relationships was short, but he knew damn well that what was happening between the two of them didn't come along very often.

They were connected, aligned, and wholly into each other.

Everywhere she touched him ignited a fire in him, and the same happened everywhere he touched her or kissed her.

Their whispers, their muted laughter, their jokes, everything created an intimacy that amplified all they were experiencing and creating. He'd never been so turned on, and he'd never felt so much lightness in his heart.

Piper pressed a kiss to the top of his head. "Make love to me, Declan. Let's do this now."

He smiled at her command, and obligingly moved over her. "I've been waiting for you to ask," he teased, even as he slid inside her.

"Oh, wow, yes. Perfect. Great." She gripped his shoulders, closing her eyes as he moved inside her.

He loved watching her face. It was so expressive, not hiding what she was feeling, how he made her feel. She was so free and unreserved right now, and he loved it. He loved that she trusted him enough to let down her guard. First, the glimpse into her past, into the life she hid from the world, and now, this moment, complete surrender physically and emotionally.

"I won't let you down, Piper," he whispered, as he began to move faster. "I swear to you, I'll never let you down." He'd let a lot of people down in his life, but not anymore. Not today. Not her.

Her eyes snapped open, and they were full of emotion. She said nothing, but she pulled him in for a kiss. There was a new layer to her kiss. More need, more honesty, more desperation.

He kissed her back even as he reached down and invited her to reach the levels he hadn't let her get to before. When she dropped her head back and gripped the sheets, intense satisfaction coursed through him. She was completely his, in this moment. Completely, and totally his, and he loved it.

One final burst, and her body surrendered completely to his siren call. The moment she orgasmed, he had no chance to stop himself from following her. He held her tight as they rode the wave together, an extended, endless wave so intense that he thought it might kill him.

But what a way to go.

TWENTY-TWO

Piper jerked awake, startled, but she wasn't sure why. She opened her eyes to find Angel on her bed. Her first thought was that Declan had woken at some point, gone to his house to get his dog, and then come back. He could have stayed at his house, but he hadn't.

He'd come back to sleep with her.

What did that mean?

Angel suddenly let out a low growl, and Declan put his hand on her back. "Quiet, girl," he said softly. "I need you to stay here and keep Piper safe while I go check it out."

Um, hello? He was awake? "Keep me safe?" Piper asked. "What's going on?"

Declan leaned over Angel's back, and she could see he was dressed. "There's someone outside," he said. "I'm going to go check it out. Stay here with Angel."

"What?" She bolted upright. "You can't go out there. That's what they do in horror movies and then get chopped up."

"Right. They should call the cops. I'm a cop."

"But—"

"It's what I do." He stood up. All business. All focused.

"It's what you used to do. Do you even have a gun?"

159

"It's at my house, but I'm good." He walked to the door. "Stay here. I'll be back." And with that, he was gone, closing the door behind him.

Piper lunged for her clothes, getting dressed as fast as she could. Her heart was hammering. It felt like the night she'd been shot, and she didn't like it. Roman couldn't have gotten there already. But what if he'd told the rest of her family, and they'd told the wrong person? Shit, shit, *shit*. She shouldn't have called him. She should have been smarter.

Or maybe it was Dick. Maybe he'd realized his wife and kids were gone, and he'd figured out that she was involved.

Real alarm shot through her. If Dick came for her, it wouldn't be a stray bullet that got her, like last time. It would be a bullet with her name on it. Or a knife. Or whatever it took to get her to reveal where his wife had gone.

Her heart started racing. She yanked her sneakers on as she heard the front door close.

Had that been Declan going out, or someone else coming in?

Angel was on her feet now, watching the door alertly. She hadn't taken her gaze off it since Declan had gone outside. Did she hear someone, or was she just looking for Declan?

Piper pulled on a sweatshirt, locked the bedroom door, then went to the window. She slid the curtains aside and peered outside. It was dark, and the outdoor lights were on. She couldn't see anything.

What if Declan got shot? What if Dick found Declan first and realized that Declan had been involved as well?

Fear shot through her, startling her at its intensity. *She cared if he got shot*. More than because he was a human being. Because it was Declan out there.

Suddenly, for the first time, she understood what Kitty had been talking about. The fear of being married to a cop and wondering if every day he was going to die.

She hadn't felt fear like this since she'd left her family. The raw fear of violence that she wouldn't see coming. That he wouldn't see coming. That could tear her life apart again.

Movement caught her eye, and she looked again. Someone was moving in the shadows, along the side of the walkway. It was too dark to tell if it was Declan.

Fear gripped her, and panic closed around her throat.

She yanked the curtain shut and backed away from the window, looking around the room. Angel hadn't moved from the door. Piper had to distract herself or she would freak out.

Take action.

"Angel. I don't like you being the first line of defense," she said. "I don't want you getting shot for me."

Angel whined and thumped her tail, but didn't give up her vigil.

Piper looked around the room, then grabbed a lamp, unplugged it, and flattened herself against the wall by the door. If someone came in, they'd be looking at the dog, not her. It would give her time to hit them with the lamp. She preferred throwing can openers from a distance, but she had to protect the dog, so up close and personal it would be.

"Ready," she whispered to Angel. "Let me know if a bad guy is coming."

Angel didn't take her gaze off the door, her big ears perked and listening.

Piper watched the dog as she waited, her heart pounding.

"I forgot how much I hate feeling unsafe," she whispered to Angel.

The dog didn't even acknowledge her. She was standing stiffly now, her gaze riveted on the door.

What did she hear?

Piper leaned her head back against the wall, watching the dog closely. Angel would tell her before someone reached the door. Angel would know what or who was on the other side of the door. If it was Declan, or if someone had gotten past him.

"This is not okay, Angel," she whispered. "I can't handle this."

Angel ignored her, clearly quite able to handle it.

Dammit. This was all supposed to be behind her.

Twenty minutes later, Declan paused on Piper's front step, doing a final scan of the night.

The evening was still and quiet, with the only sounds being ones that belonged in the night. Crickets. Bats. Owls.

Whoever it was had left.

Declan hadn't gotten an ID on the intruder, but he'd seen their silhouette. Not enough to even identify the gender or size, but enough to know that a person had been skulking around his property.

The intruder had disappeared into the night when Declan had gone after them, and he'd heard a car engine roar to life before he could reach the street. He'd seen the taillights disappear, but it had been too dark to see anything else.

But someone had been there, and he didn't like it.

He also didn't like the fact that whoever it was had shown up hours after he'd called an old contact, after he'd opened the door to his old life.

He let himself into the carriage house and locked the door behind him. He scanned the interior of the house, listening, feeling it. After a long moment, he was certain no one had entered the house.

Whoever it was had definitely left.

Declan jogged up the stairs and headed toward the bedroom. "It's Declan," he called out. "Everything's fine."

Piper opened the door, and Angel bolted out, wagging and barking. He dropped to one knee to hug his dog, but he didn't take his gaze off Piper. "You okay?"

She leaned against the door frame and folded her arms over her chest. "I now understand what your mom was telling me."

He frowned. Agreeing with his mom never meant anything good. "About what?"

"What it's like to worry that each time might be the last time I see you."

Shit. "It wasn't like that. Whoever it was took off. Probably just a kid scouting out the house."

"But I didn't know that." She shook her head. "I can't imagine what your mom must have felt with your dad and then you."

Guilt settled in his gut. And anger. He'd heard it too many times. "Okay." He didn't feel like arguing. "I'm going to sleep on the couch to keep an eye out." He turned and walked away. He felt like shit doing it, his old ways surfacing the moment that things turned, but he couldn't stay here and listen to this, after listening to it for so many years.

"Declan?"

"What?" He didn't turn around. He knew he was shutting her out, like he used to do with Diana, but it didn't matter. He wasn't dealing with this again.

Piper didn't answer.

He kept walking, waiting for her to finish.

When he got to the top of the stairs, he turned around. Piper was still standing in the doorway.

"What?" he asked again.

She frowned. "Thank you for going to the rescue."

He shrugged. "It's what I do. What I'll always do." He headed down the stairs, but as he took the first step, his knee tweaked. He caught the railing before he fell, but he didn't look back when he heard Piper suck in her breath.

He didn't want to be weak.

He didn't want to be judged.

He just wanted to go back to being alone.

TWENTY-THREE

What had just happened?

Piper stood in the doorway, listening to Declan stalk down the stairs to the living room.

Sudden anger boiled through her. After spending the night in his arms, she deserved more than to be walked out on. She wasn't that woman anymore who would accept that treatment and go hide in her room. She deserved more. "Declan!"

"What?"

"Wait a sec!"

He turned toward her as she ran down the stairs. "What?"

"That was so rude!"

His eyes narrowed. "Rude? I was *rude*?"

"Yes." He was rude. She was mad. It was a perfect storm. "I told you that I was scared, and then you just turned around and walked away!"

He stared at her. "You told me that my mother was right about the shit I put her through being a cop. And you defended her treatment of my father. I've spent my whole life listening to that judgment, and I don't need to take it from you."

She blinked, startled by his response. "That's not what I said!"

"It's exactly what you said." He turned away and headed toward the couch, turning his back on her again.

"No, it's not, you big oaf! What I said, if you were listening, was that I almost died when my brothers got tangled up in some stupid deal with their drug dealer. They came to the house and took me hostage and I almost died! And I thought my brothers were going to die! And sitting there in my room, alone, wondering if you were going to die or if Dick was going to come after me, made me relive it all again! And you walked away like a complete jerk. You're my fiancé, and we just made love, and you don't get to do that to me."

He spun around to face her, shock on his face. "You literally didn't say that."

"In my head I did! And you just heard your little, whiny inner voice being blamed for being a cop! If you had taken one second to get over it, you should have heard all the subtext and at least asked me what was really going on! You should have realized it wasn't about the pancakes!"

He stared at her. "Pancakes?"

"Yes! One day my brother came into the house, and he lost his mind because we were having pancakes, and we hadn't told him. And then we later realized that he was in trouble with his drug dealer, and that's why he was so upset. But he couldn't tell us, so he freaked out about the pancakes. It wasn't about the pancakes! It never is, and you should know that. You're a cop!"

He continued to stare at her. "Your family is a bunch of drug dealers?"

"They were, and loan sharking and all sorts of other low-level crime stuff. That's not the point! Oh my God! You're such a man!" She spun around and stormed up the stairs.

"Piper."

She whirled to face him. "What?"

One hand was on the railing, and he'd taken a step toward her. He looked intense. "Why did you walk out on your fiancé?"

"Because he was an abusive douchebag who was cheating on

me, and I didn't realize it until the last minute. Because I was so desperate to feel safe that I just let him sweep me up. But he's a terrible man with a lot of power, and he's very good at making people believe he's a good man." She put her hands on her hips. "There. Happy? You know all my terrible secrets. Piper the wedding planner has so much violence and poverty and *crap* in her past that she has no business running around in the elite circles trying to make dreams of happily ever after come true!"

She turned and sprinted up the stairs, so angry she could barely think. She stalked into her room, slammed the door shut, then dove onto the bed. She crawled under the covers and pulled them over her head.

The tears started to fall almost right away, but she ignored them.

Instead, she grabbed her phone and called her brother again.

He answered quickly this time. "Piper?"

"I just want you to know I left home because I couldn't live around a bunch of criminals anymore. I was scared that one day I would be killed because of the stuff you and the others were into. I left because as much as I hated that life, I knew I was too scared to leave you behind and I'd never have a different life unless I just cut all of you off, because I love you, and love is a trap!"

He swore. "Piper, I swear I'm so sorry. We're sorry. But what I didn't tell you earlier is that your leaving was a trigger for me. I knew why you left, and I walked away from that life the day you left. I own my own business now. It's a legit business. I have nothing to do with any of that life. And it's because of you. You were right to leave."

She was silent for a moment, stunned by his response. "Really? You…have a business?"

"Really."

"What about the others?"

He hesitated. "It's trickier with them."

She nodded. "Did you tell them I called?"

Again, a hesitation. "No. I didn't know what they'd do."

"You mean, come after me?"

"Yeah. You have money, right?"

"I do." Dammit. Her brothers would still come after her for money. That told her a lot. But Roman was different. He always had been. "You should come visit sometime."

"Seriously?"

"Yeah."

"I'd like that."

She could hear the smile in his voice, and something eased in her chest. "I'll text you my address."

"Great. Thanks for calling back."

She nodded. "You can call me, too."

"Will do." He paused. "Trip is here. I'm going to go."

"Right. Bye." Just as Roman was hanging up, she heard the sound of her youngest brother's voice. *Trip.* Her chest ached at the sound of his voice. He'd been fifteen when she'd left. What had he done? What had happened to him? Suddenly, she wanted to know.

But if Roman thought he shouldn't know that Piper had called, then Trip couldn't be in a very good place. She tossed the phone on her pillow and curled into a ball. Her chest hurt so much. A heavy ache.

The door opened, and she closed her eyes.

Angel jumped on the bed and poked her nose in Piper's ear. "Not right now, sweetie." Piper pulled the blankets over her head. "Just give me a second."

The bed shifted again, and she thought Angel had jumped off.

Then the covers flipped up, and Declan slid in behind her.

Piper stiffened as he nestled up behind her and wrapped his arm around her stomach.

"I'm asleep," she said.

"Liar." He pressed a kiss into her hair. "I'm sorry."

Her heart tightened. Damn him for apologizing unconditionally. It made it impossible for her to stay righteously indignant. "It's not your fault," she admitted grudgingly. "It was unrealistic for me to expect you to read my mind, at least this early in a relationship," she added. "A few months in, different story. But at this point? It was a little much."

He laughed softly. "I'm a cop. I should be better at subtext. I overreacted, and it messed with my instincts."

She looked down at his hand around her waist. "I was scared tonight," she said quietly. "I was scared for my own safety, and I was scared for yours. I didn't realize I would react that way. I was fine at the country club dealing with Dick, but it was different here. Tonight. Old trauma, I guess."

He pressed his face into her hair. "Fear makes people angry sometimes," he said. "I should have realized that. I'm an ass."

This time, it was her turn to laugh a little. "It was a little bit of an ass move to storm off downstairs after we'd made love," she admitted. "That's never going to go over well with a woman."

"Yeah, I know." He was quiet for a minute. "I wasn't the best husband. I was entirely focused on my career." He took a breath. "Diana told me she wanted a divorce the day before she died."

Piper closed her eyes. "Oh, wow."

"Yeah. I never told anyone until now, but the guilt?" He whistled softly. "Haunted me for years. Still does. Was she off her game because of the divorce? Was she distracted because of me? Did I get her killed because I wasn't the guy she deserved?"

Piper heard the guilt in his voice. It wasn't anguish, though. She could tell it was still there, but it was distant. He'd processed a lot. "That's a lot to carry."

"Yeah. I don't like that I walked out on you tonight. I don't want to be that guy anymore." He pressed a kiss to the nape of her neck. "Thanks for calling me out on it. I don't always realize. Patterns can be invisible sometimes."

She sighed. "It's impossible for me to still be mad at you right now."

He chuckled. "That was my goal, of course."

"It worked, but I'm not happy about it."

"If it helps, your story about your drug-dealing family knocked me right off my self-righteous platform."

She grimaced. *Crap.* One night of mind-blowing, fake-fiancé sex and she was spilling secrets she'd protected for seven years? "Yeah, about that. I know that as a cop, it's probably an issue hanging out with a woman with a background like that, so it's cool if you want to call off our deal. I just ask that you don't tell anyone—"

"It's not an issue."

She closed her eyes, her chest tightening. Dammit. She hated how happy she was that he didn't care. "You don't need to lie to me—"

"It's not worth it to lie," he said. "I don't give a shit about your family's activities. When I was younger, I might have been spouting some high and mighty ethics, but life is so much more complicated than that. You're you, the woman you are right now, and I like her."

The tension that had been gripping Piper for so long, for all the years she'd been here, suddenly loosened its grip. She'd hidden her truth so carefully for so long, it suddenly felt like she could breathe, not having to hide it from him. "I've never told anyone except Maddie," she said. "I've been so sure that I'd lose everything I've worked for if people knew my past."

"Honestly, some of the clientele you serve would probably care, but I think you know by now I'm not like them."

"But you're a cop. And you're from this fancy world. So it would make sense that you would care about my family."

"Well, now you know I don't care."

Dammit. Why did that feel so good? Their relationship wasn't even real. Why did she care what he thought about her? She had to stay focused on the big goal, her career. She rolled over to face him. "You promise you won't tell anyone?"

Declan frowned. "Yes, but you don't need to be ashamed. People who know your value won't care."

"I'm not ashamed. I'm strategic."

He raised his brows. "That's what you call it?"

"Yes." She lifted her chin. "I need to impress the ones who don't know my value, who would care. So, my past has to stay invisible. It's what makes sense."

He sighed. "It's bullshit to fake who you are to impress others. It's not a way to live."

She stiffened at his high and mighty world view. He was a man from money. He could never understand where she was coming from or how important it was what other people thought of her. "It's my way to the career I want. And I'm not *faking* who I am. I'm just keeping my irrelevant past on a need-to-know basis, and pretty much no one has a reason to know. Even you, but you got me mad enough that I told you, which puts you in the doghouse, to be honest."

He grinned unrepentantly. "You're interesting when you're mad at me. I learn all sorts of stuff about you. Like the can opener. Your family history." His smile faded. "Your ex."

Crap. She'd been hoping he'd forgotten about that. Didn't the man forget anything she wanted forgotten? His mind was like a freaking steel trap. "You can let that go, thanks."

"Don't think I can," he said. "I'm an alpha male, which means I get protective. You're my fiancée, and that makes me get itchy when I find out a guy has been abusive—"

"I'm your fake fiancée, and it was one time, the day before our wedding." She cut him off. "Look, Declan. I don't want to be protected. I don't want to be obligated to you. I just wanted to get my career sorted out so I can move to New York and—"

"New York?" He let out his breath. "Right. I forgot about that." He rolled onto his back and clasped his hands behind his head. "You're moving to New York."

"Well, not yet, but hopefully soon." She felt his withdrawal, and had to fight not to scoot across the bed toward him. "Declan, I appreciate your support. I do. But I don't need it, and I don't want it. I just—" She paused.

He turned his head to look at her. "You just what?"

"I just want to be free to live my life."

He narrowed his eyes. "How are you not free?"

"I don't know. I just felt...I mean...you got all protective of me. And I was feeling weird when I thought you were in danger. I just think...maybe we're too compatible to be fake engaged. I mean, what if I start to like you? The sex was great. Maybe it's too great."

Declan stared at her as if she'd lost her mind. "Are you falling for me?"

"What? No!" She snorted. "That's ridiculous. The last thing I want is a relationship. I've been engaged twice, and that's enough. I certainly don't want anything real with us."

"Twice?" His brows went up. "Who else?"

"A guy back home. I was running away from him when I left, as much as my family."

He stared at her. "So, you're a two-time runaway bride?"

"Three actually. I was unofficially engaged to Nathan Hold when I was seventeen, but then he got arrested for stealing a car and that was that. Didn't last long."

Declan started to laugh. "You're a three-time runaway bride?"

"It's not funny."

"It's a little funny."

She poked him in the chest "It's not at all funny."

"It is." He caught her finger. "You can't see that it's a little funny? And when we break up, it'll be the fourth time. That's practically all-star status."

"Oh, God. I didn't think of that." She grimaced. "Let's get married and then divorced. That might be better. I'm in the business of having weddings actually happen, not breaking off engagements." Crap. She hadn't thought that through.

The smile dropped off his face. "Married?"

Her heart started fluttering at the serious look on his face. "I was kidding. Clark showed me I'm never getting married. Don't look so scared."

"I'm not scared. I liked being married. Until I fucked it up."

The raw, vulnerable weight of their conversation seemed to

close around her. This was so much more than a fake relationship kind of discussion. They shouldn't have had sex. It was impossible for her to remain emotionally distant after great sex. And apparently, he was having the same problem, which made for even more trouble.

Getting emotionally involved didn't serve her. It made her make stupid decisions and almost marry terrible, awful men. The part of her that didn't agree with being alone and single forever was trying to get all soft and mushy about Declan. That part of her loved how he was being vulnerable about his marriage, and protective about her. That part of her wasn't thinking strategically, and it wasn't keeping her own well-being in mind.

Declan sighed and brushed his hand through her hair. "You look terrified, Piper."

"I am."

"Why?"

"Because this whole thing between us—" She gestured back and forth. "—it wasn't supposed to be anything more than a fake engagement. We weren't supposed to have sex, or have conversations about anything that matters."

He caught her hand. "So, we became friends. That's okay."

"But we had sex. That's different than friends."

"Friends with benefits. There's actually a name for it."

How did she say it? How did she admit she was falling for him? She'd basically told him, and he still didn't get it. Probably because he was so far from falling for her that it didn't even cross his mind. Oh, God. Embarrassment flooded her. What was she doing? She was being an idiot. Doing the same thing she'd done three times before, and falling for a guy when she shouldn't.

This time, she wasn't going to make the mistake.

This time, she was going to realize it first.

She took a breath. "I'm not going to fall for you."

He raised his brows. "I'm very fall-able. It's nothing to be ashamed of."

She glared at him to keep her snicker at bay. *Stay focused, Piper.* "Your ego is unmatched. It must be great to be you."

"It is when I'm lying here with you."

"Don't!" She hit his chest. "Just don't be like that. I'm not falling for you, but when you make adorable, sweet comments like that, then I want to, and I don't want to, so you can't be like that. You need to be the grumpy, distant landlord again."

He clasped his hands behind his head and regarded her thoughtfully. "Can't."

"Why?"

"Because we had sex. And we had dinner with my mom. Those two things make an indelible mark on a person. I see you as a human being, one that I like. Plus, you helped me save a woman. Again, bonding. And my dog likes you, which raises your likeability even higher."

She glared at him. "Why are you being like this?"

"Because—" He paused.

"Because what?"

"I don't want to fall for anyone either," he said, after a pause. "After Diana, I was done. I've been done for a long time. But you make me want to live again."

Oh, no, no, no, no. She was not taking responsibility for his well-being. "Because I'm great at sex," she said, trying to keep the conversation light.

He studied her much too intensely. "You are great at sex."

"Right. So are you. What a team." She was feeling so restless, so vulnerable, so on the verge of saying and feeling things she shouldn't. "Look, Declan, I'm just...I want us to not get emotionally involved. Can we do that?"

He pursed his lips. "You want us to keep having sex and being fake engaged, and friends, but not be emotionally involved?"

She nodded. "Yes."

"No emotional involvement?"

"Correct."

He studied her, and for a moment, she thought he was going

to refuse. And if he did, she would have to cancel their deal, because she was already in over her head…and over her heart. She needed boundaries.

He finally raised his brows. "You realize that's the stereotypical dream of every man, right? Great sex with fake emotional commitment?"

She relaxed into laughter, relieved by his response. "I'm highly sought after by amoral jerks everywhere. It's really a glorious life I lead."

"I bet." He cocked his brow. "Lucky for you, I'm emotionally unavailable for life, but willing to keep my adorable, fake fiancée sated sexually."

She grinned. "You're such a good guy."

"Right?" He leaned over her and gave her a wicked smile. "How about I show you exactly how great of a guy I am?"

Desire coiled in her belly, a desire that was light and free, not weighed down with obligation, fear, or emotion. Just fun anticipation. "That sounds like a great idea—"

He cut off her sentence with a kiss designed to set her on fire.

And it did.

TWENTY-FOUR

Declan was an hour into Thursday night's shift at the bar when Aiden leaned over the bar. "Declan."

"What?" He didn't look up from the beer he was pouring. He was on edge, and it was taking all his discipline to stay focused, to not snap at the patrons. Usually, idiots at the bar didn't bother him, but tonight, every word was getting to him.

"Take a break."

"I'm fine."

"It's not a choice," Aiden said. "Take a break."

Declan looked at his friend. "I'm fine."

"Let Chaz work the bar for a bit. It's slow. It'll be good for him."

Chaz, their new bartender, looked alarmed. "What?"

"You've got it." Aiden slapped the bar. "Let's go, Declan. My office. Now."

Declan shoved the beer at the jerk who'd just called him something that would have gotten the guy arrested if Declan had been in his cop uniform, then strode after Aiden. He followed Aiden into his office, standing restlessly while Aiden sat down at his desk. "Close the door and have a seat, Declan."

Declan closed the door but remained standing.

Aiden leaned forward. "What the hell's going on with you tonight?"

Declan frowned at him. "What do you mean?"

"Part of the reason this bar is so successful is because my bartender is coveted by every customer who's attracted to men, plus half of the ones who aren't. Everyone else wants to be you, or at least be your friend. But tonight, you've got no charm. I need the charm. Where's the charm?"

Declan blinked. "I'm not charming."

Aiden grinned. "No, you're not. You're the crankiest bartender I've ever had, actually, but you've got this edge to you that attracts people. And the last few days, you've been a hell of a lot more fun. Until tonight. What's going on? Trouble with the fake fiancée?"

Damn. Declan let out a breath. "I'm fucked," he admitted.

Aiden leaned back and clasped his hands behind his head. "What's going on?"

Wearily, Declan sank into the chair beside Aiden's desk. "Truth?"

"Hell, yeah. I'm selling less alcohol every minute that you're back here, but I'm afraid you're going to start crying into the beer and that's not going to help my sales, so lay it on me. Let's clear it."

Declan laughed softly. "You're super dramatic for a guy."

"I'm a bartender. I can turn on whatever mode I need to deal with whoever's drinking at my counter. Or crying, as the case may be, like with you. So, what's going on?"

"I'm not crying."

"I know. I'm giving you shit because I'm fun like that. But you still have to tell me what's going on, or I'll fire you. And then it'll get awkward between us, which is a sucky way to end a decades-long friendship. So, don't make me fire you. Talk to me."

Declan laughed softly. "You've fired me a bunch of times already."

"Yeah, but I never meant it. Tonight I will. It's a 'nineteen strikes and you're out' deal. This is nineteen." He leaned in. "All kidding aside, what the fuck is going on with you tonight? You can't shake it, and that's not like you." He paused. "Your interview is tomorrow. Is that it?"

Declan blinked. "Hell. I forgot about that."

"Then what is it?"

Declan ground his jaw. He'd been friends with Aiden for a long time, and they'd seen each other at their most raw. And helped each other through it. He met his friend's gaze. "It's Piper," he admitted. The minute he said it, his insides seemed to settle, as if they no longer had to shout to be heard.

Aiden raised his brows. "Things are going badly with her?"

"No, hell, no. It's fantastic. But..." He started laughing. "Ironically, Piper wants empty sex and a fake engagement. Just fun times and lies. She gave me a speech about it."

Aiden narrowed his eyes thoughtfully. "You believe her?"

"She meant it." Fuck. He knew she did.

"But is she telling herself the truth? Because you keep telling yourself that you want to go back to being a cop, and you're lying to yourself. People do that."

Declan scowled at Aiden. "I don't need that shit from you."

Aiden sat back. "I've known you for a long time, right?"

"Yeah."

"Well, I know you don't want to work at this bar."

Declan grimaced. Was it that obvious? "I appreciate the job."

"I know. But you don't want it anymore. That's fine." Aiden grinned. "I also know you don't want to go back to being a cop."

"Now, that's not true—"

"And I know you like this girl enough that she's worth pursuing."

Declan braced his elbows on his knees and looked at his friend. "I don't want sex without connection with her. I want it all."

Aiden grinned, a big shit-eating grin. "That's fantastic. Hell, yeah!"

Declan shook his head. "It isn't. I'm not ready for more, and I don't know that I ever will be."

Aiden nodded. "I get it," he said. "But the good shit in life usually doesn't come when you're ready. It comes before, and then you get ready in a hurry or you miss it."

Declan ground his jaw. "It doesn't matter if I want it or not. She doesn't want a relationship." But hell. He'd been cranky as hell ever since he'd agreed to keep emotions out of it.

"Right," Aiden agreed. "And then she proposed to you, slept with you, and won your heart. You really think she doesn't care?"

Declan stood up, pacing restlessly, thinking about that question. "All she wants is to get out of town. She deserves more than to have me fall for her and try to keep her here." He understood what drove her. He knew she needed to leave.

"Oh for hell's sake, Declan, that's just a bunch of excuses. You're fucking terrified. I get it. But you're a cop, man. Cops learn how to keep going in the face of fear. You going to run and hide, or are you going to step up and stop hiding like you've been doing your whole fucking life?"

He looked over at Aiden. "My whole life?"

"Yeah. It's time for you to start living, and to stop trying to do what you think your dad might like, or your mom might not like. Or what Diana might have wanted. Go out and live, Declan. I see that spark that's flickering right now. Don't fucking put it out. Just don't." He stood up. "You lost your chance with Diana. Don't lose your second opportunity. You're lucky to get a chance for love twice." Then he walked out of the office and yanked the door shut behind him.

Declan stared after his friend for a long moment, the words rattling around in his mind. Love her? Love Piper?

He wasn't ready to love her. Or anyone. He just wasn't.

Maybe he needed to get out of their deal. Call it off. Get out before he couldn't. Get out before he fell in love with her and wrecked everything for both of them.

End it?

Fuck. That didn't feel good.

He didn't want to end it.

Which meant that he needed to.

Now.

His phone dinged, and he pulled it out. A text from Piper.

He stared at it for a long moment, then opened it.

I'm at dinner with a potential client, and the bride's mom is being super hostile about Clark. Any chance you can swing by and charm her?

He closed his fist around his phone.

He needed to text her that he was out.

That was the only option.

The best option.

He texted her back. *I'm out.* The moment he sent it, regret bit deep.

Hell. Was he running away? Was Aiden right? But she'd been shot. *Twice.* She was leaving town. She wasn't interested in a relationship. She was wrong for him in every way.

He needed to be out.

She texted back right away. *Out? You're out somewhere? What does that mean? Is that a yes?*

Declan laughed softly. Leave it to Piper to be so focused on her dream that she didn't even notice that he'd just broken it off. She *was* a bride protector, and she cared more than anyone he'd ever met. One of the many things he loved about her—

Shit.

He did love her.

He'd loved her for a long, damned time. Probably since the day she'd rented his carriage house.

He took a moment to breathe it in, and he wasn't surprised how terrifying the thought was. But he was surprised that it also felt good. Alive. Real. He hadn't thought he'd love again. But he did. So, what was he going to do about it?

Declan?

He stared at her message. He couldn't keep going with her and agree to keep it distant. He'd never been built like that, and especially not now.

If he stayed in this sham relationship, it was with one purpose, to see if it could be real…which would break the promise he'd made to her.

He'd broken a lot of promises to Diana, because all he'd cared about was himself and what he wanted.

Maybe it was time to be a better man. To help Piper and *not* try to make it more. To respect what she needed and wanted from him in a way he'd never done with Diana. Of course, Diana had wanted a present, loving, communicative husband, and Piper wanted the opposite. Piper wanted the old Declan, and he didn't want to be that guy anymore.

Poetic justice, Diana would probably say.

He laughed softly. He got what he deserved: a chance to be about something other than himself. It kind of sucked, but it also felt weirdly good to become more. To give someone else what they needed because he could. Yeah, this was good. It felt right.

He was doing this, and he was doing it how Piper wanted. *Text me the location, and I'll be there.*

Yay! Thank you so much! You're the best!

Her joy made his decision right. He'd had no idea it could feel so good to make someone else happy, when there was nothing else in it for him, other than breaking his fucking heart again.

He was a cop.

He could handle pain.

He was born for it.

TWENTY-FIVE

By Saturday night, Piper was finally beginning to grasp the magnitude of her idiocy.

"Wait a sec," Tori leaned in, grinning. "You banned Declan from emotional intimacy, and told him empty sex was all that was allowed?"

Piper grimaced as she picked up her glass of wine. She'd wrangled an invite to a fundraiser that had potential clients. Declan had needed to work at the bar, so she'd brought her friends as her dates. "I did."

"And how is that working out for you?" Maddie was sitting on a couch, snuggling with her service dog, Violet.

"Great. It's exactly what I need. He bailed me out the other night at a client meeting. He was pure charm. It was perfect." She scanned the room, looking for her targets for the evening, but she was having trouble summoning the fire that usually drove her.

It had been a long, desperate week, and she was four clients short of the four she needed by Sunday night. The two she'd come to see hadn't arrived yet, and it was getting late.

Tori raised her brows. "Sweetie, we've known each other since we were all broke and living in a loft together. I know when you're tossing out a bunch of lies."

"I agree," Maddie said. "Talk to us, babe."

"It's just work—"

"Liar." Keira shook her head. "We've seen you work-glum for the last year, and this is different."

Piper looked around at her friends. "The truth?" She sighed. "Telling Declan I wanted only empty sex hasn't worked out that great for me."

Maddie burst out laughing. "No shit. Really?"

"That's so weird," Keira said. "Most women really thrive when they ask a hot, charming guy who likes them to put those emotions away and just have meaningless hammertime instead."

Tori was openly laughing. "Babe, you need love so much that you got engaged to Clark. Why would you think that you could have naked time with Declan and not care about him?"

Piper couldn't help but grin. "It seemed like a good idea. I was starting to like him and—"

"What?" Keira hurled a napkin at her. "Shut up! You're falling for him?"

"I knew it!" Maddie clapped her hands. "I opened the flood-gates for love when I got engaged to Lucas. Yay!"

Only Tori didn't laugh. "That makes sense, then," she said. "You don't want to get trapped like you did with Clark, but if you like Declan and then he likes you back and starts being a decent guy, then what defenses do you have?"

"Exactly!" Piper sighed. "He's not nearly as grumpy and irritating as I was expecting him to be. He's really messing with my plans."

"Men will do that," Keira agreed.

"Sometimes, it's all right," Maddie said. "I wasn't ready for Lucas, but it turned out great."

Piper looked at Maddie desperately. "That's what scares me. I thought you were going to be single forever, and Lucas came in and he changed everything for you. I don't want that, and Declan…" She paused. "He makes me want it."

Understanding filled their faces. "Terrifying, huh?" Maddie said.

"It's not just that." Piper bounced her foot restlessly. "I've made such stupid mistakes in the past when it comes to men, and I don't trust myself. I have to focus on my career, and not get trapped again."

There was silence for a moment, then Tori frowned. "Mistakes, plural? Who else besides Clark?"

Maddie looked away, not letting on that she knew about Piper's past, but suddenly, Piper was so tired of hiding. Declan hadn't judged her, and he had every reason to.

These three women were her heart. Why had she spent so long hiding from them? "I was engaged twice before. I bolted both times."

"What?" Tori's eyes widened. "When?"

"Back home." She took a breath. "And I grew up in a family of drug dealers. Gamblers. My dad's in prison. My brothers were in and out. I have scars from being shot."

Maddie smiled at her and gave her a thumbs up.

Piper took a breath, and she felt like a thousand pounds of weight had fallen from her shoulders.

"Shot?" Keira said. "Like, with a gun?"

"Yes." Piper shrugged. "Twice."

"Damn, girl," Keira said. "You're a freaking survivor. To make it all the way from that world to this one? I'm so impressed."

A warmth settled in Piper's chest. "Thanks. It's been a long road, made easier by you guys, of course."

Tori frowned. "Why didn't you ever tell us this before?"

"Because that past would ruin my career. I had to leave it behind."

Keira nodded. "I get that. There are things in all our pasts that we don't want to ever look at again." She reached over and squeezed Piper's hand. "You done good, girl."

Sudden tears filled Piper's eyes. She'd spent so long hiding, and Declan had unlocked her secrets. "Don't tell anyone," she said. "You guys still love me, but it would kill my career."

The three women exchanged glances, but it was Tori who spoke. "Anyone who thinks less of you because of where you came from and what you have overcome doesn't deserve you."

Piper started laughing. "That's basically what Declan said."

"The man's right," Keira said. "Keep him around. He's good for you."

"I can't keep him," Piper said. "He's just temporary."

Maddie was rubbing Violet's ears. "Do you really want him to be temporary? I fought against Lucas for so long, but the truth was that I wanted him. Us. I wanted to trust him."

Piper rubbed her finger where her engagement ring from Clark had sat, where Declan's ring now twinkled. "The truth that I don't trust myself. I don't trust my instincts. I've been wrong so many times, and I had no idea until I was about to marry them."

"So, plan the wedding, then," Maddie teased. "If you bolt, you know he's wrong. If you don't, then maybe magic sparkled into your life."

Piper tensed at the thought of getting married. "I can't. I can't—"

"Hey," Tori put her arm around Piper's shoulders. "It's okay, sweetie. No one is making you marry him." Her eyes were full of understanding, but the sympathy felt disempowering.

Piper didn't want sympathy. She wanted to be strong, capable, and badass. She wanted to feel confident, not steeped in fears and stress. She needed to find her own power, and not link it to Declan or any other man. "I just need to get some clients," she said. "Then I'll be able to focus."

Tori drummed her fingers on the table. "Look," she said. "Why would you try to get all these clients for a woman who might fire you anyway? Why don't you get them for yourself and open your own business?"

God, she wanted to. "My name is tainted right now. I have to leverage someone else's name right now." How had she gotten to this point? She'd worked so hard for so long to be independent, and yet, after all this time, she was still dependent on someone else for her job, her dreams, and her money.

Wow.

That was depressing.

She lifted her chin. "I'm not giving up." She stood up. "I'm going to go mingle. I've never given up before, and I'm not now."

"Damn straight," Tori said, bouncing to her feet. "I'll help. There must be brides out there that we don't know about. We can find them."

"We sure can." Maddie hopped up, and Violet did the same.

"I'm in!" Keira picked up her purse. "The Loft Squad is in business. Let's go."

Piper grinned as her friends took off across the party, all of them headed in different directions. She was so lucky—

"Hello."

She turned sharply at the sound of a man's voice, and she saw Dick standing directly behind her.

TWENTY-SIX

Dick's eyes were cold, his jaw hard, his face cool.

Oh, shit.

Piper quickly called up on years of practice from her childhood and schooled her face into a charming smile. "Hello. Can I help you?" she asked, pretending not to recognize the abusive sociopath she'd helped Jessie and her kids escape from.

"You were planning a party with my wife on Wednesday night."

She blinked, trying to appear confused, then brightened. "Oh, right. Jessie. Is she all right? She hasn't been responding to my texts. I need to put some deposits down, but I can't go forward without her okay." Could he feel how fast her heart was racing? She felt like she was ten again, trying to stall some jerk while her brothers raced out the back door, leaving her alone to protect their home.

Dick narrowed his eyes, studying her. Sudden realization gripped her. He suspected that Piper had helped Jessie escape. Oh...*shit.* "If you tell me where she is, I'll forget I met you." His face didn't promise the respite.

Oh, God. Oh, God. The menace pouring off him was surreal.

He was like one of the enforcers from her childhood. A man who liked violence and had no qualms using it to solve his problems. And Jessie had been married to him?

Piper lifted her chin, sudden conviction rushing through her. Jessie had escaped her life, like Piper had escaped hers. There wasn't a chance in hell Piper was blowing it for Jessie. Screw Dick and his belief that he could intimidate her into backing down. *Never.*

She'd been through too much in her life to be afraid of *him.* She frowned, trying to appear confused. "I don't know where she is. I'm trying to find her." Behind him, Tori came into view and raised her brows in question.

Of course Tori would have read Piper's body language and realized something was wrong. Girlfriends were the best.

Piper immediately gave the signal they'd created when they were all in their early twenties, single, and adventurous. She tapped her right eyebrow five times with her index finger.

Tori's eyes widened, and then she sprinted over, just as Dick leaned in. "Tell me where she is or—"

"Girlfriend," Tori said, as she grabbed Piper's arm. "Your darling Captain Hawk is getting antsy." She shot a non-apologetic look at Dick. "I gotta steal her. Sorry!" Then, without giving him a chance to respond, the two women turned away and strode off, shoulders back, heads high, walking with as much power as they could summon.

"What was that?" Tori muttered as they wove their way through the party.

"The asshole from the other night. He recognized me."

"Oh…shit." Tori didn't turn around as they made their way through the party. "Did he threaten you?"

"Of course." Piper used the mirror over the bar to look behind her, but Dick was already gone. Crap. Where was he? She didn't like not knowing where he was. "I don't think he knows my name."

"He'll ask around and get it pretty quick if he wants it." Tori was tight beside her. "Let's bail."

The minute she said that, Piper stopped. "No."

Tori gave her a look. "I know you're desperate for clients, but—"

"No. It's not that." She put her hands on her hips. "I can't let him drive me out of here. He travels in these circles. I'll see him again. I have to act innocent. Like I have nothing to hide."

"You do have something to hide," Tori said. "You literally helped his wife escape. A guy like that has access to his wife's accounts. He probably went on her computer and saw that there were no messages about his party. He knows you lied, and right about now, he probably has your name. Another three minutes, and he'll know where you live."

Piper's spine tingled, but it wasn't with fear. It was determination. "I have mace."

Tori nodded. "We all do." All four of them had pasts that had taught them how to be tough, how to be strong, how to defend themselves. "No being alone until this is settled, though, okay? Always with one of us."

Piper nodded. "I'll have Declan stay over, so you guys are off night duty."

"Maybe stay at his house?"

Piper raised her brows. "If Dick breaks into my house to come after me and Declan, then his future will be done. I want to tempt him."

"Do you?" Tori put her hands on her hips. "Do you, really? Because this guy is bad enough that his wife hired Eliana to get her out of there, and the Harts were needed to help with the extraction."

Piper took a breath. "No one helped my mom. This is my turn."

Tori stared at her. "Your mom? You mean, your mom needed protection from your dad? What about you? Did you need protection, too? Did anyone help you?"

Piper shrugged. "It was complicated." She paused as she caught sight of Dick again. He was speaking to a woman she'd met at Kitty's fundraiser, and they were both looking at Piper. The woman nodded and said something. "He knows my name." *Shit.* For all her bravado, she wasn't feeling very safe right now.

Dammit. She hated feeling unsafe. She'd fought so hard for a life where she felt safe, and in one altruistic move, she'd ripped that away from herself.

"Complicated? How complicated?" Tori's face was sad. "What else haven't you told us, Piper? You know you have all of our hearts. We'll help any way we can."

"I know, but sometimes dredging up the past doesn't serve. All that matters is what we do with the life we have now. I refuse to be stuck in my past."

Dick pulled out his phone and called someone, still watching her.

Tori was also following him in the mirror over the bar. "I'm a little worried for you right now," she said. "The Harts need to provide protection for you."

"Eliana makes women disappear. I'm not going to disappear from my life." She pulled out her phone. "I am, however, going to call Declan for a ride home."

Tori grinned. "What happened to making it sex only?"

"I think guarding my body is part of sex, don't you? Nothing personal here." She texted him. *Declan. I need a ride home. Soon, if possible.*

Her phone rang almost instantly, Declan's name flashing on her screen.

Tori raised her brows. "That was quick. He must have some super Piper sense about your well-being."

Piper tried not to care, but a part of her settled at the sight of his name. "He doesn't know me well enough to notice the undercurrent of terror in my text."

"No?"

"No." She answered the phone. "Hi."

"What's going on? What's wrong?" He didn't waste time with preamble.

Her throat tightened at his questions. He *knew.* He paid enough attention that he'd picked up on her tension through a freaking text. She could hear the noise of the bar behind him, and realized he'd called her without even taking time to step away from the bar. "Dick."

"Dick?" He paused for a second. "You want sex?"

Horror shot through her. "Oh, God. No. I didn't mean that." She started laughing, that freakout kind of laugh that combined with building terror. "I was referring to that guy Dick from the fundraiser the other night."

"Oh. I was going to make a joke about sex, but I need to follow this Dick train first. Why are you talking about him?"

"Because he's here, he threatened me, and now he's watching me and talking on the phone. I'm a little concerned he has his heavyweights heading to my car or house right now to kidnap and torture me until I reveal her location. I have my friends here, but I don't want to drive home alone."

Declan swore. "Stay in the ballroom. Do not step away for any reason. Aiden! I'm leaving!" The background sounds of the bar faded, and she knew he was outside.

Her heart tightened. He'd run from the bar for her. God. She'd never had a man be the one to keep her safe before. It felt… foreign. And wonderful. "I'm at the Diamond Plaza Hotel."

"Got it." He paused. "GPS says I'll be there in thirty minutes. When does the party end?"

She looked around. "People are leaving already."

"Fuck. Are you near the bar?"

"Next to it, yes."

"Give your phone to the bartender."

"What?" She stiffened as she glanced at the bartender. He was quite tall, muscled, and looked like he could deal with any drunk who caused trouble. "No. I can handle this. I'll ask him to stay with us myself."

His truck roared to life. "Piper. Don't fucking do that to me."

She heard the edge of desperation in his voice, and suddenly realized what she'd done to him, dragging him back into a situation like the one that had haunted him, calling him when she was in danger. "Shit, sorry. I didn't mean to drag you into this—"

"Do you think I'd prefer that you didn't call me, but this time, when I broke into your house, you *were* actually dead on your kitchen floor instead of meditating? Is that what you think I want? Because let me clarify things for you. I'm a born protector, Piper. I *need* you to call me and ask for my help any time you're in danger. Never apologize. Got it?"

She took a breath. "Yeah, okay."

"I request that you give your phone to the bartender, Piper. Please."

She felt the iron willpower it took for him not to demand she hand the phone over, and she settled. She could say no. He would never force her. But she knew how bad people could be, and so did he. "Okay."

She waved to get the bartender's attention and held up her phone. "Would you talk to my fiancé, please?"

The bartender gave her a look that said he was so tired of rich people, but he nodded, because he was paid to cater to her. "Sure." He took the phone. "Hello. How may I help you?"

Piper watched as he listened. His eyes narrowed, and he looked at Piper, and then scanned the room. "What does this guy look like?" He asked Piper.

She looked in the mirror and described him.

The bartender's gaze settled across the room. "Got him." He turned away, turning his back to Piper while he continued to talk to Declan.

Tori leaned over. "Update?"

Piper filled her in while the bartender went back to mixing drinks, still on the phone with Declan.

"Damn, girl," Tori said. "Declan checks all the boxes, doesn't he? Dropping everything to keep you safe?"

"I don't have a checklist."

"No, but if you did, he'd fill it in nicely." Tori sat down next to her. "I'm going to text Maddie and Keira. I want them here with us. There is power in numbers."

Piper nodded. "Thanks." She saw Dick leaning against a pillar, watching her. His phone was in his hand, dangling from his fingertips. He wasn't even pretending not to watch her. He was stalking her, trying to intimidate her. Dammit. This wasn't a one-time thing. These were his social circles, and they were hers.

He would never stop until he had his wife back, or had finished his business with Piper.

Tori squeezed her arm. "In it together, girl. We always are."

While Tori texted, the bartender handed the phone back to her. "Piper, my name is Myles Bolden." His voice had an interesting lilt, an accent she couldn't quite place. Cajun, maybe? His skin was dark brown, his eyes impenetrable, his energy focused and all business. Gone was the annoyed bartender. His tone was gentle, but there was an edge to it. "I'm your bodyguard for the next thirty minutes."

Piper took a breath. "All right."

He looked at Tori. "You're her friend?"

Tori cleared her throat. "Yes, I'm Tori."

"So, this man has seen you with Piper?"

Tori glanced at Piper. "Yes."

"Then you're under my protection as well. If you have other friends here, tell them to stay away."

At that moment, Maddie and Keira raced up. "We're here," Maddie said. "Lucas's plane is landing in a few minutes. I'm going to call him, and get the Harts on this—"

Tori and Piper met gazes and turned toward each other, blocking out their friends. "You guys need to go," Piper said softly, not looking at them.

"What? No—"

Myles leaned in. "If Dick sees you with Piper, you both become his target. Stay at the bar, but go to the other end and pretend you don't know Piper and Tori. Do it now."

They stared at Myles. "Wow," Maddie said. "You're like a Hart with that intensity."

He raised his brows. "I'll take that as a compliment. I've met a few of them through the Stocktons, and they're good people."

"You know the Stocktons?" Maddie said. "I'm marrying a Hart! The Stocktons will be my family, too."

Myles eyed Maddie. "All the more reason to keep you out of danger. To the other end. Both of you. Now."

"Right. Got it." Maddie grabbed Keira's arm, but didn't look at Piper or Tori. "See you guys across the room, where we can stare longingly at each other."

"Stay safe," Piper muttered. "Please."

"Always."

Piper wanted to hug them as they hurried away. She wanted to grab hold of her friends and keep them close. They were her rocks, her anchors, the only family she felt like she had, and she had to let them go.

Tori put her arm around Piper's shoulders. "You think he saw us with Maddie and Keira earlier?"

Piper looked at her. "Crap. Maybe."

Myles frowned. "If he saw you together earlier, they could be in danger, too. I'm telling them to stay at the bar as well until Lucas can get here." He raised his brows at Tori. "You engaged to anyone handy as well?"

Tori snorted. "I'm engaged to myself."

"Independent woman. I like it." Then he turned and strode to the other end of the bar.

Tori stared after him. "That man exudes pure danger. He's not a bartender. At least not in his soul."

Piper smiled at the way Tori was watching Myles. "He's very rugged."

"He is, isn't he? I feel like a woman could get lost in a swamp, and he'd plunge in, wrestle a few alligators, take down some poachers, and then cart her right out of there without even getting bitten by a single mosquito."

Piper leaned on the bar, grinning at her friend. "Damn, girl. You're attracted to him."

"I definitely am," Tori said, dragging her gaze off him. "That is so unexpected. I need to hydrate more."

Piper chuckled. "Hydrate?"

"Yes. Hydration is the magic elixir for all ailments, including being attracted to dangerous bartenders with secret lives and too much muscle."

"What about part-time bartenders who are ex-cops, dog whisperers, and obscenely wealthy? Does hydration work for that too?"

"Damn straight it does."

Piper grinned and raised her hand. "Myles! Can we get a couple waters?"

"Make it a pitcher," Tori called out. "A pitcher for each of us!" She sat back as Myles nodded. "Dammit. Even his nod is sexy. This is no good. No good at all." She looked at Piper. "Our friendship is ruining me, Piper. It's your fault I know his name and spoke to him."

"Well, you guys made me start thinking of Declan as a man, not a grumpy landlord, so it's payback."

Tori made a face. "I hereby recant all attempts to make you notice Declan. It's very disconcerting to be attracted to a man after a self-commitment to a life of being solo."

"Right?" Piper relaxed a bit, relieved that at least one of her friends understood how stressful it was to be thinking about dating again. "After this is over, let's go on a girls trip."

"To an all-women resort," Tori said. "No men allowed."

"Absolutely." Piper glanced in the mirror over the bar. At first she didn't see Dick anywhere, and she relaxed slightly. Maybe he'd left. Maybe they'd overestimated the level of threat he was. Maybe—

She suddenly saw him off to her left. He was leaning against the wall, holding a glass of wine.

Watching her.

He met her gaze in the mirror, and raised his glass to her in a toast.

She jerked her gaze off him and looked at Tori.

Her friend squeezed her arm. "We got this, babe. You know we do. And we have Declan, Myles, the Harts, and the Stocktons, too."

"I know." She was grateful for all of that, but at the same time, it came with a cost. Having to rely on protectors meant she was losing the most important thing.

Her freedom.

Then she saw Declan sprint into the ballroom, and her entire body shuddered with relief. She hadn't realized how scared she'd been until she saw him. He was in jeans and a black t-shirt, and he looked rough and dangerous, a man who even a guy like Dick would have to notice.

Declan's gaze found her immediately, and relief flooded his face when he saw her. He strode across the floor, and didn't stop when he reached her. He simply grabbed her around the waist, hauled her against him, and kissed her like a man who wanted the entire world to know that he claimed her, that he was protecting her, and that anyone who wanted to hurt her would have to go through him to get her.

It was arrogant, testosterone-laden, and raw, potent fire.

She knew he was kissing her for a purpose, and not because he actually was desperate to kiss her, but that didn't matter.

It was a kiss that broke every single shield she had against him.

TWENTY-SEVEN

This was what he was good at.

This was his zone of genius.

But when Declan walked into Piper's kitchen after patrolling her property and ensuring it was safe, he felt like he was in quicksand.

She was sitting on her couch with his dog, her feet tucked under her and her arm around Angel. She'd ditched her dress in exchange for jeans, sneakers, and a sweatshirt, and she was holding a can opener in her lap.

A fucking can opener.

Because no one was going to get to her if she had a damned can opener.

Piper.

He hadn't been able to stop looking at her, touching her, kissing her since he'd walked into the Diamond Plaza Hotel ballroom and seen her sitting at the bar with Tori.

The drive to the Diamond Plaza Hotel had felt like the longest fucking drive of his life. The images going through his mind had been graphic, shit he hadn't seen in his head for years.

When he'd seen her, all he'd been able to think about was

getting to her. Touching her. Kissing her. Reassuring himself that she was safe.

He was completely fucked.

He'd already known he was falling for her, but when he'd gotten that text, the fear that had gripped him was like a punch in his gut. And his heart.

Piper looked over at him. "Everything okay outside?"

"Yep." He shut the slider and locked it, then pulled the curtain closed and set the alarm. "You sure you want to stay here?"

Lucas had taken Maddie, Keira, and Tori to a hotel, and he was staying with them until they figured out if Dick was going to target them, but Piper had wanted to come home, and Declan had gone with her. Obviously. "We could at least stay at my house. I have a better security system there. And a shower that isn't ripped up."

She shook her head. "This is my home. I can't let him drive me out."

"I know. I get that." Declan walked over and sat on her coffee table, facing her. His gun was in a holster on his hip. It had been years since he'd worn his gun. It felt weird as hell, and, at the same time, it felt like home. "I made a couple calls to former associates to see what they can dig up about Dick. Dylan is doing the same."

Dick had disappeared when Declan had shown up, which had probably been good.

Declan hadn't been in a frame of mind where seeing Dick would have ended well.

Piper took a breath. "See, so we're good."

His jaw flexed, and she could feel tension radiating off him. "I don't like this."

She leaned forward and put her hands on his thighs. His pulse jumped at her touch, and he had to fight to stay still.

"Thank you for helping me," she said. "I know you don't want to be here."

"I want to be here. I just wanted it to be under different

circumstances." He looked behind her, checking the slider, his gaze then sliding to the windows. On maximum alert. Every muscle in his body was taut, every nerve firing. "Men like Dick are bullies. He doesn't want to deal with me. I don't think he'll try anything with me here. That's why I parked my truck in front."

"And why you kissed me like you owned me at the hotel."

He paused, surprised by her comment. She thought that kiss had been for show? It had been his undeniable truth breaking free of his control. "It probably helped back him off," he said, evading a direct answer.

He'd promised her no emotional involvement, but he was long past that. The question was how long he could hide it from her.

Aiden had been right. Declan wasn't built for casual. He was built to go all-in, and he'd thought he had only one chance in this life.

But by some incredible gift, he had another. He wasn't going to blow it this time, at least not yet. He had to give Piper space. He knew it. But, *hell*. Tonight had nearly undone him.

Piper put her hand on his thigh. "You're bouncing."

He stilled his leg. "I'm restless."

"I can see that." She studied him. "I was scared in the hotel, but the minute you got there, I felt calmer. I feel good now."

She was resilient as hell. He loved that about her. "Good. I'm glad I can give you a break from being scared."

She scooted closer to him. "How can I help you? Is it your past that is getting to you?"

Fuck. She was so close, and she smelled so good. He didn't lean in toward her. "No."

She raised her brows. "No?"

"It's not my past. It's *you*, Piper. You're the one in danger, and you're in danger because I asked you to help. I'm on full alert to keep you safe. It's about no one, but you." His voice was raw and rough, deeper than he'd intended.

She put her hand on his face, and he sucked in his breath. "Declan," she said softly. "In case I forget to thank you later, thank you for coming tonight. Thank you for rushing out of work, for kissing me like a madman, and for staying here with me. This is obviously more than a fake engagement situation, and I want you to know that I realize that, and I appreciate it."

He put his hand over hers, holding her palm to his cheek. He didn't give himself permission to respond, because what he wanted to say would break the rules he'd agreed to, and it would scare the crap out of her. "I'm glad to do it," he finally said.

Glad to do it. What kind of platitude was that?

"Do we stay up all night, then?" she asked. "Like the movies?"

He managed a smile. "No. I'm too old to stay up all night now. I'll probably fall asleep and shoot myself in the foot. Dick isn't going to come with me here. We'll lock the door to your bedroom. It'll be fine."

"And tomorrow?"

He shrugged. "I'll be your shadow until we figure out what is up with Dick. Dylan is working on it, so my job is just to keep you safe." He grinned. "Apparently, I'm a very devoted fiancé with no life except to follow his gorgeous woman around."

She raised her brows. "As it should be. Women rule the world."

"Agreed." He realized his leg was bouncing again. "To bed, then?" The moment he said it, heat poured through him. He might not be able to tell her what he was feeling, but the bedroom was a place where he didn't have to hold back with her. Passion? Heat? Love?

He could channel all of it into his lovemaking.

Mischievousness flashed in her eyes. "On one condition."

He leaned in, need pulsing through him. Need to get close to her. To hold her. To lose himself in her. "What's that?"

"You have to kiss me like you did at the bar."

Heat flashed through him, and he grinned, a slow, pleased grin. "You liked that, did you?"

She slid her arms around his neck. "I really did."

Hot damn. "That's just the start, sweetheart. I can level up from there. You want hot? I'll give you hot."

She grinned. "I want hot. Really, really hot."

"Then you shall have it, my dear."

He leaned in to kiss her, a no-holds-barred kiss that ripped through the last shields around his heart.

The moment Piper kissed him back, he knew it was over for him.

He was lost to her. In every possible way.

She could destroy him.

She could save him.

Either way, he was in it until the end.

TWENTY-EIGHT

Piper opened her eyes to the faint glow of dawn. Declan was in her window seat, shirtless and in bare feet. One knee was up, and he was scanning the outdoors. His whiskers were thick, and his hair was tousled.

She tucked her pillow against her chest, watching him. There was something so intimate and casual about the way he was sitting quietly, as if he was simply breathing in the morning while letting her sleep.

He was so male that he literally made her toes curl, but there was so much depth to him. So much complexity.

"Morning, sweetheart," he said, not even looking over at her.

"Hi." She hugged the pillow closer. "Can I ask you something?"

"Sure."

"How did the interview go?"

"I told you. Fine. I'll hear from them probably next week."

She sighed. "I know you said that, but that's not what I want to know. How did you feel about it? How was it to be back?"

He shrugged again. "Fine."

Frustration ground through her. "I know it wasn't just fine, Declan. Why won't you tell me how it really went?" They'd just spent half the night making incredible love, and she was feeling raw and vulnerable. She needed to connect with him on a deeper level.

He finally looked over at her. "You said you didn't want things personal between us. I can't answer that question the way you want it without going to places I agreed not to go." There was no judgment in his tone. No attack. Simply truth.

She sighed and flopped back on the bed. "That's why you've been avoiding talking about it?"

"Yep."

More proof that she was an idiot? Did she really think she could do this without getting personal with him? "I want to know."

He was silent for a moment.

"Declan?"

"Well, now I'm not answering because I don't want to talk about it. You called my bluff."

She giggled and rolled back onto her side so she could see him. "Tell me one thing."

He was looking out the window again. "They changed the color of the paint on the walls. It used to be off white. Now it's more like ecru."

"Because you're a paint color expert from doing your house?"

"Yep."

Piper patted Angel, who was curled up on the pillow, then she grabbed the comforter, wrapped it around herself, and padded across the room. She crawled onto the window seat with him and tucked herself against his side.

He immediately put his arm around her, pulled her against him, and kissed the top of her head, making her smile.

"What was good about being there?" she asked.

He took a breath. "You're very persistent."

"I am. One thing. One good thing about being there."

He was quiet for a moment, but his arm was still tight around her shoulder. "The people. I forgot how many friends I have there.

I walked away from that life and left everyone behind. It felt good to see them."

She spread her palm on his stomach. "I was very alone when I first moved here," she said. "Loneliness can be devastating."

"I'm not lonely." But his arm tightened as he said it. "At least not right now, while I have a gorgeous, naked woman tucked up against me."

She laughed softly. "Name one bad thing about being there."

"I could feel the energy of the building pressing down on me. It felt like I was suffocating."

Piper was startled by the rawness of his answer. It was so honest, and she was touched that he trusted her with it. "Did it go away after a while?"

"No, but it felt familiar. I think it was always like that, but I didn't notice. I notice now." He shrugged. "I'm sure I'll get used to it again."

"But do you want to?" She knew she was pressing at him, but she wanted to know. She felt like there was so much boiling inside him, and he had no way to relieve the pressure.

Silence for a long moment, then, "It's who I am, Piper. It's in my soul."

That wasn't a yes, and she knew it. "It's a part of your soul, yes, but maybe its time has passed. Maybe it's time to listen to another part of your soul."

"And build houses?" He laughed softly. "Bartend? Nothing else moves me like being a cop. It makes my heart beat."

Sudden sadness filled Piper. Sadness that he was going to go back into a dangerous job, but also sadness because she knew he didn't want to go, and he knew it, too. But it was the only path he knew. She wrapped her arms around his torso and rested her cheek on his chest. She didn't know what to say, because there were no answers.

He leaned his chin on her head. "Why do you want to be a wedding planner so badly?" he asked. "Why is it your soul?"

She smiled at the memories his question evoked. "One of my mom's jobs was waitressing for a high-end caterer. She was always working these fancy weddings and parties. I would go with her and sit in the corner. We would pretend the party was for us, and that we were the guests of honor. It was the best part of my life, when we got to go be with fancy people and pretend we mattered."

His arm tightened around her. "You do matter."

She watched the colors of the sky change as the sun woke up, evolving from a dusky orange to a vibrant pink. "My dad used to beat my mom up. And me. And my brothers."

"Fuck, Piper—"

She cut him off. "It's okay. He's in prison now. When I got old enough to understand, I asked my mom why she stayed with him. She believed she didn't have a choice. She got pregnant and married at seventeen. She didn't have a high school diploma, and he controlled the money. She believed she was trapped, and that it was all she was good enough for." She touched her necklace. "She hid her tips for years to buy this for me for my sixteenth birthday. She gave it to me, and made me promise that I would get out of that life. That I would escape the way she hadn't been able to. I told her I would start my own wedding planning business, and she would come work for me, and we'd be powerful, rich women who no one would ever control. We'd make weddings that were real fairytales, not the shotgun trap that she'd had."

As she spoke, her throat got tight, and the words started to slow.

Declan wiped a tear off her cheek. "You're trying to earn the money to bring her to Boston?"

"No. She died a few months after my sixteenth birthday, and I've been trying to keep my promise to her ever since." She looked down at her hands. "She wanted freedom of choice for me, Declan. The ability to choose who I wanted to be with and how I wanted to live. And I almost married two different jerks in town, and then I almost married Clark. All three men were a betrayal of the dream she had for me, and now, I've screwed up even my business." She leaned her head back against Declan's shoulder. "I have to make her proud. I have to be the woman she wanted me to have the chance to be," she whispered. "I can't let her down, and I'm about to do exactly that."

To her surprise, she started to cry.

Real, wrenching sobs that were years of failure, of trying, of apologizing to the woman who had given everything up for her kids.

Dammit. Piper worked so hard to be strong, to keep going, and she was caught unprepared for the sudden onslaught of emotion.

"Oh, sweetie." Declan pulled her into his arms, and she let him, burying herself against him, letting the strength of his embrace and the warmth of his body keep her body from breaking apart, shattering into fragments of guilt and shame, which she fought to get back on track.

"My whole life, I've dreamed of weddings, of that fairytale, of giving women what my mom never had," she whispered through the tears. "But I think I also really wanted it for myself. I didn't want to be strong and independent. I wanted a prince charming who would take care of me, but you know what?"

He moved his hand and began rubbing circles on her back. "What?"

"When you want someone to take care of you, you make stupid choices, like the three men I almost married. There's no way to have it all. I just..." She sat up, forcing herself to hold herself up. "I just need to do it by myself. I can't lean on some man because then I'll be trapped like she was. I have to do it myself. I have to, because she couldn't." She stood up, surprised to find her hands were shaking. "It's fine. It's fine. I know today is Sunday and I don't have any clients, but I'll find a way. I always do. Because my mom was tough, and she taught me how to be tough, and—"

Suddenly she was crying too hard to talk, which was super annoying because she didn't want to waste time crying.

But she was doing it anyway.

Declan stood up, pulled her into his arms and kissed her gently, slobbery tears and all. "Piper, you're an absolute freaking badass. Your mom would be so proud of you."

"She wouldn't! She would be sad, because I'm still not free, and I'm about to fail. This was our dream, Declan. Hers and mine. And I'm about to fail completely."

"You're not going to fail."

"I know." She lifted her chin, wiping her cheeks. "I'm not. Because the only way to fail is to give up, and I'm not giving up. I'm giving up men and getting married, but I'm not giving up on creating the life I promised my mom I'd lead."

He watched her thoughtfully. "What about Maddie? Or the other Harts? Their weddings would put you right back in the game."

"No. I won't use them that way."

"They love you—"

"And I love them too much to use the most important day of their lives for my own advantage." She turned away. "I'm going to get back on the internet. I'll find more people I'll—"

He caught her arm. "Piper," he said softly. "You're a treasure. You have the biggest heart full of love and courage. You don't need to spend your life trying to fulfill your mom's dream. All she wanted was for you to be free to make your choices, not her choices."

She stared at him. "You're trying to live your dad's dream."

Something flashed in his eyes, but he ignored her statement. "Your mom's dream was freedom for you," he said. "Not necessarily to be a top-level wedding planner, right? That was simply the path she saw, but it's the ending that matters."

Piper shook her head. "It was our dream. We were going to do it together. All of it." She stepped away and sat down on the bed, wrapping the comforter around her. "I'll think of something." But what? She'd worked so hard all week.

"Can I help?"

She looked over at him, and suddenly she wanted to cry again. "I can't ask for help."

"You can." He walked over and then crouched in front of her, his hands on her knees. "Piper, getting help from others doesn't take away your freedom. Sometimes, it's necessary. I want to help. You matter to me."

She heard the earnestness in his voice, and realized he meant it. She did matter to him. Her throat tightened again. "Thanks," she whispered. "That feels good."

He smiled and rubbed her thighs. "Is that a yes? You'll let me help?"

She sighed. "Only because I'm down to my last twelve hours, and you look so good without a shirt on."

He laughed. "All right. I need to make a call." He pulled out his phone and dialed, winking at her as a woman's voice answered. "Hi Mom."

Mom? He'd called Kitty? She shook her head.

He ignored her. "Piper needs your help. I'm going to put her on." He held out his phone. "You're family now, Piper. Let my mom help."

She put her hands behind her back. For heaven's sake, they were already lying to Kitty about being engaged. She couldn't use that lie to get her help. "No, I can't—"

He put the phone in her hand and walked out of the room.

Damn him. See? This was why no good ever came from getting married. Men were a pain in the ass.

"Piper? Are you there? Piper?"

Piper sighed and put the phone to her ear. "Hi, Kitty."

"What's going on? How can I help?"

"It's nothing—"

"You little liar. I've had enough of that crap, and I'm not tolerating it from you."

Piper couldn't help but grin. "What crap is that?"

"Not asking for help. For heaven's sake, Piper, women support women. Do you know how many women I've supported trying to make it in the music business? I started my own label run by women and signing only women artists, because women need to support women. So, this isn't about Declan, or your pride. It's about you. Talk to me, and don't leave anything out."

Piper paused. "You started your own record label?"

"Of course I did. You think I'm going to sit around and be old and bored? No chance. Talk to me."

"I'm not trying to become a singer."

"One more smart-ass comment from you, and I'm coming over there and moving into your guest bedroom for the summer. You want that? No? Then talk."

Piper started laughing. Kitty had all the boldness and fierceness that Piper and her mom had always pretended they had. Her mom would have loved Kitty. "All right, but don't judge me."

"I've already judged you. Too late for that. And since I'm talking to you, you know what my conclusion is. So, what's up, buttercup? Give this old lady a purpose."

Piper felt hope for the first time in a long time. Kitty was everything she'd dreamed of being. A woman who had found her power, unapologetically. "All right, Kitty. Let's do this."

"Amen, girl. Let's go."

TWENTY-NINE

T wo hours later, Declan was sitting at the empty bar at the country club, watching as Piper and his mom chatted over breakfast with some women that his mom knew.

It had taken his mom less than an hour to come up with a suitable potential client for Piper, as he'd expected. She'd brokered the intro, and now she was sitting back, arms folded, looking very pleased with herself.

His mom looked across the room at him, then winked. He grinned and raised his bottle of water to her.

At that moment, his phone rang. He pulled it out, and saw it was Dylan Hart. He immediately answered, watching Piper as he spoke. "Declan here."

"It's Dylan. I've sent people scrambling to track down Dick. His record is spotless. He may pay someone money to keep it clean, or he may be one of those guys who keeps his bastard side hidden inside his own family."

Declan relaxed his shoulders slightly. "You don't think he'll come after Piper?"

"I didn't say that. I said we can't find any evidence to indicate he will, but as we both know, some monsters hide in plain sight and no one knows. What about you? Did your contacts come up with anything?"

"I haven't heard back yet."

"All right. I'm going to send some folks to set up shop with Tori and Keira for the next few days so they don't have to stay in the hotel with Lucas and Maddie." Dylan paused. "If you bring Piper to our ranch, we can guarantee her safety."

Declan watched Piper lean in to speak with the bride and her mother. Piper's excitement was so genuine and infectious...and suddenly he realized that the wedding planner dream might have been the one created by Piper and her mom, but it was now fully in Piper's heart.

She cared so much about making these women's dreams come true. He could see it in every move of her hands, her smile, the way her face lit up. This was her zone of genius, her gift. She was gorgeous while she was talking, because her spirit lit her up.

Damn. She had to do this.

"Declan? You there?"

He forced himself to turn away so he could focus on Dylan. "Piper won't hide. She's in the middle of a crisis with her business. She can't walk away."

Dylan laughed softly. "I get that. You good to stay with her for now?"

"Yeah. For sure."

"All right. I'll be back in touch soon." Dylan paused. "Thank you for helping the other night. This is our situation, and we'll do whatever it takes to ensure the safety of Piper and her friends. We fucked up by allowing her to get identified, and we'll own it."

Declan rubbed his head. "Yeah, well, I fucked up by asking her to help." The guilt had been weighing on him constantly. If something happened to her—

He looked over, and his gut went cold when he saw the table was empty. All four women were gone. He hung up on Dylan instantly, and called Piper as he sprinted across the ballroom, looking around frantically. "Piper!" he shouted.

He'd promised not to make a scene and scare the bride and her mom, but all bets were off when she disappeared. "Piper!"

She didn't answer her phone, and fear gripped his throat as he sprinted toward the main doors. He burst out into the hallway, and it was empty.

"Piper!" He took off down the hall, racing toward the parking lot. Fuck. Fuck. Fuck. "Piper!" He burst out the front doors, and saw the four women standing by a Porsche, chatting amicably.

The bride was getting into the driver's seat, and her mom was walking around to the passenger side.

Hell. He stopped and bent over, his hands on his knees, fighting for his breath. He couldn't breathe. His head was pounding. His knee was screaming.

Swearing, he sat down on the curb, bracing his forearms on his knees as he watched Piper and his mom say their farewells.

Hell. They were safe. Completely fine. And he'd nearly lost his mind.

His phone rang. Dylan. He answered it. "Sorry about that. I lost sight of Piper for a minute. Had to handle it."

Dylan whistled softly. "Does she know how you feel about her?"

"I don't feel any way about her. I'm her protector."

"Liar," Dylan said softly. "Your voice is shaking."

Declan cleared his throat. "Just out of breath."

"From running for two minutes? No." Dylan paused. "You ready for her? For this?"

"No."

"You going to do it anyway?"

Declan watched Kitty and Piper wave good-bye and stand arm in arm, watching as the Porsche drove away. They were both laughing and giggling. They looked happy, like partners in crime. "She doesn't want to get involved with me. Or anyone."

"Neither did my brothers, but the best thing they ever did was do it anyway. I didn't believe any of us had a chance until I saw them make it work. You've seen Maddie and Lucas. You going to walk away from that?"

"It's what she wants, so yes."

"Or she's so scared that she can't even let herself dream."

Declan ground his jaw. "She's not scared. She's determined."

"Hell, man. Are you for real? We're all scared. All of us. Piper walked away from three weddings, right?"

Declan didn't ask how Dylan knew. The man ran a detective agency. "Yeah."

"You know why her dad's in prison?"

Declan took a breath. "Don't tell me. It's Piper's story to tell."

"Well, I'll just say that growing up the way she did, if she's not scared shitless to trust anyone, then she's not a human being. And you have your own crap. She's Maddie's best friend, which means she's an amazing human being. And we like you, so that means you're a good guy, but you walk in shadows too. Maybe it's the first time either of you met someone worth trusting. Don't walk away without giving it all you have."

"I'm giving it all I have."

"Are you?"

Declan tightened his grip on his phone as Piper and his mom neared. "I gotta go. Keep me posted."

"Will do." Dylan didn't even hesitate at the change in subject. "See ya."

Declan shoved his phone in his pocket and stood up as the women approached. "How'd it go?"

"Great!" Piper's eyes were sparkling. "I loved her. She's wonderful."

Kitty beamed at him. "Piper is fantastic. She lights up the world."

Declan smiled. "She does," he agreed.

"If Piper were a singer, I'd sign her to a contract immediately," Kitty said. "That kind of passion, fire, and talent is the secret combo to success." Kitty turned to Piper. "I loved how you told her that your schedule was filling up and you needed an answer tonight. Well done."

"Thanks." Piper grinned. "I didn't sound desperate?"

"You sounded confident. I loved it." Kitty looked at her watch. "We have ten minutes until the next one arrives. I'm going to run to the ladies room. Piper?"

"I'm all set. I'll meet you in the café in five."

"Ah…" Kitty looked meaningfully between them. "You want a little private time with Declan. I get that. See you in a minute, my darlings." She blew Piper a kiss and then headed down the brick walkway, pausing to chat cheerfully with the landscapers, as she always did.

Declan watched her go. "Thanks, Mom."

She was already through the doors and didn't hear him.

Piper touched his arm, her face glowing. "Thank you so much for calling her. It's amazing what having her recommendation does. I don't have to prove myself. My capabilities are assumed, and all I have to do is show up and be me. Plus, your mom has amazing ideas!"

Declan grinned. "You're welcome." He paused. "I can see your passion," he said. "This is your dream. I understand now. It lights you up."

Piper nodded. "It does. I want to be the creator of fairytales. It's my gift."

"I can see that." He paused, Dylan's words gnawing at him. "You know, with my mom's help, you may not need someone else's business to get clients. Maybe this is the break to go out on your own."

She stared at him, and there was no mistaking the longing in her eyes.

"Maybe go into business with her," he suggested. "With my mom."

"Holy crap." Piper said. "That's a great idea. You think she'd do it?"

"She likes to invest in women, so yeah, maybe."

"Kitty!" Piper whirled around and raced into the club. "Kitty, wait."

Declan shoved his hands in his pockets and strode after her. His mom and Piper going into business together? It was a brilliant idea. It would probably work.

But putting his mom and Piper together?

He'd felt Piper pull away from him from the moment he'd suggested it. The idea made her powerful and independent, and she wouldn't need him anymore. Not for her career, and not even for support. Fake fiancé job over. She'd have it all. Hell, she would even have a mom to do the business with. Kitty was his mom, obviously, but he could tell she'd already claimed Piper.

What did that leave for him? What would Piper need him for?

Nothing.

Which meant she had to *want* him.

But she didn't. Not for the full ride, at least.

He thought of Dylan's advice as he pulled open the front door and strode inside. What if she did want him, but she was holding back because of fear?

And what did *he* want? He loved her, yeah, but did he want more? Could he afford more? Could he risk that leap? It had taken him years to recover from his last one.

Ahead of him, he saw his mom and Piper talking animatedly, and he stopped, watching them.

Piper was drifting out of his reach as he stood there. All he had to do was nothing, and the engagement would fade. His mom probably wouldn't even be disappointed, because she'd have Piper either way.

They turned and hurried down the hallway, still chattering animatedly.

Piper was stepping into her power, and she deserved it.

If he told her he loved her, if he decided he wanted more, would that screw up everything for her? Steal from her the very dreams that were finally coming alive for her? Would she think that the deal with Kitty would disappear if she turned him down?

Would she feel like she couldn't say no to him, and then, on their wedding day, she'd have to run from him, the way she'd had to run before?

Fuck. He wouldn't do that to her.

But…he loved her. He absolutely loved her. His heart was whole again, alive, laughing, joyful, because of her.

If he told her he loved her, what did that mean for him? He'd told Dylan and Aiden he wasn't ready. Was that the truth? Or was he lying to himself?

THIRTY

"Do it," Kitty said. "Do it, now. You have to do it before they say yes."

Later that afternoon, Piper was sitting at her computer in her living room, with Kitty beside her. On her computer, written, but not sent, was her resignation letter. "What if the brides from today don't say yes?"

"Then we'll get more." Kitty had her feet up on the coffee table, and she was stretched back, looking confident. "You're fantastic, my darling. But if you're still working for another firm when you get an offer, she could have a case that the client belongs to her. You don't want to get in trouble, even if she's wrong."

Piper wanted to send that email so much, but she was scared.

Scared to go out on her own.

Scared to be alone.

Scared to count on herself.

Despite all her words of bravado to Declan about being independent, the idea terrified her. She was barely hanging onto her job, but it felt like it was better to hang onto it than to hurl herself off a cliff and trust she could fly.

Was a mucky pond that she knew how to navigate better than a cliff that she wasn't sure she could handle?

No. It wasn't. But suddenly, all the fears that had kept her mom stuck her whole life settled on Piper, and she felt like she couldn't breathe. "I can't send it," she whispered.

Kitty sighed and patted her knee. "You're not ready. I can see it. It's fine. Give the clients to your boss. You call me if and when you want to team up." She stood up. "I'm sure you'll get more than one 'yes' from today. It was fun!"

Piper sat back as Kitty let herself out, wishing she had the courage to call the brilliant, sassy older woman back.

Declan was in the kitchen working on dinner, and she turned to look at him, feeling better when she saw him there. He was her rock, her safety. Beside her, Angel was snoozing with her head on Piper's lap. Suddenly, all she wanted to do was curl up under the blanket, snuggle with the dog, and let Declan take care of her.

She didn't want to be brave or strong or independent. She wanted to be taken care of. To not have to summon any energy at all.

He looked up and frowned at her.

"What?" She would be so happy for him to get grumpy with her. It would be a great distraction.

"I want to interfere."

"With what?"

"Your business."

She twisted around on the couch and leaned on the back of it. "Go ahead." She'd take his interference over the noise in her head right now.

He raised his brows. "I specifically told myself to back off and let you do your thing."

"My thing feels like a failure right now," she said honestly. "I'd welcome your input."

He still hesitated, then finally put his knife down. "Fear is a bitch."

She raised her brows. "Fear?"

"Yeah." He shifted restlessly. "Fear is like a vise around your soul. It strangles you."

She stiffened. "I know."

"Here's the thing." He leaned on the counter. "Most of the time, fear isn't real. It's that voice in your head telling you to stay where it's safe and familiar. The brain craves familiarity, and it will lie to you to keep you where you are."

She lightly rubbed Angel's fur. "I don't love where I am." But his words were literally what she'd been thinking.

"I know. That's why fear is a bitch. She knows you're not fully where you want to be, but it's good enough that she can keep you there." He paused. "Your comfort zone is a bad place to be, because you can stop moving forward. It's okay, it's safe, it's enough. But it's not enough, and you know it."

She chewed her lower lip. His words made sense. They did. "My mom was stuck in fear her whole life. I don't want to let her down by staying stuck. I don't." But still she sat there. Still the email sat on her computer, unsent.

"Can I ask you something?" He was still in the kitchen, not coming toward her, but a sudden tension had come into his voice.

Piper looked at him, her heart started to race. "Yes." Anything other than thinking about how she was letting her mom down.

Declan didn't say anything.

She turned all the way to face him. "What?"

He finally looked at her. "What if you could have a relationship with a man who didn't trap you? One that lit you up, set you free, and inspired you to live the life you want? If you had that, would you still want to stay single?"

Her heart started to speed up at his low tone. "That's not what a relationship is."

He walked around the counter and strode up to the couch. He crouched behind it and rested his arms on the back of the sofa, so his face was inches from hers. "What if falling in love gave you everything you'd ever dreamed of? What if it set you free?"

"Love is a trap," she whispered.

He took her hand. "Let's pretend for one moment, that it's not.

Let's pretend that love makes you whole, and that it's fun, and beautiful, and wonderful. Would you want it then? If it was safe?"

She swallowed. "Um…"

"Just pretend."

Her mind was racing with his question. Fear was shouting at her that love could never be safe, that a relationship could never set her free, but she fought to ignore the shouting. She tried to listen to that part of her that was quiet, the part of her that wasn't screaming at her to run away. She took a deep breath. "I watch Maddie and Lucas, and I can see how beautiful it is."

Declan raised his brows, but he didn't interrupt.

"I think," she said slowly, "that if I had what Maddie found with Lucas, that it could be okay."

He laughed softly. "Just okay?"

"Well, wonderful, but admitting it might be okay is a big step for me." She paused. "What about you?"

"I believe in love," he said immediately.

She smiled. "Of course you do."

"My struggle is whether I believe in hurling myself into a meadow full of knives and flowers, being willing to risk landing on the knives instead of the flowers."

She blinked. "That's quite a visual."

He nodded. "I decided I'm willing to risk the knives."

Her heart started to pound. "What does that mean?"

"Love nearly destroyed me," he said. "I believed in love until it wrecked me." He paused again. "But you made me believe in it again."

She froze. "What?"

He met her gaze. "I wasn't ready to love, Piper, until I fell in love with you."

Her heart started racing. Panic seemed to close around her. Panic because his words made her so happy, and she knew what stupid choices she'd made around love. "Declan, I—"

He shook his head. "Nothing for you to say, Piper. I don't want anything from you. I just wanted you to know that you're loved, and it doesn't mean you're trapped. You're simply loved. You healed my heart and my soul. I don't live in darkness anymore, because of you."

Tears filled her eyes. "You deserve so much more than to live in darkness, Declan."

He inclined his head. "Darkness sucks, but you don't realize how dark it is until you're out of it." He took a breath. "If you decide you want more than our current fake-engagement-with-benefits situation, I'm in all the way. But if you don't, it's okay. Going into business with my mom has nothing to do with me. Just wanted you to know that." He stood up. "I'm going to go finish dinner."

"That's it?" She stared after him as he walked away. She was so stunned by his words. He loved her? *He loved her*. This amazing man thought she was special? "You drop that nugget and walk away?"

"I have to." He went back to the kitchen counter and picked up his knife. "I'm not going to trap you, Piper. But Dylan asked me if you were simply scared and that was why you didn't want more, or if you really didn't want more. He got me thinking, so I asked."

She took a breath. "I'm scared," she said softly. "I'm terrified."

He smiled gently. "I am too, sweetheart. But I saw my parents lose out because they were afraid to try, and I'm trying not to let that happen to me. So, I love you with no pressure."

"Declan, if I wanted—" She stopped. If she wanted what? God, she'd gone down this road before and been so wrong. Her heart was aching for him, skipping with joy because of his words, longing for him.

She trusted him. But did she trust herself?

He turned around, his brows shooting up. "If you wanted what?"

She swallowed, her hands shaking. "If I wanted—"

His gaze shot past her toward the front of the cottage. "Expecting company?"

She spun around to see a Range Rover pull up in front of her cottage. "No—" Then she yelped when she saw Dick get out.

Declan swore. "Stay here. Do not come outside, no matter what. This is mine to handle. Angel, with me." He charged the door, yanked it open. "Do not come out," he repeated. "This man targets women. He's mine." He then bolted outside, slamming the door shut behind him before she could even move.

Piper froze, her heart racing as she watched him stride up to Dick.

He didn't hesitate, because he didn't have to. He was a tall, muscular ex-cop with a gun.

The world didn't scare him.

But then she remembered that it did.

At least, love did.

Love. The man who'd rushed outside to protect her, *loved her.*

What was she going to do about that?

THIRTY-ONE

Declan had his hand on the butt of his gun as he strode up to Dick. "What do you want?"

Dick spun around to face him, a startled expression on his face. "I'm here on a social call."

"It's my property. You can talk to me." Declan struggled to keep his voice calm. This man was scum of the lowest level. The law didn't care, but Declan did.

The thought made him pause. The cops had done nothing about Dick. Nothing. Because he had power. But Declan wasn't a cop right now. Which meant he had different rules.

Dick held up his hands in a friendly de-escalation move. "Hey, sorry. I must have the wrong house. No biggie."

All the years of working to take down scumbags settled in Declan's core, all the years where he'd had to watch them walk away, because red tape set them free. All the years of terror this man had probably inflicted on those who trusted him and loved him clamped down on Declan. This man was a threat to the woman he loved.

He hadn't been able to protect Diana, but Piper?

Different. Fucking. Story.

He walked right up to Dick and stepped into his space. "I'm an ex-cop," he said, his voice low and dangerous. "I'm armed. I'm dangerous. And I'm not bound by rules anymore."

Dick's eyes widened slightly. "Are you threatening me? Because I'll call the cops."

"If you so much as go near Piper ever again, I will call in favors from people you won't want to know. You'll never see them coming. You'll never know what hit you. And no one will fucking care."

Dick stared at him, and his right eye twitched. Fear? "You're threatening me?"

Satisfaction pulsed through Declan. "You abused your wife and kids. That doesn't fly. You stop looking for them. You stop going after Piper."

"What? You liar—"

At that moment, Declan's mom's Porsche came roaring up the driveway. She screeched to a stop behind the Range Rover, vaulted out of her truck, and trotted past Declan. "I decided I'm not letting Piper off that easily," she called out. "She needs to get brave."

Declan grinned as his mom basically sprinted into the house, shouting Piper's name.

Piper was going to get a Kitty lecture. He'd had a few of those in his life, and annoying as they were, his mom was usually right. Then he saw Dick watching Kitty.

"No." Beside him, Angel growled, drawing Dick's attention to the dog. "I love the women in my life," Declan said. "I protect them, and I'm good at it. You don't want to fuck with me."

Dick narrowed his eyes. "I'm not afraid of you—"

"You should be. My first wife died in my arms from a gunshot wound during a drug raid. I know what loss is like, and I will not let that happen again. No matter what the cost." His voice was cold now, laced with an emotion he hadn't felt in a long time. Deep, dark commitment to a cause, no matter what the cost. "I got another chance, and I will spend every fucking minute protecting her from you, and anyone like you." He smiled, a cold, hard smile. "You're the kind of man who drove me to become a cop, but I'm not one anymore. I can do whatever I want. And the joy I would get from having an excuse to hurt you is indescribable."

Unmistakable fear crept into Dick's eyes, probably because he heard the truth in Declan's words. A truth that surprised Declan. He hadn't realized how much anger he had under all the grief, numbness, and guilt.

Anger felt good.

Standing up against a bully? Even better.

"Here's my suggestion," he said. "File for a divorce from your wife. Give her a good settlement. Set her and your kids free, and go get therapy. Maybe there's humanity under there. Maybe not. But if you try to find her, if you try to trap her, if you threaten *anyone*, I will find out. And then I will make myself happy by ensuring you get what you deserve."

Dick stared at him for a moment, then he turned and walked back to his Range Rover, not saying a word.

He got in, hit the gas, and then peeled out.

Declan let out his breath and shrugged his shoulders, surprised by how good he felt. How light. It was like all the rage that had been coiled up inside him for so long had finally been heard. Or maybe it was telling Piper he loved her.

Either way, he felt the best he'd felt in a long damn time.

He crouched down beside Angel. "You did good, sweetie. You're very brave, growling like that."

She wagged her tail and licked his face, making him laugh. "Yeah, right? Feels good not to be hiding anymore." He ruffled her fur. "What do you think? Should I go back in there and have an actual conversation with Piper? I might have been a little quick to bolt after my declaration." He'd told Piper it was to give her the space to not respond, but really?

He'd been afraid of her response.

But he'd been living in fear for a long time, and he didn't want to live in fear anymore. "Let's go see Piper," he said.

As he spoke, Angel turned her head, staring down the driveway.

He followed her gaze and then stood up when he saw a big food truck rolling down the driveway. It said "Lucy's Spectacular Tacos" on the side of it with a pretty cool caricature of a grinning brown-haired woman eating a taco.

He put his hand on Angel's head. "Stay with me."

They stood together as the truck rolled to a stop beside his mom's Porsche.

The man driving rolled down his window as Declan and Angel walked over to it. "I think you have the wrong address," Declan said. "We didn't hire a food truck for an event."

The man grinned at him. He had short dark hair, and a pink Lucy's Spectacular Tacos hat on. He looked about Declan's age, maybe a little older. "I'm not here to sell anything. Is this where Piper Townsend lives?"

Declan immediately stiffened and his hand went to his gun. "Who are you?" He highly doubted that Piper had hired a taco truck for a wedding.

The guy raised his brows. "Why are you asking me that? You with Piper? Trying to defend her? Are you her man?" He opened the door and jumped down. "Why'd she pick you? You good to her? Because I have connections I'm willing to unlock if you hurt her." His voice became rougher and rougher as he spoke. "She's been through hell and back. If you mess with her, you mess with me."

Oh, hell. Was this another old flame? The man was dressed in jeans, sneakers, and a t-shirt. He had a vibe that said successful businessman, not a random taco truck driver. Declan decided to deescalate instead of engage, as his years of training as a cop kicked in. "You franchised?"

The man paused, clearly startled by the change in topic. "No. I own all my trucks."

Yep. Business guy. "Tacos are big right now. It's going well?"

The man paused again. "I have four trucks. I funded them all myself. Bank won't loan to me because I used to be in prison." He added the prison with just a dash of extra gusto.

Prison? Damn. Who was this guy, and why was he after Piper? Declan nodded, assessing his visitor with extra caution. "Prison can be a tough background in business. I'm sure it took a hell of a lot of commitment to do what you've done."

The man frowned. "What are you doing?"

"Deescalating. I have a gun and I don't want to use it on you."

The man's gaze shot to Declan's hip, and he suddenly looked stricken. "Fuck. Piper's involved with a man with a gun?" He turned away and braced his hands on the hood of his truck and bent his head, swearing to himself. "It's my fucking fault. Son of a bitch. I thought she was free. And she's not." He hit the hood of the truck and spun around to face Declan. "Stay away from my sister. Just don't fucking bring her into your world. Do you understand? She got free. I will hunt you down and—"

Declan held up his hand "Wait a sec. Your sister? Piper's *your sister?*"

"Yeah." The man's fists bunched. "I will protect her, even from you."

What the hell was going on? "How did you find her?"

"She called me."

Understanding struck. "A couple days ago? She called you a couple days ago?" At his nod, Declan searched his memories for his name. "You're Roman?"

The man frowned. "She talks about me?"

Declan surveyed Roman with frank curiosity. "She told me a little, yeah." Roman might have a salty past, but Declan was getting only kind vibes from him. Protective, but kind. He was a man that Declan would trust.

Roman grinned. "Nice." He paused. "But you still need to get out of her life. She left home to get away from men like you."

Declan relaxed. He appreciated that Roman was watching out for her. "I'm an ex-cop. That's why I have a gun. Piper helped out with a situation where a woman needed to escape an abusive husband, and it's created a little danger for her. I was just dealing with the man right before you drove up."

Roman stared at him, clearly processing. "She's in danger?"

Declan would have gone with that first, too. "No. I just needed to deal with him."

"How do you know he's not coming back?"

"I don't." Declan paused. This man was Piper's family, which meant Declan wasn't holding back any truths. "But I sleep here with Piper, so if he does, I'll handle it." He tensed, waiting for Roman's reaction to his statement.

As expected, Roman's eyes narrowed. "You're sleeping with my sister?"

Declan took a breath. "I'm fake-engaged to her to help her rebuild her business, but in the process, I fell in love with her. I don't know if she loves me back yet, though." Damn. That first part felt good to admit out loud. Really good. Second part? Not so good, but that was on him, for walking away without giving her a chance to respond.

Roman stared at him. "That's a lot to take in."

"I know." Declan held out his hand. "Declan Jones. Your sister's fake fiancé, bodyguard, and landlord."

Roman finally grinned and shook his hand. "Roman Townsend. You're all right, Jones."

"Thanks. You, too." Declan glanced back at the house as he let go of Roman's hand. "I'm going to have to ask you to wait outside, though. Let me check with Piper and make sure it's all right if I invite you in." The fact she hadn't come out to see her brother could have been because Kitty had corralled her. Or it could mean she didn't want to see him.

Declan was going to make sure she had the chance to turn her brother away if she needed to. But he liked the guy.

Sadness streaked across Roman's face, but he nodded. "I understand."

At that moment, yet another car came hurtling down the driveway. Both men spun to face the visitor as the Jeep skidded to a stop. Keira jumped out. "Declan! Is Piper home? I found another possible client for her, but Piper's not answering her phone."

He nodded. "She's inside with my mom."

"Great!" Keira jogged past him. "Can you get me a taco? I love tacos. Thanks!" She ran into the house, closing the door behind her.

Roman stared after her. "Who was that?"

"A friend of Piper's."

Roman whistled softly. "I want to meet her. She's like a damned whirlwind."

Declan grinned. "Don't mess with your sister's friends. It's never a good idea."

Roman grimaced. "Yeah, you're right. I'm not going to mess up Piper's life like that—"

The front door slammed open, and Keira raced outside. "Declan!"

He spun around, alarm shooting through him at the urgency in her voice. "What's wrong?"

"Something happened to Piper! Hurry!"

Declan was running before she finished her sentence, fear gripping him like it had that night not that long ago, when his world had been shattered. "Piper!"

THIRTY-TWO

Declan burst through the front door and saw Keira in the kitchen. "Here!"

With Angel by his leg and Roman behind him, Declan sprinted through the house and into the kitchen. On the floor by the back slider were the remains of Piper's espresso maker, shattered into a million pieces. There was a new dent in the doorframe by the back door.

He realized immediately that she'd thrown the espresso machine. To defend herself? "What happened?"

"Look at the living room."

He spun around, and saw that a lamp was on the floor and a table was overturned. On the carpet was Piper's phone. "Piper!" He grabbed the phone and looked around, his heart racing. "Mom!"

He ran back through the house, searching every room, but neither woman was there either. "Shit, shit, shit."

Roman was standing still, his hands loose by his sides, energy vibrating off him. He looked ready to explode, but there was no target, so he simply stood there.

Keira looked stricken. "Do you think she was kidnapped?"

"With us in the front of the house? That would be bold."

Declan pulled out his phone and logged into his security system, his heart hammering as he pulled up the app. To give Piper privacy, he didn't have cameras installed inside the cottage, but he had them on the patio.

He logged into the system, and then swore as he watched a man walk up through the woods behind his house, walk up to the patio door, and open it. The man's face was shadowed, impossible to see. He knew where the camera was.

Declan thought back to the nighttime visitor from the other evening. Had it been the prelude to this?

A moment later, he saw Piper being carried out over his shoulder, apparently unconscious. Fear gripped him, and his fingers tightened around the phone.

"Son of a bitch," Roman said, leaning over his shoulder, watching the screen.

A second later, Kitty came charging out the door. She grabbed a plant and slammed it into the head of the man carrying Piper. He swung around, took one swing, and then his mom was down on the ground, too.

A minute later, he disappeared from the screen, carrying Piper on one shoulder and his mom on the other, heading into the woods behind the cottage.

But as he carried them away, Kitty lifted her head, looked right at the camera, and gave a thumbs up.

"Son of a bitch." He set the phone down, torn between laughing and going into assault mode. "My mom faked getting hit so that she wouldn't be left behind. She literally invited herself into Piper's abduction."

Keira grinned. "I love your mom. She's amazing."

Roman had a strained look on his face. "Your mom put herself in danger for Piper?"

"Yeah." Declan's amusement faded. "My mom is a badass, and she knows how amazing Piper is. It's been only minutes. They must be close."

"But where? We can't track Piper. Her phone is here."

"But my mom's isn't." Declan pulled up the Find My Friends app on his phone and opened it. For a long moment, his mom's location circled, and then it said unavailable. *Shit.* "She has her phone off." He sighed. "She decided to save Piper and forgot to turn her phone on."

"Or maybe their abductor wrested it out of her hands, and threw it out the window," Keira said.

They both stared at her.

She grimaced "Yeah, not helpful. Sorry. I'll call the police."

Declan went into his contacts. "I'm calling the Harts."

THIRTY-THREE

I t took Piper a moment to realize she'd just woken up in the trunk of a car.

A moving car. With someone squished in next to her, not moving.

What the hell?

She'd been in the trunk of a car a few times in her youth, thanks to her brothers, so she immediately looked for the trunk release lever. Like in all new cars, it was glowing in the dark, easy to find, but the car was moving too fast.

She'd have to wait until they slowed down.

Her eyes began to adjust to the darkness, and she could see Kitty's dimly lit face beside her. The older woman's eyes were closed, and panic clamped down on Piper. "Kitty! Are you all right?"

"Shh! I'm faking it, like they do in the movies."

Relief rushed through Piper. "We're alone. No need to pretend."

The older woman opened one eye and looked around, then opened both. "We're alone."

"I literally just said that." Piper frowned at the older woman. "You all right?"

"I am." Kitty grinned at her. "You got kidnapped!"

"Is that why we're in a car? Dammit. I was hoping it was Declan's way of having a surprise party for me. Do you have your phone with you?"

"No, don't you?"

"I can't find mine." Dammit. Piper touched her head and felt a lump in the back. "I got hit? By who?"

"Honestly, I don't know. I was looking at the computer when it happened, and when I looked up, some man was carrying you out onto your patio."

"Then how did you get in here?"

"I attacked him to save you, and then he grabbed me." Kitty sighed. "I should have thought about the fact Declan was out front and screamed for help, but in the heat of the moment, it felt very important not to let you out of my sight. Sister solidarity is powerful. You're safer with me than you would be alone."

Piper's heart tightened. "You attacked a kidnapper to save me? That is incredibly sweet."

"I'm not sweet. I'm a mom, and it's in my nature to go mama bear for my kids. And that includes you. Call me fierce, a badass, a creature of darkness, but never sweet."

Sudden tears threatened, and Piper finally couldn't keep up the lies anymore. This woman had sacrificed herself to help her. "Kitty, I really appreciate you helping me with my business and getting yourself kidnapped to save me, but I can't lie to you anymore. Declan and I aren't really engaged."

"Of course you're not. Do you think I'm a complete idiot?"

Piper stared at Kitty, the older woman's silhouette barely visible in the dim light of the trunk. "You knew?"

"My husband and my son were both cops. I have a very suspicious and logical brain. It didn't take much."

"But you went along with it?"

"Of course I did. My goal was to get Declan dating, and it worked." She paused. "And then I realized that you two are a perfect match. I was clearly a visionary when I propositioned you."

Piper cleared her throat. "We're not a perfect match—"

"Of course you are. Declan has joy in his heart. That doesn't come lightly. He lets very few people in, and he's let you in." Kitty patted her arm. "He's in love with you, my darling. Don't you know that?"

Piper took a breath. "He told me a few minutes ago." Not that she could focus on that right now. She'd been kidnapped with a national treasure, which meant she had to get herself free as well as Kitty. Who had kidnapped them?

"Declan admitted it?" Kitty hit her on the arm. "That's fantastic! Do you love him back?"

Piper grimaced. "I'm not ready for love."

"Is that what I asked? It's not what I asked."

Piper felt along the sides of the trunk, looking for something to use as a weapon. "We need to focus on getting out—"

"Hey!" Kitty grabbed her shoulder. "I sacrificed myself to save you. You don't get to blow me off, missy. Do you love my son?"

Piper stared at her. "That's what my mom used to call me when I was being sassy."

"Missy?"

Piper nodded. "She died when I was sixteen. We were going to open a wedding planning business together and I was going to get her out of her life. But she died first. And just then, you sounded like her. You reminded me of her."

Kitty's face softened, and she put her hands on Piper's cheeks. "Sweet Piper," she said softly. "You've been scrambling since you were sixteen to make your mom's dreams come true?"

Piper nodded. "I'm trying so hard."

"As a mother, I can confidently say that your mom's only dream is for you to be happy. That's it. Are you happy?"

"I love my friends," she said. "I love making brides happy. I really do."

"And what about love? Does Declan make you happy? Just be

honest. This might be our last moments before we die. Do you want an old lady to die without knowing if her son is loved?"

Resolution flooded Piper. "We're not going to die."

"We might. You never know. Do you love him?"

Kitty's voice was so warm, so full of love that suddenly, Piper's resistance disappeared. "I tried not to fall for him," she admitted. "But he's impossible not to love."

Kitty let out a little whoop. "Best news I've had in years. Did you tell him that you love him?"

"No."

"Why not?"

She sighed. "I'm scared."

"You don't think he was scared? My baby boy got his heart broken when Diana died in his arms. He's probably scared to death to put his heart out there again, but he did it for you. If you're remotely worthy of him or your mom, you'll go live with courage, not fear."

Piper almost started laughing. "You're lecturing me?"

"I am. Because when you marry Declan, you'll have a mom again, and I have to set the expectations that I'm not going to be a pushover. If you're being an idiot, I'll interfere. And if Declan is, I'll interfere there as well."

A mom again. Real tears started to threaten. "Marry him?" Piper let out her breath. "I think you're getting a little ahead of things."

"My son's heart goes in one direction. Once he falls in love, it's forever. Do you deserve forever?"

Piper heard the challenge in Kitty's voice, and she lifted her chin. "I do, actually."

Kitty chuckled. "That's my girl. You both do. Lean into it. I didn't run from your kidnapper, so you don't get to run from love."

Piper rolled her eyes. "I've been stupid about love before."

"Haven't we all? But if you keep putting yourself out there, then you have a chance of getting it right." She gave a fist pump. "This is fantastic news. I've been working so hard on manifesting love for Declan, and I did it. I'm going to call Jennifer Aniston and tell her that the Instagram video in which she was talking about manifesting was the spark that got me started."

Piper almost started laughing. "You and Jen are friends?"

"Not yet, but as soon as she realizes that I'm willing, she'll be in."

"Of course she will. Who would turn you down?" Piper went back to searching for a weapon, relieved that Kitty had gotten distracted from the marriage talk. She was stunned by the realization that she did love Declan, but when Kitty had mentioned marriage, familiar fears had clamped down.

How would she know she was choosing the right man? How did anyone ever know? "I can't believe I got kidnapped. I've always been very confident in my abilities to defend myself."

"To be fair, you were distracted by me yelling at you," Kitty said. "I take up a lot of emotional space. I'm very proud of that. Most women try to stay small, but you gotta lean into your bigness."

"Can you describe him?"

"Broad shoulders. Gray sweatshirt. Short dark hair. Jeans. Nice ass." Kitty grinned. "I only saw him from behind, and I was more concerned with your safety than noticing his features. But the ass was worth a notice. Never say women my age lose their libido."

"I'd never dare." Piper's fingers closed around a small object that she quickly realized was a golf ball. *Yes.* It wasn't a can opener, but she could do some damage with a golf ball. "See if you can find a golf ball in the corners. I found one, and there's usually more than one if he's a golfer." Clark had been a golfer, so she knew—

She froze. Clark? Her ex-fiancé? A sudden chill gripped her. If Clark had snatched her, it would be personal. How dangerous was he? She hadn't stayed around to find out, but her gut had ordered her to leave..

Kitty hit her. "What are you thinking? You thought of something."

"It could be my ex-fiancé who abducted us."

"Bad guy?"

"Maybe." She held the golf ball up to the glowing quick release lever. "He has monogrammed balls. If I can read it—" She shook her head. "It's too dark."

"We can use the flashlight on my phone."

"You don't have your phone—"

"Of course I do! You think I'd get myself kidnapped without my phone? I stuffed it in the crotch of my pants so he wouldn't search for it."

Piper stared at her. "You lied to me when you said you didn't have it?"

"Of course I did. I had to pressure you into admitting you loved my son." Kitty shuffled, then swore. "Dang it. My phone's off. Declan hasn't been tracking us. We'll have to stay alive longer—"

The car suddenly took a hard right turn, slamming them against the side of the car. Another turn, then a hard stop.

Then Piper heard the unmistakable sound of a garage door closing.

Locking them in.

And Declan was nowhere close.

THIRTY-FOUR

Declan's pulse jumped when he saw his mom's location pop up on his phone. "She turned her phone on." He dropped a pin to the location on his GPS. "I'm going to get them!" He took off for his truck, Angel right beside him.

"I'm coming too," Keira said. "That's my girl."

Roman didn't even bother to say anything. He just tore after Declan and beat him to the truck.

Declan leapt in, Roman got in the back, and Keira got in the front beside Angel.

He hit the gas and tore down the driveway as he called Dylan. "Got a location." He read it off. "Can you look it up?"

Dylan already had a local team mobilized, and he'd been working on the security video to see if he could identify the man who'd taken Piper and his mom.

"Hang on."

Declan shot out of his driveway and hauled the truck to the right. "We're twenty minutes away." Crap. So much could happen in a split second, let alone twenty minutes. His heart was pounding, and his palms were sweaty. "Are you closer?"

"I don't have anyone closer," Dylan said. "My guys are twenty-two minutes out."

"Fuck!" Declan hit his palm on the steering wheel.

"Should we call the cops?" Keira said.

"No. If they show up and alert this guy, they might push him over the edge. We have to just get in there quietly." He pushed his speed harder, then swore when he saw Keira wrap her hand around the door handle to brace herself.

"Piper's been in these situations before." Roman was leaning over the seat. "She can handle herself."

"Never thought I'd be grateful that she had such a hellish childhood." Declan hit a corner too fast, and for a split second, his right wheels came off the ground.

"Slow down, my friend," Roman said. "Piper's got this."

"I don't want her to have it by herself. I want to help her."

"You won't save her by flipping the damned truck."

Declan glanced in the rear-view mirror. Roman looked as calm as he sounded. Roman's calmness irritated him. "You ever lost anyone you loved because you were too late to save them?"

Roman met his gaze. "Yeah. I have."

Declan blinked, surprised by the emotion in the other man's voice. He wanted to ask what had happened, but now was not the time. But he suspected that Roman understood in a way no one wanted to be able to understand. "Then you know that I have to get there. Now."

"I do know that. But you can't. So you have to pull your shit together and get there alive, and with a plan."

Declan glared at him. "Shut up."

Roman grinned. "I feel ya. But you still need to stay under control."

Declan eased his foot off the gas ever so slightly. His head was pounding, and fear was gripping him. *I'm coming, Piper.*

"Did you just say you love Piper?" Keira asked, looking over at him.

"Yeah." Sixteen minutes away. So fucking long. What was happening to them? The only two women he cared about. He was such an ass for keeping his mom pushed away and walking away from Piper like he had.

"Did you tell her that?" Keira asked.

"Yep."

"What did she say?"

He shrugged. "She didn't really answer. But I walked away so she didn't have to. Figured I didn't want to hear her response."

Keira sighed. "She's afraid to trust her judgment when it comes to men."

"I know—"

"If she could see the raw terror on your face right now, she wouldn't worry whether she can trust you."

Raw terror. That's what was trying to overtake him.

At that moment, Dylan came back on the line. "The house belongs to Clark Houston. You know him?"

"Her ex-fiancé?" Keira groaned.

Fear gripped Declan. If her ex-fiancé had kidnapped her, it could be bad. Shit. "You must have someone closer than I am."

"I don't, but I'm doing a search on Clark to see what I can find. I'll call you back in a minute." Dylan hung up, and Declan tossed his phone in the console.

He gripped the steering wheel with both hands, his foot pressing down on the gas. "You ever been to his house, Keira?"

"Yep. It's in a gated community. You'll never get through."

Declan settled down in his seat. "My truck has a reinforced grill. I'll get through. Trust me."

Fifteen minutes.

An eternity.

THIRTY-FIVE

"What do we do?" Kitty whispered. "Attack him? Bribe him? Claw his face off?"

Piper heard the car door slam, and her heart started to race. She frantically tried to think of all she knew about Clark. Assuming he meant to cause her harm, what was the best way to stave him off? "Text Dylan that I think we're with Clark."

"Got it. Will do. Who's Clark?"

"My ex." God, she had the worst exes. "He's the one who taught me never to trust a man again."

"That's a stupid lesson. My son is fabulous. Unlearn that shit right now."

Piper almost started laughing. "Don't make me laugh. This is serious business right now."

"Only if you make it serious." Kitty elbowed her. "Let's have some fun with this."

"Fun?" She listened to the footsteps coming toward the trunk. "You're insane."

"I'm not insane. I just know that the best ideas come when I'm having fun. Plus, it deescalates. I've been a cop's wife for too long, plus a celebrity, and going in aggressive usually isn't the best choice."

"No?" Piper raised her brows. "What's the right choice, then?"

Kitty grinned. "Pretend we're drunk and we have the giggles. It'll get him totally off guard and then we can attack him when he's not looking."

"Drunk giggles? You want us to fake drunk giggles? That's insane—"

The trunk flew open, and Piper found herself staring at the man she'd almost married.

His face was chiseled and model-worthy, his muscles sculpted, his blue eyes blazing. But as she stared into them, she saw that they were cold. Ice cold. No warmth. No laughter. No vulnerability.

Nothing like Declan, who was so full of warmth and depth, even though he'd hidden it for so long. How could she ever have thought Declan was an anti-social grump? He was vibrating with passion, unlike Clark, who was…just…a lump.

"Whoohoo!" Kitty tumbled out of the trunk and landed on Clark's foot. "That was fun!"

Piper bit her lip as Clark looked down at Kitty, a surprised look on his face as Kitty wrapped herself around his leg and began singing the newest Taylor Swift song.

Her voice was stunning. "Holy crap, Kitty. Your voice is amazing!"

"I know! I'm a star!" Kitty sat up and leaned against Clark's leg, belting out the next verse.

"What is that? What is she doing?" Clark kept staring at Kitty, and Piper realized that Kitty's plan was working.

Clark wasn't a hardened criminal. He was a stupid, arrogant jilted man who was jealous of her new fiancé, and therefore susceptible to manipulative ex-pop stars with as much sass as sense.

"That's Kitty Jones. She's famous."

"I know who she is. That's why I brought her." Clark stepped back and pulled out a gun. "Both of you, on your feet."

Piper froze, her heart stuttering. "Since when do you have a gun?"

"Get out of the car, Piper."

Kitty stopped singing, and she scrambled to her feet. "Guns are dangerous, young man," she said. "Put that away."

Clark pointed the gun at her. "Get in the house. Now."

Piper gripped Kitty's arm, squeezing it, begging her not to get herself shot. "Let's go, Kitty."

"Party time!" Kitty burst into more songs, and she started dancing her way through the garage.

There was no way Piper could do that. No way she could fake being oblivious, drunk, and dumb.

She'd spent her life disempowering herself and running away, and she was over it.

Instead, she shoved her hand in her pocket and wrapped her fingers around the ball, then turned to face Clark. "Kidnapping us is a felony. Jail sucks, Clark. I know that. You don't want to wind up there."

He narrowed his eyes and walked up to her. "You humiliated me, Piper. Dumped me at my wedding. And then you got engaged to a *cop*."

Piper stiffened and pulled her shoulders back. "You don't get to have me, Clark. You hit me."

"Once! One fucking time! I made a mistake!"

"No." Power was coursing through her, power she'd never felt before in her life. The power to stand up for herself, to finally understand herself. It was so clear what Clark was. She saw him now. He was just a bully, and he'd swept her into his web because she'd been too afraid to stand on her own.

Not anymore.

"Look, Piper." He softened his voice. "I told you I'm sorry. Let's try this again. We're good together. You know we are."

God, how she'd convinced herself she loved him. How she'd

sat at his family's dinner parties and pretended his life was the one she wanted.

She glanced over at Kitty, who was spinning in circles, still singing, and her heart softened. That was the people she wanted. The life she wanted. Real people with flaws and truths and huge hearts.

Like Kitty.

Like Declan.

Like her friends.

She faced him. She didn't need to trick him into leaving her alone. All she had to do was give him the honesty she'd hidden for so long. "My father is in prison for murder," she said, admitting a truth that had never before left her lips.

His eyes widened. "What?"

"My brothers have all been in prison for dealing drugs. I was shot twice in a drug deal gone wrong. My family is dirt poor and dedicated criminals. My whole fancy life is a lie, Clark. I grew up in a trailer park. My brothers are still dangerous, and I came up here to get away from them because if I'd stayed, I'd be dead by now."

He stared at her. "You're lying."

"I'm not lying. I've hidden who I was this whole time because I wanted to fit in, and be accepted, but you know what? I don't care about the people who won't accept me for who I am."

"I accept you," Kitty called out. "Even if your dad did murder someone. You didn't, so hugs to you! Or did you?"

Piper's heart swelled at Kitty's response. "I haven't killed anyone yet," she called out. "But it's in my genes."

"Of course it is, dear," Kitty said cheerfully. "Once a killer, always a killer. Did you know I also grew up in a trailer park? My mom was a gorgeous singer, but she had to be an exotic dancer to pay for our food and rent. I bought her a lovely mansion when I was twenty-one, because money can buy your way into any social circle."

The disgust that curled Clark's lip lit a fire in Piper like she'd never felt before. She poked Clark in the chest. "Never, ever look at Kitty like that. She's amazing."

"He can look at me however he wants. I don't care! Money and power make you immune to little gnats like him." Kitty was spinning around a pole in the middle of the garage. "My mom was a great pole dancer. I wonder if I remember any of her moves?" Kitty began working the pole with an expertise that was extremely impressive.

Piper almost started laughing at the shocked look on Clark's face. "Yes, Clark. Your garage is being used for exotic dancing by my new business partner."

"What?" Kitty stopped. "We're in?"

Piper started laughing. "How could I not team up with you? You're amazing."

"Yay! That's fantastic. We're going to make brides everywhere the happiest women on earth!"

Clark looked at Piper. "You're opening your own bridal company? With a stripper?"

"I'm not a stripper! I'm the daughter of a stripper. I'm a pop star, incredibly wealthy and connected. Oh, and I'm trailer trash too," Kitty said cheerfully as she bounded up and tucked her arm through Piper's. "We're in the wedding planning business."

He looked back and forth between them. "No one will hire you, Piper. *No one.* I'm going to make sure the world knows exactly who you are. You're finished. I'm calling the papers to tell them about your past. I'm calling the cops. You stalked me, and I'm filing for a restraining order." Then he spun around and stalked out of the garage into the house, making sure to slam the door behind him.

Kitty put her hands on her hips and stared after him. "Did you know we're stalkers? I had no idea."

Piper said nothing. She just wrapped her arms around Kitty and pulled her into a hug. "Thank you," she whispered. "Thank you for accepting me."

Kitty laughed and hugged her fiercely. "You're a treasure,

Piper. Imagine if you'd married him? That monster can't accept you for who you are. How could you marry him?"

"I couldn't." Piper tucked her arm through Kitty's and headed toward the garage door. "Was all that true about your childhood?" Piper pushed the button to open the door.

"You bet." Kitty shrugged. "When you're a pop star, colorful backgrounds are an asset. I never hid who I was. If people don't like me, they aren't worth my time."

Piper hugged Kitty's arm more tightly as the door rolled open. "My mom taught me that we had to hide our truths in order to be accepted into these circles."

"There are some who will never accept you," Kitty agreed. "You have to decide whether that matters."

Piper stepped out into the late afternoon sunshine, looking around at the beautiful landscaping. She'd loved Clark's house. It had been the one she'd always dreamed of. But as she looked around, she saw heartless perfection. Not the artistic, heart-felt beauty of Declan's home. "I always thought it mattered."

"And now?"

She looked at Kitty as they began to walk down the driveway. "I told Declan the truth about my past. And then he fell in love with me."

Kitty smiled. "Of course he did."

"And you don't hide your past, and yet all those brides were so excited to work with me when you told them I was great."

Kitty grinned. "This is true. What does that teach you?"

"That it's time to stop hiding." She paused as a big, black pickup truck sped down the quiet street toward them. "Declan's driving very fast."

"He's terrified you're about to die in his arms," Kitty said, waving cheerfully at the truck. "I'm sure this has been a very traumatizing half hour for him. Normally, I would be very upset, but I think maybe this is going to work out exactly the way I want."

Piper's heart tightened, and she waved at the truck as well. "Your son is a good man."

"He is. You love him?"

Piper smiled. "I do."

The truck skidded to a stop beside them, and Declan launched himself out of the truck. "Piper! Mom!"

"Hah! He said your name first. Good boy," Kitty chuckled.

He raced toward them, and Piper saw the expression on his face. Raw, unfiltered emotion that went right to her heart.

This man would never hurt her.

He'd die before he'd hurt her.

"Go get him," Kitty whispered, elbowing her in the back.

Piper broke into a run. "Declan!"

He reached for her, and caught her as she jumped into his arms, locking her legs around his waist. She threw her arms around his neck, holding tightly as he pinned her against his chest. "Fuck, Piper," he whispered. "I was scared shitless."

She pulled back so she could see him. "I love you, Declan. I love you with all my heart, and I'm still scared, but I don't care. I'm not going to run this time. Not from you. Not from us. Not ever."

His face softened, and pure love filled his eyes. "I'm in it as long as you'll have me, Piper. I love you, too."

"I want you for all of it."

He grinned. "You've got it." He kissed her again, then framed her face. "This whole thing with you getting targeted by Dick and then getting kidnapped has showed me that I'm done with any kind of life like that. I'm not going to be a cop. I'm not going to do work for the Harts. I just want to build a life with you."

She smiled, her heart dancing. "I would have loved you no matter what, but I'm thrilled not to have to worry about bad guys in our lives. What are you going to do? Build houses?"

He shook his head. "I think I'm going to start investing in businesses, like my mom does."

"Businesses? Like what?"

"Like a taco truck franchise. I thought I'd start there. We need more tacos in this world, and I like the idea of supporting businesses that have trouble getting funding. Helping out where help is needed. Like owners who have been in prison, for example."

She blinked. "Taco trucks? You want to invest in a taco truck franchise owned by an ex-convict?"

Before he could answer, Angel jumped up, knocking against them. They both laughed, and Piper slid down his body to hug the dog. "And you, too, sweetie. You've made me into a dog person!"

"Piper!" Keira came racing up. "What happened? Are you okay?"

"Keira?" Piper stood up, bracing herself as Keira launched herself at her. "Oomph."

"Don't ever get kidnapped again. Do you understand?"

"I won't. It's a one-time thing." Piper laughed and hugged her friend, her heart contracting as she watched Declan walk over to his mom and envelop her in a huge, long hug. *Yes.* "I—"

She stopped, frozen, as she saw her brother get out of the truck. "Roman?"

Declan turned and walked over. "You want me to make him leave?"

She shook her head silently as tears filled her eyes. It had been so long. Roman had been a scrawny, dangerous criminal when she'd left, and now he was tall, muscular, and presentable. He looked so non-criminal. It almost made her miss who he had been, but then he smiled, and it was the same cocky, mischievous unapologetic smile he'd always had.

He paused, looking hesitant. "I barged in on the rescue mission," he said. "I had to come see you. I missed you, sis, and I wanted to tell you that I love you, and I've got your back—"

His voice was so familiar. He was home to her, the good home. Her mom. Belonging. Family. Being accepted. "Roman!" She held out her arms, and he grinned.

They both broke into a run, meeting each other halfway. She buried herself in the arms of her brother, no longer the little sister who made herself small to survive, but as a strong, powerful woman ready and able to stand on her own...but she didn't need to.

She held out one arm to Keira, Declan, and Kitty. "Family hug," she said. "Everyone in."

And then, like the old days with her mom and her brothers, before everything had gotten so bad, she was squished in the middle of a love sandwich with the family she'd chosen: friends, lover, bonus mom, a great dog, and her big brother.

She met Declan's gaze and he smiled. A special, warm smile just for her.

Yes.

Her days of running were over.

THIRTY-SIX

"Paris!" Tori jumped through the doorway onto the Hart's jet and put her arms in the air. "You're getting married in Paris! What the heck?"

Piper burst out laughing, unable to contain her joy. "I know, right? Freaking Paris!"

"In six days!" Tori ran into the plane and swept up Piper in a hug. "I'm so happy for you, Piper! You're glowing!"

"I know!" Piper hugged her back. "I was worried I would feel panic as the day got closer, but it's been only happiness. I'm so excited."

"Then you know it's right." Tori set her bag on the floor and looked around. "Holy crap, girl. This plane is fantastic. I'm so happy that Maddie married into this family and that makes us honorary members."

"I know. It's amazing."

Tori danced across the floor and dove onto one of the gorgeous, leather couches. "Remember when we were going to steal a private jet? This is so much better than having a quick joyride and then spending years in prison."

"It was still a good Plan B." Piper peered out the window, and her heart leapt when she saw the rest of her friends getting their bags out of the SUV that Declan had hired to pick them up. "How did you get inside so fast?"

"Sexy Myles said he'd get my stuff."

"Sexy Myles?"

"Yes!" Tori rolled her eyes. "You remember the bartender from the party who bodyguarded us briefly? Remember how he mentioned he knew the Stocktons and the Harts?"

Piper raised her brows. "I do."

"Well, he's the one who picked us up. He looks even better in the daytime out in the wild. He's clearly dangerous and capable, and I have no time for that. But I do have time for him to get my bags."

Kitty appeared in the doorway. "The party can begin now." She was decked out in diamonds, black rhinestone leggings, platform shoes, and pink sunglasses.

Piper burst out laughing. "You look fantastic."

"I know." She sashayed onto the plane, followed by Maddie and Keira.

Piper hugged them all, but then there was a shriek from the back of the plane.

She spun around and saw the two Hart sisters, Meg and Bella, pop out. "Surprise!"

Piper's heart tightened when she saw them. Meg and Bella were fantastic, and they were already getting swept up into their circle of friends. "You guys are on this flight?"

"We hitched a ride from Oregon," Bella said, bounding into the room and hugging Piper. "We didn't want to miss out on the fun. The rest of the Harts are coming straight from Oregon in a couple days, but we cleared our schedules to come early."

Piper felt so loved, and it was wonderful. "That's fantastic."

"Right?" Bella put her hands on Piper's shoulders as everyone settled in and found their spots. "I have a question for you, and you have to feel free to say no. No pressure just because we're basically family now."

Piper nodded. "Sure. What's up?"

"You know how I run a restaurant on the dude ranch vacation part of the Hart Ranch?"

"Of course. You're an amazing cook."

Bella grinned. "Thank you. I know I am." She took a breath. "I'm really jealous of Lucas starting a life out here with Maddie and you guys. He got me thinking. After the season is over in Oregon for the dude ranch, I'd like to come out here and do a catering business. I was thinking of maybe working with you and doing some weddings. What do you think?"

Piper stared at her, sudden tears filling her eyes. "A catering business?" Exactly like it had all started with her and her mom.

"Yes. I know that when you and Kitty book places that have kitchens, you have to use their staff, but what about the others? I know you're trying to make your services accessible to brides who don't have a lot of money, so I'd love to do those weddings. I don't need money. I just love the idea of being involved in the fairytales you create. What do you think?"

Kitty leaned over Piper's shoulder. "I think it's fantastic. I'm in."

Piper grinned. "Me, too. I'd love to work with you." Bella was so much fun, but there were also a lot of shadows in her eyes. Like the other Harts, Bella had a traumatic past, and she had made it clear she wasn't interested in dating. She wanted to build her own business, and Piper totally understood that.

Relief flashed in Bella's eyes. "Awesome. I was afraid you'd say no." She took a breath. "It's terrifying to think of leaving the ranch, but I have to do it. Thanks for letting me land here."

Piper hugged her. "You always have a home with us, Bella. Always."

Bella nodded. "Thanks," she whispered. "I love my brothers, but having sisters is special. I'm so grateful Maddie brought you all into our lives."

"Me, too." She hugged Bella again, and laughed with so much happiness when Kitty threw her arms around both of them.

"Hug the bride," Kitty yelled.

Piper shrieked with laughter as her friends tackled her, giggling and laughing. There was so much joy bubbling through the plane, her heart was so full. She'd thought she had it all when she'd had her three friends, but now? More and more amazing people kept coming into her life, including their fifth friend from the loft days, Ella, who was meeting them in Paris.

"Any space left in here for men?" Lucas appeared in the doorway, along with Declan's friend Aiden, and his brother Eric.

And behind them was Roman. Her heart tightened when she saw him. He'd named his taco truck business after their mom, Lucy, and her amazing tacos. Every time she saw that truck and her mom's face smiling at her, she felt like her mom was sitting on her shoulder, hugging her.

Roman winked at Piper, and then his gaze sought out Keira, as it always did whenever he was in town. Nothing had happened between them, and Keira hadn't noticed him watching her, but the undercurrent was strong.

Would anything ever happen?

She wasn't even sure she wanted it to. She was just getting to know Roman again, and she wasn't sure she wanted to jeopardize it by having him date one of her best friends.

Maddie waved Lucas over, and the other women settled on the couch, focused on girl time, not man time.

As the men walked in, Declan appeared in the doorway. He was wearing jeans, sneakers, a t-shirt, and a baseball hat. He looked rugged, casual, and insanely hot.

That was her man. *Hers.*

His gaze met hers, and he smiled, a private, wonderful smile just for her.

The joyful chaos in the plane faded away, until it was just Declan. Piper smiled as he walked across the plane, his gaze intent on her, fully focused only on her.

He locked his arm around her back, and pulled her in for a delicious kiss that had no jellyfish undercurrents whatsoever. This kiss was intimate and special, despite the hubbub surrounding them. "I still think that flying over by ourselves would have been fun," he whispered between kisses. "There's a full bedroom in the back."

She grinned. "That's for the honeymoon."

He raised his brows. "You think we'll make it to the honeymoon, then?"

She draped her arms around his neck. "Definitely." She paused. "Declan Jones, I love you with all my heart. I wasn't ready for you, but I got you anyway, and I'm so grateful every day of my life that we were both brave enough to try."

His face softened with pure love. "Piper, you're my light, and I'm so excited for life with you." He touched her diamond necklace. "Your mom is chuckling, right now. Heading off to Paris to get married with a whole bunch of people who love you? And a thriving business. And a great guy, if I do say so myself."

She laughed. "My mom would have loved you. She's definitely chuckling with joy right now." Her phone rang, and they both laughed when she pulled it out to look at it. "April," they said together.

April had dumped her fiancé, and she'd hired Kitty and Piper to put on a girl power party for her instead. Their business had quickly taken on the energy of Bride Protector, and parties for women to celebrate themselves and their female friends had started to become a thing, and she and Kitty were the ones always hired to run them.

Fairytales that were about more than falling in love and getting married. They were the fairytales of falling in love with yourself first and celebrating that.

Finding her own power was where it had all started for Piper, and it was the foundation of all she had.

It was her friends who had decided that Declan was the one for her, and they'd been right. Because no one could do it alone. Everyone needed a posse, including women like her who simply wanted to wake up in the morning and feel capable of tackling her life and her dreams.

Declan silenced her phone. "April is just going to have to wait until you get back."

Piper smiled. "You know I'm going to text her back as soon as I have a chance."

Declan grinned. "I know. You'd never let down one of your girls, friends, or clients. And that's just one of the many things I love about you."

Piper knew he was telling the truth. Declan would never, ever try to make her small or hold her back. He was fully supportive of who she wanted and needed to be, and of her plans for the future.

And at the same time, she loved who he was becoming. His business with Roman had lit him up, and he was actively searching for small businesses to fund, focusing on those founders who had trouble securing funding from traditional resources, including those with a prison history, both men and women. He was vibrant and alive, and she never had to worry about him facing bullets when he was at work.

Clark had been arrested. And after a thoroughly unfriendly and threatening visit from the Hart lawyers, Dick had given Jessie her freedom.

And that was just the start. So much ahead of them, all of it fueled by love, freedom, and friendship.

Want to know what happens when Keira suddenly needs the kind of help that only a sexy ex-con can offer? Or when Bella meets the cowboy who challenges everything she believes in? Order your copies now of *When We Take a Chance* (Roman and Keira), and *A Rogue Cowboy's Kiss* (Bella & the absolute *last* cowboy she would ever want to fall for!). New to Stephanie Rowe? Grab a copy of Maddie & Lucas's story, *A Rogue Cowboy's Heart,* or keep reading for an excerpt!

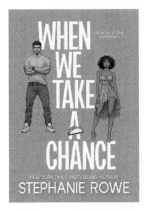

(Mr. Inconvenient, Book #2)

All's fair in love and tacos. Except, of course, when the tacos are made by an irritatingly attractive ex-con fighting for redemption.

Keira Vogel is intentionally single, unintentionally broke, and on the rise. Yes, she's a little stuck, but the plucky entrepreneur has plans...until her not-so-pretty past finds her. Now, she's in danger, her business is at risk, and the only one who can help her is Roman Townsend, the ex-con, taco-trunk-owning brother of her best friend.

Roman Townsend knows he brings a load of trouble with him. He knows he doesn't deserve a second chance. And he isn't about to get entangled with his sister's classy, upscale bestie, no matter how compelling he finds her.

But when Keira needs a little bodyguarding help, it's Roman's chance to be the man he's never been. But to be who he wants to be, he has to keep his hands off the sassy, irreverent Keira. But the closer they get, the more he realizes she might be everything he's ever wanted...and never thought to dream of.

Keira's been thoroughly burned by love, and this body-guarding situation is business only. But there's something about this gregarious, muscled taco genius that makes her want to heal his shadows...the same shadows that almost ruined her before.

Worth the risk? No.

Dangerously tempting? Absolutely.

Treat Yourself to *When We Take a Chance* **today!**

———

Want to know when Stephanie's next book is coming out, or when she's having a sale? Join her newsletter at www. stephanierowe.com.

———

Do you love the feel-good sisterhood of *When We Least Expect It***? If so, you'll love the hilarious** *Mia Murphy* **mystery series, which features three of the coolest women alive!** It has a little romance and lots of corpses, chaos, and unexpected twists. Get started with *Double Twist,* or skip ahead for sneak peeks of *Triple Trouble* and *Top Notch!*

What about heart-melting, fun, small-town romance? A new *Birch Crossing* **is available!** Leila Kerrigan is back in town with no time for the rebel who stole her heart long ago...but now he's playing for keeps. Treat yourself to *Secretly Mine* today or skip ahead to a sneak peek! It's a connected standalone, so you can enjoy it without reading any of the other *Birch Crossing* books (but you'll probably want to go back and read the others when you're done)!

New to Stephanie's cowboy world, and want more heart-melting cowboys? If so, you *have* to try her *Wyoming Rebels* series about nine cowboy brothers who find love in the most romantic, most heartwarming, most sigh-worthy ways you can imagine. Get started with *A Real Cowboy Never Says No* right now. You will be sooo glad you did, I promise!

Are you a fan of magic, love, and laughter? If so, dive into my paranormal romantic comedy *Immortally Sexy* series, starting with the first book, *To Date an Immortal*.

Is dark, steamy paranormal romance your jam? If so, definitely try my award-winning *Order of the Blade* series, starting with book one, *Darkness Awakened*.

Keep reading for sneak peeks of Stephanie Rowe books! You might find your next binge-read right here!

SNEAK PEEK: TRIPLE TROUBLE

A MIA MURPHY MYSTERY

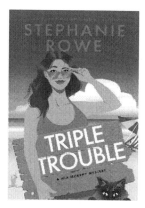

"So much darn fun!" Five-star Goodreads Review (Penny)

CHAPTER ONE

X.

I stared at my phone, stunned at the text that had just come in from an unfamiliar number. My brain immediately shouted at me that the X meant bad things, bad, bad things.

Then I remembered that I wasn't ten years old in the middle of a con with my mom. She wasn't standing on the other side of a luxurious room crowded with celebrities, holding up two crossed fingers, giving me the X sign that meant "abandon the con right now because it's going south."

I was, in fact, a grown woman who had walked away from that life and my mom ten years ago. I was currently standing on my dock in the gorgeous morning sunlight on a beautiful Maine lake, going over my list of all the must-do items still undone prior to the grand reopening of my new marina.

Not a celebrity or con in sight. And definitely no mom.

I took a breath. Wow. My head had gone to old places in an alarming hurry.

I grinned at my massive rescue cat, who was perched on the end of the dock, his tail twitching in anticipation of the next unsuspecting fish to swim past. "It's all good, King Tut."

He ignored me, but I knew that the love was still there.

My life was great. I had friends, a home, and a marina that I was determined to turn into a success. I looked down at my phone again, studying my list. The landscapers were due to finish today, and—

A second X popped up.

My heart sped up, and I sucked in my breath. *What the fudge?*

Tentatively, almost terrified of getting a response, I texted back. *Mom?*

I got an immediate, automated reply stating that the phone number was not in service.

I felt both relieved and weirdly sad. Of course it wouldn't be my mom. I hadn't had any contact with her since I'd left her when I was seventeen. Granted, I'd always felt that she knew exactly where I was and what I was doing, but even if that were true, why would she be texting me *XX* after all these years?

One X had meant abandon the con. XX had meant that it was getting dangerous and to get out as soon as possible. Get out? From my own home? That made no sense. But I couldn't help but take a more careful look around me.

The lake was relatively quiet, but there were a few boats

around. Across the cove was Jake's Yacht Club, with its upscale blue and white awnings. Staff in their navy shirts and khaki shorts were strolling around helping customers. Everyone was calm. No danger that I could see.

I studied each driver of the boats that were near me, but I recognized everyone. No one new.

I turned around to examine my marina. The painters were working, the landscapers were making things beautiful. The front window that had been shot out my first week, almost killing one of my new besties, had been replaced, so the big plywood board was gone.

Everything was coming along well.

But despite all the warm fuzzies surrounding me, I could feel panic starting to build in my chest. I'd been relaxed for days, so the sudden descent into panic was throwing me. I was out of practice being on guard for my life.

I looked at King Tut again. He was my gold-star surveillance system. He'd sacrificed morals, pride, and common decency to save me more than once. "King Tut!"

He didn't take his gaze off the lake.

I took a breath, trying to get my head back into focus. The fact King Tut wasn't concerned meant there wasn't a threat. Granted, it could also mean that he was so deeply immersed in predator mode that he had no mental space for anything else...

My phone dinged again. My heart jumped, and I looked down.

X.

Three Xs.

Three Xs meant *get out fast, no matter what it takes.*

I looked around again, the hair on the back of my neck prickling even as I tried to talk myself out of freaking out. It was a few Xs. There was nothing special about an X. Anyone could type an X. Glitches could produce Xs with zero effort.

I was at home at my marina. What could possibly be so

dangerous that I needed to get out as fast as I could? My mom's messes hadn't been mine for a very long time.

Then my gaze settled on Vinnie, the sometime-gang-leader-ish guy who was currently acting as my unofficial bodyguard, due to the fact that my real one had been murdered (by a person unrelated to me and my life). The feds still couldn't figure out who had put surveillance cameras in my marina, so Vinnie had taken over keep-Mia-alive duty.

It had never once occurred to me that the spying had anything to do with my mother. I'd assumed it was connected to my ex-husband, who was currently in federal prison for being a drug kingpin. I'd put him there, and his mom had tried to kill me for it.

Vinnie was standing in the parking lot, his arms folded as he scanned the area. He looked dangerous and armed, despite the fact he had already admitted he would never shoot anyone for me, due to his aversion to a life of guilt and trauma, and things like that.

But at six-foot four, muscular, and wearing just the right amount of bling for a gang leader, he looked like a deadly force, so I doubted anyone would try while he was around. Plus, honestly, after spending so long looking over my shoulder, I'd gotten used to the possibility of being a target.

I was chill now.

Except, apparently, when being triggered by my past.

I looked down at my phone again, trying to think of a reply that might help me figure out if the sender was my mom.

My mom had been a code person, because living a life of crime had taught her that paper trails were never good for the criminal.

I tried to remember something from the code we'd used, but all I could think of were the made-up symbols that we'd created, none of which were on the keyboard of my phone (go figure, right?). I couldn't quite recall how any of them went together anyway.

I did remember the symbol for my name, though.

I quickly knelt on the dock, dipped my finger in the water, and then drew the symbol on the wood. I took a picture of it then texted it to the number.

Again, an immediate reply that the number was not in service. Then, right after that, another text came through. *XXX.*

Alarm shot through me, the kind that she'd triggered in me so many times as a kid. *Run, Mia, run!*

"King Tut," I shouted. "Let's go. Now." I didn't know where to go, but I had to get out, and get out fast. I had no idea what was happening, but I liked my life too much to be willing to die. "Vinnie," I shouted. "We gotta go!"

Vinnie started running toward me, but King Tut ignored me. I ran to the edge of the dock to get him. Leaving my cat behind didn't qualify as "no matter what." He was my family, and there was no way I was leaving him. "King Tut! We gotta go—"

He shot off the dock and dove into the water, disappearing under the surface. "Hey!"

I immediately jumped in after him, knowing that sometimes King Tut vanished for hours once he got under the water. I didn't know where he went, but wherever he came up for air was out of my sight. It used to freak me out, but I'd gotten used to it.

But now was not the time to lose my cat for hours. The late June water was warming, but still a shock to my system as I hit the lake. I immediately ducked under, searching the crystalline water for my black cat.

I didn't see him.

I stood up, water dripping off me. Vinnie was already at the end of the dock. "What's happening?" He looked alarmed.

"Where's King Tut? Can you see him? We need to get out of here, but I need to get him first!"

"King Tut?" Vinnie pulled off his sunglasses and scanned the water.

At that moment, I heard the roar of the lake patrol boat. I whirled around and waved my hands at Devlin Hunt, the too-handsome-for-anyone's-good cop who was driving it. "Stop!" I shouted. "King Tut's under the water! Turn off your propeller!"

Because we'd done this drill many times since I'd bought the marina a few months ago and discovered that my cat was an avid underwater hunter, Devlin immediately shut his boat off and leaned over the edge to search the water.

For a long moment, there was silence as the three of us scanned the water for my baby.

"There!" Devlin pointed close to the beach, and I sloshed through the water toward where he was pointing, my heart pounding.

"Something's wrong!" I shouted as I hurried after King Tut. "I'm in danger!"

"What?" Devlin stood up and put his hand on his gun. "What's going on?"

"I don't know!" I saw a black shadow under the water, and I lunged for him. My hands wrapped around King Tut's waist, and I dragged the yowling beast out of the water. "I need to go!" I started running toward the shore. I had no idea what the danger was or where it was coming from, which made me even more alarmed.

Just as I reached the shore, fighting to hold into a sodden ball of long-haired anger, an extended-cab pickup truck shot into the parking lot. I knew that black truck. It belonged to one of my two best friends, Hattie Lawless, a seventy-something chef who ran a café in my marina and raced cars on the side. "Hattie!"

She hit the brakes and the truck skidded to a stop. She jumped out, grabbing my shoulders as I ran up. "What's going on? Why do you look like you're freaking out?"

"A triple X! I think my mom sent me a triple X!"

"Is that porn?" Hattie looked intrigued. "I had no idea your mom was into porn. I mean, not surprising because she's a wild card, but porn? Can I see it? I assume it's girl power porn, right? She seems empowered."

"Porn?" I stared at her. "No. It's our signal that the con has gone south, and we need to run."

"A con?" Her eyebrows shot up. "You're running a con with your mom? What con?"

"I'm not. I mean, that I know of. But I got this text from this random number, and it could have been her, and—"

"Wait a minute." Hattie put her hands on her hips. "Mia Murphy. Pull yourself together. You're not running a con. You own a marina in the charming town of Bass Derby. You don't engage in illegal activities, except to help others. And you haven't heard from your mom in over a decade. Whatever you think is going on, isn't."

I grabbed my phone and handed it to her as Vinnie ran up. "See?"

Hattie took the phone, and the two of them peered at it. "This?" Hattie frowned at me. "Some random text from a number that doesn't even work? You're freaking out about *this?* How do you know it's her?"

"I don't *know* it's her, but what if it is? What if there's something going on and she's trying to warn me and—"

"Hey!" Hattie cut me off. "Take a breath, girlfriend." She held up her hands palm up and inhaled. "Deep breath. Channel your inner river."

I blinked. "My river?"

"Yes. A calm, scenic river. Tranquility. Peace. Serenity. Imagine chiseled, charming men lined up on the banks, singing about how wonderful you are."

I stared at her. "Seriously?"

"Yes. Imagine their deep voices, singing 'Mia is a badass. She rules the world!' Maybe they're even dancing for you, some manly, synchronized beauty. How can that not feel good? Breathe in. Breathe out."

Devlin finally caught up to us. "What's going on?"

"Keep channeling your river, Mia. I got this." Hattie held up my phone. "Mia thinks this text is from her mom, signaling that the end of the world is upon us, and she must run away. To where? She doesn't know. From what? Also unknown."

Devlin took the phone and frowned at it. As he studied it, I found my pulse slowing and my panic easing. Devlin was a local cop in the small town of Bass Derby, but I was pretty certain he had a black ops background.

His buddy, Agent Hawk Straus, who I called Griselda to reclaim my personal power, was the FBI agent who had coerced me into a two-year-undercover sting against my ex. When I'd moved to Bass Derby, Griselda had asked Devlin to make sure no one from my ex's life assassinated me. He trusted Devlin with my life, which means I did, too. With Devlin standing by my side, no one would be able to get to me.

Plus, the river visualization had been surprisingly helpful.

I took the deep breath Hattie had wanted for me, and she nodded her approval as she studied me. "It's not like you to freak out like that," she observed. "You're very unflappable when it comes to danger like assassins, guns, and other imminent threats to your life. Why are you having a fit over this?"

Devlin looked over at me. "Hattie's right. This could easily just be some random text."

They were right. I usually was pretty calm. A childhood of crime had inured me to the small dangers in life. In fact, it had instilled in me an affinity for a high-risk life, which I tried to suppress as much as possible. "I know. It's just…well…it's my *mom*."

"It's probably *not* your mom," Hattie said.

"I know. I just meant that she triggers me." I let out my breath again. "The purpose of the triple X code was to get my attention when I wasn't taking things seriously. She would use it to freak me out and get me to do what she needed me to."

Hattie cocked her brow. "That sounds a little manipulative."

"When you're a criminal, sometimes you can't mess around." I looked over at Devlin, who was frowning at me. "What?"

He held up my phone. "I'm going to have Griselda, I mean Hawk, track this number and see what he can figure out."

I nodded. "Okay, great. Thanks."

"But in the meantime, I agree with Hattie," he said. "Keep an eye out, but we're already on alert, so I don't think we raise the alarm any higher. Unless you know something else?"

I looked at the three of them, and buried my chin in King Tut's soggy head. "You know, I think you guys are right. It makes no sense that my mom would be telling me to run from here." My tension eased even more. "It was an old trigger, I guess."

"We all have those," Devlin said softly.

I knew he understood. He'd been in a gang when he was a kid, so I imagined he had his own share of childhood land mines that came up from time to time. "Thanks."

He nodded. "It's all good, Mia." But he continued to study me. "You do look like hell, though."

"Thanks." Not too long ago, Devlin had declared his interest in dating me. On the same day, Griselda had made the same announcement. They were besties. Griselda had warned me off Devlin. Devlin had warned me off Griselda. I didn't want to ever date anyone again.

It was awkward.

And yet somehow, I'd agreed to have dinner with Devlin tomorrow night. Umm...

Hattie peered at me. "You know, you do look haggard. It can't all be from that text."

"Mia was up all night working on the marina," Vinnie offered. "She's freaking out about having it ready in time for her grand reopening."

Empathy flashed across Hattie's face. "Sweetie, it looks amazing. It's going great."

"I know, but it's just that I have to overcome the marina's reputation and mine. Do you know that the sheriff came over here with some woman a couple days ago? She'd lost her diamond ring and accused me of taking it, due to my criminal history and all."

Devlin narrowed his eyes. "I didn't know about that." No one in the entire town was impressed with our sheriff, not even the mayor, who had hired him. She also happened to be his mom.

"Well, the lady found it under her own bed," I said.

"Which you could have put there," Hattie said. "It doesn't exonerate you."

I looked at her. "How is that helpful?"

"Just wanted to remind you of your awesomeness. Just because someone doesn't appreciate your specialness or sees it as a threat doesn't make you any less awesome." She put her arm around my shoulders. "You need a vacation."

I sighed. She'd offered this trip about forty times in the last two weeks. "I can't take a vacation. I'm opening my marina in ten days."

"And yet, you were ready to abandon it all forever, because of a random text," she said.

I grimaced. "So I freaked out a little."

"A lot," Vinnie said. "You dove in after your cat like he was about to be murdered."

I tightened my arms around my soggy cat, who was now purring and happy to be snuggled. "I thought he was in danger."

Hattie put her hands on her hips. "As I have told you repeatedly, I'm going to visit my cousin Thelma for a couple days to celebrate her birthday. Come with me. It's a five-star island resort on the coast of Maine. You'll come back rested, refreshed, and ready to receive all texts with a clear mind."

I wanted to go so badly, because having friends was a precious new treasure, and I loved every second of it. But setting down roots in my new town was critical for me, and getting accepted by the town was more difficult than I'd expected. I had a lot riding on this grand opening, and I needed to be here working, not on vacation. "I already told you I can't. I have the grand opening—"

"If the triple X *was* from your mom, then leaving for a couple days seems like a great idea as well," Hattie interrupted.

Huh. "You're not wrong about that," I admitted slowly.

"And Lucy's coming on the trip," Hattie said. "Girl bonding. You know you love it."

Aw...Lucy was going, too? Now I really wanted to go. The

three of us had become such a tight trio since I'd moved to Bass Derby.

"I think it's a good idea to go," Devlin said. "Get off the grid for a few days while we figure this out."

I looked at him, both disappointed and relieved at the idea of missing our date. "Our dinner?"

He grinned, looking pleased that I'd even remembered we had plans. "I don't know about you, but I'll still live in this town when you get back. We'll figure it out."

I bit my lip. The idea of stepping away from the marina for a couple days did sound good. I was drained, I loved Hattie and Lucy, and a little part of me was worried that the text really had been from mom. "Is the resort cat-friendly?"

"I don't think so, but hang on." She pulled out her phone and made a call. "Beau. It's Hattie."

Beau Hammersley was a reclusive, wealthy mystery writer who claimed to hate the world, except for me, my mom, and Hattie. I suspected he liked people a lot more than he claimed, but I adored him either way.

"Mia needs to leave town for a couple days because her mom might have just sent her a cryptic text about danger. Can you come over and grab King Tut and watch him?"

I grinned. Beau was obsessed with my mom. He'd run across a documentary on the infamous Tatum Murphy when he'd been researching one of his books, and the obsession had been born.

Hattie hung up the phone. "He'll be here in a few seconds. He's around the corner. He's out boating."

My arms tightened around King Tut. "I don't want to leave King Tut behind—"

"Yo! I'm here!" Beau came flying around the corner in his boat, shouting and waving his arms. He sped up to the beach and ran his boat right onto the sand. He leapt out and came racing up. He was wearing his bejeweled sandals, denim shorts, and his tee shirt with the bloody dagger on it. His hair was ratty from the wind, and the only sign of wealth on him was the brand of his sunglasses. "Your mom's in danger?"

I almost started laughing at his delight about my mom being involved. "I don't know. Maybe."

Hattie pointed to King Tut. "Mia needs King Tut safe."

Beau eyed the cat. "Tatum might come to check on him?"

"She might," I agreed. Who knew what my mom might do? No one. Checking on my cat was as possible as anything else.

"Then he's safe with me." Beau held out his arms. "Come on, King Tut. Let's go." The reclusive mystery writer liked to put on a tough persona, but in his heart, he was a good man. If he said he'd keep King Tut safe, he would. He'd do whatever it took. After decades as a mystery writer, the man had ideas about danger, death, and murder that no one wanted to know.

King Tut gazed at Beau and didn't budge from my arms.

Beau met his steely gaze. "I have caviar."

King Tut immediately leapt out of my arms, raced down the sand, then jumped into Beau's boat. He sat down on the bow, flicked his tail, and gave us all a sullen, serious glare with his unblinking yellow eyes. Even with his black fur still dripping with water, he looked huge, menacing, and dangerous.

"Damn, girl." Hattie grinned. "If you decide not to go and deprive that cat of Beau's caviar, you will never be safe from that feline again."

"I need to channel King Tut's attitude for my next villain," Beau said. "Look at that threat. It's brilliant. Subtle. Unyielding. And yet disarming in that kitty-cat ball of soggy fluff. It's almost diabolical. I love it! He's my new muse. Get me his life jacket, and we're off."

I bit my lip. "I've never been without King Tut since I rescued him."

Hattie put her arm around my shoulder. "King Tut will be safe away from the marina, and you'll be safe too. Plus, both of you will have fun."

"I think it's the best call," Devlin said. "Give me a couple days to figure out what's going on." He looked over at me. "I'll keep an eye on the marina."

"I will, too. I know what the contractors are supposed to be doing, and I'll manage it," Vinnie said. "I'll sleep in the spare store-front. It'll cost you, but I'm worth it."

I looked at the three of them, and my heart got all mushy. These were my friends, people who cared if I died, cared if my cat was safe, and cared about my marina. I might not have had my breakthrough with the rest of the town yet, but I'd found a little niche of home, and I appreciated it with all my heart.

The truth was, I did want to go with Hattie and Lucy. I wanted to go with every fiber in my being. "How long's the trip?"

"Three days and two nights," Hattie said. "The ferry leaves in four hours, though. We need to hurry. How fast can you pack?"

I looked over at her, and suddenly, I knew she was right. They were all right. Those texts might not be from my mom, but they were the impetus I needed. I was supposed to go on this trip, and I wasn't going to miss it. "Fast."

Want more *Triple Trouble*? Get it today!

SNEAK PEEK: TOP NOTCH

A MIA MURPHY MYSTERY

"I was catapulted into the story and remained captivated until
the end!" ~Five-star Goodreads Review (Elizabeth)

CHAPTER ONE

FRIDAY NIGHT WAS THE KIND OF DARK that was every assassin's
dream, which meant that it wasn't exactly the perfect weekend-
starter for me.

The rain was hammering so loudly on the metal roof of my
marina that even an entire army of drug dealers firing assault

weapons could have snuck up on me without me hearing them.

I'd been outside checking for assassins for almost twenty minutes, which was more than enough time to get absolutely drenched, thoroughly chilled, a little freaked out, and up to my ankles in mud and puddles.

And yet, I couldn't remember the last time I'd been so happy. If ever.

Whistling cheerfully, I sloshed through the flooded parking lot behind the marina, finishing up my nightly pre-bedtime property check for assassins. As had been the case for all four nights since I'd arrived in Bass Derby, Maine, there were no professional killers lying in wait to pop me.

Witness protection? Who needs witness protection? Hah. No one would bother to follow me here.

Sure, I'd had a couple amateur murderers pointing guns at my face this week, but I was alive and they were in jail, so yay for me. More importantly, they'd had nothing to do with my ex-husband's drug empire, the one I'd spied on for two years and then testified against, in a move that had made me all sorts of popular with his slightly bitter and vengeful family. My former in-laws hadn't followed me to Bass Derby (so far), so I was calling my decision to move here a win.

Equally delighted to be traipsing around in a cold downpour was King Tut, my massive rescued/purloined Maine Coon cat. He was trotting happily beside me, his ears nearly flattened to the side of his head from the rain.

I grinned down at him as we rounded the corner on the backside of the deck that stretched across the entire front of the marina. "Pretty great, right?"

He didn't answer me. Instead, he froze in place, one paw raised mid-step. His body went stiff. His tail went still, except for a tiny flick at the end, and the fur on his back went up, his gaze fixed on the latticework lining the backside of the deck.

I shined my flashlight in the direction he was looking, and I saw a hole in the latticework that I hadn't noticed before. A gap big enough for a human.

Alarm shot through me, and the hair on the back of my neck stood up. Had that been there since I'd moved in? Or had someone made that hole tonight?

Fear started slithering down my spine, and I scowled. I was so over being scared. "I'm sure it's fine," I said aloud. "What are the odds that someone came here to kill me?"

Low. The odds were super low.

But not zero.

Which meant I needed to check it out. Discovering an assassin while I was awake and only a few feet from my car gave me marginally better survival odds than discovering an assassin while I was asleep in my bed.

When it came to death, I needed any additional edge I could squeeze out. "If someone explodes out of there with a gun, you kill him."

King Tut ignored me. In fact, he still hadn't moved from his stiff-legged, puffed-out-fur stance, which was really creeping me out. Was he in predator mode or defender mode? I really hoped there was some creepy crawly under there that King Tut was going to have for dinner, and not an assassin who was going to dump my precious body in a gully somewhere.

I took a breath. An assassin hired to kill me wouldn't bother to lie in wait. I had no skills. They'd just walk up, pop me in the head, and collect their paycheck. So it was probably fine. If it wasn't, I'd be dead already.

But I still had to check. Because, you know, in case I was wrong.

"It'll be fine. I'm very good at evading being murdered." My voice sounded confident, but my heart starting pounding as I crouched down and shined my light under the deck, keeping my weight balanced so I could leap up and bolt for my car if I needed to.

The beam illuminated an old wooden barrel on its side, tucked up close to the entrance, blocking my view under the rest of the deck. It was wet from the rain, making the beam of the flashlight reflect back at me.

I grimaced and bent lower, angling my light to the sides to try to see around the barrel. There were several cement blocks, old boards, a couple canoe paddles, a half-buried keg, and other abandoned junk that was impossible to identify in the dark night.

What I could tell, however, was that there was plenty of space for a hit man to squeeze past the barrel and retreat into the shadowy recesses of the 100-ish-foot-long deck. The puddles obscured any possible footprints, leaving me with no way to tell if someone had recently crawled under there.

I tried to listen for movement, but all I could hear was the hammering of the rain on the wooden deck slats, against the metal roof of the marina maintenance building, and into the puddles surrounding me.

Short of crawling through the mud to the back of the deck, I had no way of knowing if a professional killer was hiding under there in waterproof pants, waiting for me to nod off to sleep.

Crawling under there didn't feel like the best choice at this time. Or any time, for that matter.

King Tut crept past me and slithered past the keg. His feet disappeared into the puddles, but he didn't make so much as a ripple, despite his snowshoe-sized paws. He suddenly lifted his head, his body tense as he stared into the dark underbelly of the deck. He went utterly still again, except for the twitching of the tip of his tail.

I knew that stance. He was about to launch. Fear shot through me. "Wait, don't—"

He hissed and shot under the deck and out of sight. I could hear scuffling and yowling. And…was that a curse? Had someone just *cursed*? The hair on my arms stood up—

A hand came down on my shoulder. "Mia."

I screamed and leapt up, cracking the back of my head on the underside of the deck. I hurled the flashlight at my assailant and ran, racing for my car as I tried to get my keys out of my pocket—

"Mia! It's me!"

I knew that voice. "Hattie?" I stumbled to a stop and whirled around.

The silhouette of Hattie Lawless, the seventy-something race car driver who leased space in the marina for her local eatery, Hattie's Café, loomed in the darkness. She held up her hands. "It's just me. Relax."

"Relax? I've had four people try to kill me in the last three weeks." I put my hands on my knees, bending over as I tried to catch my breath. "I thought we decided you weren't going to surprise me like that anymore."

King Tut shot out from under the deck and sprinted past me into the marina store, carrying something in his mouth. A dead animal? Crud. I hoped he didn't put it in my bed. But yay for a dead animal and not a murderer. Unless it was my potential murderer's hand. King Tut could definitely take off a hand.

"We didn't agree I wouldn't surprise you." Hattie sloshed through the puddles as she headed toward me. "We agreed you wouldn't try to kill me if I did. There's a difference, and I'm pretty sure that hurling a metal flashlight at my head violates our pact."

"I don't think that's what our agreement was, and you're well aware that I'm a little jumpy when people sneak up on me." I'd kept my pickpocketing, con-artist childhood hidden from Hattie, but she'd recognized me from the news as the ex-wife of Stanley Herrera, drug kingpin.

I'd spent two very stressful years as a spy for the FBI gathering evidence on him, and now that he was in prison, I was trying to pretend I had a chance at a normal life. I was on day four as the new owner of the Eagle's Nest Marina in Bass Derby, Maine, seizing my chance for the friends, home, and the life I'd never had.

So far, Hattie and my mail carrier, Lucy Grande, had helped with the friend goal. The law-abiding life? Not so much. Murder will do that. But I was hoping day five would be the charm. Or I had been, until Hattie had snuck up on me, mostly because I couldn't think of a single innocuous reason for her to be in my parking lot at midnight in the middle of a storm.

She held out my flashlight. "Either way, you have terrible aim. My head thanks you."

"I have great aim when it counts." Like when an assassin, or a hot police officer (oops), was sneaking up on me. I tucked the flashlight in my pocket, no longer needed now that we were under the floodlights from the marina. "What's up?"

"We have a situation."

"We do?" I tensed. We'd had a lot of situations in the last few days, but I'd thought they were over. "What happened?"

"I'll tell you on the way. Hop in." She pointed at her truck, which was idling, headlights on, in my parking lot. Attached to her truck was a boat trailer, which was half-submerged in the lake. Lucy, fresh off almost being arrested for murder, was strapping a small, worn-out motorboat to the metal struts.

Apparently, they'd been busy while I'd been sneaking around my property checking for professional killers. Good to know that the rain on my metal roof could drown out that much noise. That made me feel safe.

Lucy waved enthusiastically. I narrowed my eyes in suspicion, but waved back.

They were both way too cheerful for being in my parking lot in a storm in the middle of the night. Something was definitely up. I was getting a bad feeling about this situation. "Is that my boat on your trailer?"

"Yes, mine are too big. Let's go." Hattie started heading toward the truck.

I put my hands on my hips and made no attempt to move. "That boat has a leak. It's been sinking all week."

Hattie sighed and turned to face me. It was raining so hard that her jacket was glistening, and her cheeks looked like they were coated in glass. "The boat's not sinking. It just has a month's worth of rain in it, because you haven't bailed it out. It'll be fine."

I folded my arms over my chest. "Fine for what, exactly?" I might have known them for only a few days, but I already knew better than to blindly trust any of Hattie's plans.

Hattie set her hands on her hips, looking impatient. "A little trip to Dead Man's Pond."

Going to a place called Dead Man's Pond at night during a storm in a sinking boat sounded like a fantastic idea. "Why would we be doing that?"

She blinked as the rain hammered her cheeks. "We're going to rescue some old ladies."

"Seriously?" I wasn't sure I believed her. Hattie already knew me well enough to know there was no chance I'd refuse to help rescue some senior citizens from a storm. "Who needs rescuing?"

"You remember Bootsy Jones and Shirley Kincaid?"

"Of course I remember them." Bootsy and Shirley were part of a group of senior sewers-for-hire called the Seam Rippers. Last I'd seen them, they were dressed up in leather, blasting heavy metal music, and drinking margaritas. They were absolute spitfires, and there was no way I could snuggle down and sleep while they were stranded somewhere. *If* they really were stranded. "Why are they out on the lake? Were they camping?"

Maybe they weren't really in trouble. Maybe this was a front for going out drinking with the ladies…or something more nefarious that she was hiding from me.

"They were hunting a ghost."

I stared at her. "Ghost? Did you just say *ghost?*"

Hattie nodded. "The ghost of the man that Dead Man's Pond was named after. Jack the Ripper."

Jack the Ripper? Because that was charming, innocuous nickname. "Was he a serial killer?"

"Never proven."

I looked over at Lucy as she jogged up. "Is she serious?"

"Totally. It was never proven." She grinned. "According to

Hattie, the Seam Rippers got hired to make a fundraiser quilt for the Halloween fest in October, so a few of them decided they needed to get in the spirit. It's difficult to channel proper Halloween mojo when it's Memorial Day."

Ohh... I could see where this was heading. "They decided to commune with a ghost? And they chose a serial killer's ghost?"

"It's for Halloween," Lucy said, with just a wee bit of sarcasm that my highly tuned senses were able to pick up. "What good are *friendly* ghosts?"

"No good," I agreed, with equally subtle sarcasm. "Deep, debilitating terror is the only way to channel Halloween. Or even just everyday living. Fear is such a great motivator."

"Right?" Hattie nodded. "See, Lucy? Mia gets it."

Lucy raised her brows at me. "Does she?"

I grinned at her wise skepticism. "Of course. I love fear. It's super fun."

"You young 'uns are such wimps. You're lucky to have me around to toughen you up." Hattie gestured impatiently. "They hired Glory Starr, a ghost whisperer from Portland, to take them out tonight. Bootsy texted that they're stranded. They've been out there for hours, but they're running out of tequila, so Bootsy called for a rescue."

Lucy and I exchanged knowing glances.

"So, basically, they waited until midnight to call for help because they were having too much fun until now." It wasn't surprising. I'd met the Seam Rippers. Why abandon fun if you don't need to?

"Pretty much." Hattie grinned. "When that alcohol wears off, there are going to be four very cold, very wet, close-to-death old ladies on that pond, unless we go save them."

I believed her now. Given what I knew about the Seam Rippers, it made sense. But... "You want to rescue them in a sinking, old boat? Why not call Devlin?" Devlin Hunt was a local police officer who also carried the honor of being Lake Patrol. He was capable, charming, and distractingly attractive. "Saving people on lakes is literally what he's paid to do."

"Why delegate when we can do it ourselves?" Hattie asked.

"A lot of reasons, actually."

Lucy tucked her hand around my elbow and leaned on my shoulder. "Come with us, Mia. It'll be fun."

"You'll be the hero that you long to be," Hattie said.

I eyed the blue-haired senior. "I don't long to be a hero."

"Yeah, me either, but sometimes we get what we get." She started toward her truck, sloshing through the puddles that were getting deeper by the moment. "Let's do this. The girls are waiting."

I glanced at Lucy. "You realize there's no way this little adventure is going to turn out fine, right?"

She grinned, despite the rain dripping off her hood onto her cheeks. "It involves Hattie. What could possibly go wrong?"

Hattie started honking her horn at us and flashing her high beams.

I sighed. "A lot. Definitely, a lot."

Lucy raised her brows. "And you'd want to miss that?"

"Yes. Absolutely." But as I said it, I started walking toward Hattie's truck. Because who was I kidding? I totally wanted to go. Lucy and Hattie was already becoming friends, and, although I was committed to a law-abiding life, I'd never been able to shake the need for adventure that had been trained into me by my infamous, con-artist mom.

Lucy laughed. "Me, too." She slung her arm over my shoulder. "Have I told you how happy I am that you moved to Bass Derby?"

I pulled open the door as Hattie yelled at us to hurry up. "Me, too." I paused before climbing into the truck. "One promise, though."

Hattie raised her brows as Lucy squeezed into the back seat. "What's that?"

"No murder. No dead bodies. Nothing illegal." That last one

was critical. I was desperate to leave the world of crime far behind me.

Hattie grinned. "That's an easy one. Nothing fun like that is on the agenda. A murder would be great, right?"

"No!" Lucy and I spoke at the same time.

I shook my head as I climbed in. "What's wrong with you, Hattie? Seriously."

"Nothing. I'm flawlessly fantastic. As always." She hit the gas before I'd even gotten the door closed, leaving me dangling out of the truck for a terrifying moment before I got the door yanked shut.

Yep, this was definitely going to go well. I had a good feeling about it. Really, I did.

Want more *Top Notch*? Go *here* to get it now!

SNEAK PEEK: A ROGUE COWBOY'S HEART

CONTEMPORARY ROMANCE

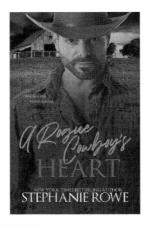

★★★★★ ""OMG!!! The best yet!! Stephanie has outdone herself! I am in love with this book." Five-star Goodreads Review (Cindy A)

The rules are simple for reclusive cowboy Lucas Hart. Make sure Maddie Vale is safe, and then disappear before she even realizes he's there. But some rules need to be broken.

Lucas Hart had found her.

Madison Vale.

And she was a shock to his very core.

He hadn't known what to expect when he'd come after her. None of the Harts had. Until this moment, she'd been only a memory for his brother Jacob, and a name and address on a piece of paper.

And now…she was in front of him.

And he realized he hadn't remotely expected *her*.

The way she spoke to her friends was pure warmth and loyalty.

The way they hugged her showed how much they loved her.

The bond between the foursome was real and powerful, the kind of loyalty that the Harts lived and breathed every moment of their lives.

Madison was sexy as all hell in that red dress, and her sneakers made him grin. Her brown skin was insanely beautiful, and the intricate braids cascading down her back were a literal work of art. Sassy. Beautiful. Bold.

He liked her immediately, which surprised him. He didn't like many people. Trusted even fewer. But the energy between Madison and her friends hit right in the core of what made him get up every day. Love. Loyalty. Commitment.

She seemed like she had it all together.

His job was done. He'd seen her. He'd made sure she was all right. Now he was supposed to walk away and let her resume her life. His family was on alert. If Madison ever decided to unlock her past and started asking questions, the Harts would know and they would come forward.

But a family meeting had convinced the Harts not to confront her, because every single Hart had a past that they wanted to leave behind. Each Hart understood in their core that it would be cruel and brutal to force Madison's past on her unless she wanted it, because none of them wanted that to happen to them.

Jacob had wanted to come find her, but he'd asked Lucas to do it instead, not trusting himself to keep his distance once he saw her...also fearing that if Madison saw Jacob, she'd recognize him, and be sucked back into her past without the Harts even saying a word.

So, Lucas was here.

And Madison was fine.

Time to leave.

But he didn't move.

Because he couldn't take his eyes off her dog, and the bright orange Therapy Dog vest she was wearing.

They were at a black-tie affair in a five-star hotel. And yet Madison had a massive pittie by her side, even on the dance floor. She almost always had a part of her touching the dog, and the dog's vigilance to Madison was constant.

As Lucas watched, the dog suddenly rose to her feet and put her huge paws on Madison's chest, as if she'd sensed something was wrong with her owner.

Dammit.

At what point did he interfere? Madison's life was clearly fine. She had friends, a business, and a support system.

But that orange vest on her dog was a blaring alarm that all was not well with the woman who had haunted his brother for so many years.

Madison suddenly turned her head and looked right at him.

Lucas stiffened, shocked but also not shocked, by the jolt of electricity that shot through him when his gaze met hers. He already knew that he was drawn to her energy, but the eye contact felt like she'd fucking climbed into his chest and lit a fire.

Fuck.

Walk away?

Walk over to her?

He hadn't expected anything complicated, which had been incredibly short-sighted. He knew damn well what a traumatic childhood did to a person, even as an adult.

He realized that he'd hoped that she'd escaped unscathed, getting yanked out of that life at such a young age.

But the dog told other stories.

Madison said something, and immediately, her three friends all turned to look at him.

None of their faces were friendly, which he appreciated. He was accustomed to everyone idolizing him, wanting something from him, pretending to be his friend so they could get to his money or his family.

It was refreshing as hell to see four women studying him as if they were debating whether they needed to pull out their guns and take him out back into a dark alley.

Yeah. *Good job, Madison.* Friendship like that was everything.

The women didn't take their gazes off him, but he could see their mouths moving as they discussed him. He wished he could read lips, but all he could do was watch their body language and their facial expressions to realize that they were deciding how to handle him.

He contemplated continuing to stand where he was and let them choose whether to approach him, but he was in the middle of a crowd. He didn't like crowds, and he didn't want his conversation with Madison to be overheard.

He shook out his shoulders, surprised to discover that his heart had actually sped up. Nerves? Anticipation? Didn't matter. His connection with Madison had been opened. He'd been careless enough to be seen watching her, and now he had to handle this.

What he was going to say, he had no idea.

But he'd spent his life in survival mode, adjusting on the fly, so he was in his zone of genius.

Except as he started walking toward Madison, and saw her stiffen, he suddenly felt like he was about to step into a world he had no idea how to navigate.

He didn't like that feeling at all.

At. All.

But there was no going back.

Buy *A Rogue Cowboy's Heart* now to see what happens when they finally meet!

SNEAK PEEK: SECRETLY MINE

CONTEMPORARY ROMANCE

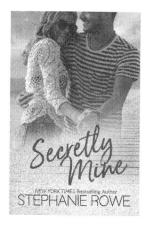

"Exquisitely beautiful!! All the feels. This is a do not pass up
book. Perfectly written :)." ~Five-star Goodreads Review
(Jann)

*She's back in town with no time for the rebel who stole her heart
long ago...but now he's playing for keeps.*

Dash Stratton had just picked up his welder when he heard his name hollered from the front of the house.

Recognition flooded him, and he swore, spinning around. That voice sounded familiar, but there was no way Leila Sheridan would be at his house, bellowing his name.

But he'd thought he'd seen her in that car outside Wright's.

That was twice in the span of an hour.

What the hell was going on?

She, whoever it was, shouted his name again, and something prickled along his skin. He would have sworn it was Leila.

He set down the welder and strode out of his studio. He jerked his sunglasses down over his face, and headed across the lawn around the side of his house, moving with an instinctive urgency.

He practically sprinted around the side of the house, and then stopped dead, stunned.

Leila Kerrigan was in front of the house, her hands on her hips, staring right at him.

Emotions flooded him, so many emotions he couldn't sort them out. He couldn't take his gaze off her. She was a woman now, not a scrawny, scared eighteen-year-old. She was wearing shorts and sneakers, and a blue tank top, looking like she was ready for a day on the lake, like the old days.

She had curves now she hadn't had before, the curves of a woman. Her sunglasses were on top of her head, revealing those glorious blue eyes and dark lashes that he'd begun to think he'd imagined.

She sucked in her breath. "Dash."

"Fuck." He grimaced. That was all he could think of to say after all this time. "I mean, what the fuck are you doing here?"

Her eyes widened. and he swore under his breath. "Sorry. I'm just stunned to see you in my front yard. You look great." Suddenly, he realized why she was there.

She wanted a divorce. The time had come.

Fuck. This time, he meant it.

A cute little frown furrowed between her eyebrows. "You don't know why I'm here?"

Double fuck. Had her lawyer served him? Had he missed an email? "No."

"You don't know about Bea's will?"

He narrowed his eyes. Bea's will? Not a divorce? He was annoyed by the relief that shuddered through him. "What about it? I know I got the house, because she told me many times that's what she was doing." He frowned. "What did she put in there for you?" Was there something at the house that was for Leila? He hadn't seen anything with her name on it, but Bea might have hidden it well. "Do you need me to find something for you?"

Leila stared at him, then understanding dawned on her face, and she burst out laughing. "I swear to God, I'm going to kill Eppie. And Clare!"

Ah...Eppie. He knew what kind of chaos she could cause. "What did they do?" Eppie was as much trouble as Bea had been.

"Clare gave me a letter for you." She fished around in her back pocket, then held up a folded envelope. "I suspect she explains it here."

He didn't move. If it was a letter from Bea, he didn't want to read it, hear her words, feel her presence. It was too soon for him. "You explain it."

Leila waved the letter at him. "No, thanks. Here."

Swearing under his breath, Dash walked over to her to take it, but as he neared, he felt like his world was spinning. Leila Sheridan was back, and she was unfinished business. *His* unfinished business.

He took the envelope, and his fingers brushed against hers, sending a shock reverberating through his system. Yeah, the attraction was still there, but this time, she wasn't an eighteen-year-old he had to protect from a piece-of-shit stepfather.

She was a woman, and their age difference no longer mattered like it had when she was barely eighteen and he'd been twenty-five.

When his hand touched hers, she sucked her in breath and jerked her hand back. "Letter," she mumbled.

"Letter," he agreed, as he took a step back, folded it, and put it in his pocket. "I'll read it later."

Leila's brows went up. "You need to read it now."

"I'm good. You need anything from me?"

She stared at him. "You're as stubborn and difficult as you were back then."

"Probably."

She folded her arms over her chest. "Read the letter, Dash."

"Nope." There was no chance he was reading Bea's words right now. He missed her like hell, and he wasn't in a place to read a letter she wrote to him in front of Leila. Or anyone. Or even himself. "Anything else you need?"

She stared at him. "Really?"

"Yeah. Whatever you need." This conversation felt awkward and distant, nothing like how he'd envisioned it might be all the times he'd thought about her over the years. "Want a drink? I have water and beer." And other stuff he didn't feel like mentioning.

"Water?"

"Yeah."

She put her hands on her hips. "Dash."

"Leila."

She sighed in aggravation. "Bea didn't leave you the house. She left *us* the house."

Dash stared at her. "Us?"

"Yes." She pointed back and forth between them. "You and me. Co-heirs. We have to both live in the house together for thirty consecutive nights before either of us can do anything with it. I'm moving in now."

"No." His amusement fled. Oh, wait, he hadn't been amused by anything about her sudden appearance. "It's my house. I've been living here for the last six months. She told me it was mine, repeatedly." He'd been counting on this house, and not just for himself.

"Well, it's also half mine. I need the money from selling it, and we can't sell it until we both live here together for thirty days."

Sell it? No one was selling this house. He couldn't afford to buy out Leila. He swore under his breath, then pulled out his phone and called Clare.

She answered on the first ring. "You read the letter?"

"I'm co-heirs with Leila, and we have to live in the house together for thirty consecutive nights before we can do anything with it?" It had to be wrong. It didn't make sense.

Clare sighed. "Yes, look, I'm sorry I didn't tell you, but Bea's will specifically said Leila had to be the one to tell you."

All thoughts of his attraction to Leila vanished in a surge of irritation. He ground his jaw. "So it's true?"

"Yes, it is."

He glanced at Leila, who was watching him, chewing on her lower lip. Why did she look so damned adorable chewing on her lip like that? Why did he care? He didn't have time for this. "I need this house. You know I do."

"Thirty days, Dash. You can have it in thirty days, as long as Leila agrees to give up her share."

Fuck. He couldn't afford to buy her out. "What else is in the will that you didn't tell me? There's more, isn't there? More games that Bea put in there?"

Clare cleared her throat. "It's a rather complicated will, but that's the gist of it."

He swore under his breath. "Clare—"

"Look. You could probably contest some of the provisions, but it's *Bea,*" Clare said softly. "You loved her. She loved you. Don't you want to let her do this her way? Would you deprive her of that joy?"

"No." Dash rubbed his forehead and cursed again. Bea had changed his life in many ways, standing by him when his parents disowned him. He'd spent the rest of his life giving back to her, and he couldn't stop now just because she was gone. "I'd never let her down," he admitted grudgingly.

"Bea spent a lot of time planning this," Clare said. "It's her gift to you. Not just the house, but all of it."

Dash looked at Leila. Was Leila a gift that Bea had decided to hand him? Another chance at the woman he'd let go? He ground his jaw. A year ago, co-habitating with Leila to compete for the house would have been very different than now.

Now, it didn't work for him. "Clare, she wrote the will before—"

"No, she didn't. She updated it afterwards."

That stunned Dash into silent. "She wrote it *after*?" After his whole life had changed. Rocked to its foundation. Shattered into a thousand pieces that he was still struggling to put back together. She wrote the will *after* that had happened? *What the hell, Bea?*

"Yes," Clare said. "It's your choice, Dash. You can contest it, and drag Bea's last moments of joy into question, or go with it."

He sighed. "You're very manipulative."

Clare laughed. "I know. You're welcome. Eppie and I have to confirm every night's sleepover, so you'll see a lot of us."

Roomie. Living with Leila Sheridan for thirty days. Thirty days in which to convince her to give him her half of the house. Not sell it to him. *Give* it to him.

Fuck. He didn't like needing charity from her. Bea's promise to give him the house had been his key to getting free. To have that compromised... *What the hell were you thinking, Bea?*

He didn't have a backup plan. He'd put everything into this house on the assumption he would get it.

And in those thirty days, he also had to avoid having Leila ask for a divorce. And...he to resist the temptation that she'd been to him for a long time.

Three bedrooms.

One and a half bathrooms.

One shower.

Hell. This was going to get rough fast.

And a part of him was looking forward to every minute of it.

How hot does it get when Leila moves in? And what secret is Dash hiding? Treat yourself today to *Secretly Mine,* and fall in love with Dash and Leila today!

A QUICK FAVOR

Did you enjoy Piper and Declan's story?

People are often hesitant to try new books or new authors. A few reviews can encourage them to make that leap and give it a try. If you enjoyed *When We Least Expect It* and think others will as well, please consider taking a moment and writing one or two sentences on the etailer and / or Goodreads to help this story find the readers who would enjoy it. Even the short reviews really make an impact!

Thank you a million times for reading my books! I love writing for you and sharing the journeys of these beautiful characters with you. I hope you find inspiration from their stories in your own life!

Love,
Stephanie

ABOUT THE AUTHOR

NEW YORK TIMES AND USA TODAY bestselling author Stephanie Rowe is the author of more than sixty published novels. Notably, she is a Vivian® Award nominee, a RITA® Award winner and a five-time nominee, and a Golden Heart® Award winner and two-time nominee. As the author of more than sixty novels, Stephanie loves writing sassy, smart heroines and the men who win their hearts. She has written for Grand Central Publishing, Harlequin, HarperCollins, Sourcebooks, and Dorchester Publishing.

www.stephanierowe.com

Printed in Great Britain
by Amazon

53248914R00175